Fatal

MW00436697

A Karina Cardinal Mystery (Book 2)

By Ellen Butler

A Karina Cardinal Novel

K.C.

Power to the Pen

Power to the Pen
PO Box 1474
Woodbridge, VA 22195
PowertothePen@ellenbutler.net

Trade Paperback ISBN 13: 978-0-9984193-6-7
Digital ISBN 13: 978-0-9984193-5-0

Categories: Fiction, Thriller & Suspense, Mystery, Amateur
Sleuth, Police Procedurals

Cover Art by: SelfPubBookCovers.com/RLSather

"Unfortunately, money in politics is an insidious thing - and a loophole in our campaign finance system was taken advantage of with money going to existing or new 527 groups with the sole purpose of influencing the election."

- Olympia Snowe

Chapter One

"Excuse me, Senator Kollingwoods," I interrupted, pausing the senator's tirade against one of her fellow colleagues for the pejorative comments he directed at her on the Senate floor. Her frustration was not out of line; however, my quarry, the reason I'd been skulking around the Capitol offices, exited the men's room and was walking away at a fast clip. "I see Senator Harper and must speak to him."

Senator Kollingwoods turned to follow my gaze as Harper turned the corner. "I'll just bet you do," she said with a smirk.

"Thanks for your time." I edged past. "I'll provide those research stats to Marianne tomorrow."

"Give him hell, Karina," she called as I strode around the corner.

Lucky for me, my target had been halted for a moment by a staffer, and I caught up with him as he entered the elevator labeled SENATORS ONLY.

"Senator Harper," I called out.

His milky blue gaze showed no surprise at my approach, and he waved me into the car. "Ms. Cardinal, I've been wondering when I'd hear from you. I'm headed over to the Russell building."

The doors closed behind me, and the elevator operator, an elderly African-American man dressed in the requisite navy-blue blazer and striped tie uniform, pressed the button that would take us to the basement.

"Did you have a nice weekend, Arnold?" Harper asked the elevator operator.

"Yes, Senator. My oldest granddaughter came home for the weekend."

"She's a sophomore this year?" The senator's wheezing breaths filled the small car.

"Yes, sir."

"Remind me, what college is she attending?"

"University of Maryland."

We ended our descent with a slight bump. "Give my best to your wife."

"Will do, sir."

The elevator spit us out not far from the entrance to the underground passageways connecting the Capitol to the Russell, Dirksen and Hart Senate office buildings. For an overweight man in his early seventies, he walked at a relatively brisk pace, and my sensible heels clacked against the aged russet stone flooring. Fortunately, my height provided an advantage when walking with taller men and I could easily replicate their stride.

"How'd you get past security?"

"I came over from Dirksen with Senator Kollingwoods."

Either he preferred not to talk over my noisy heels or his own pace was too much for him, because he slackened his gait. The heavy breathing continued, and I was relieved he slowed us down. "You want to know why I voted against the bill," he stated.

"I don't understand. You voted for it in committee, and on the Senate floor the first time. Why?" We exited the drab putty-colored walls of the Capitol basement to enter the bright white halls of the tunnel system.

"You know why."

"The amendment?" I clarified.

"Amendment? Try amend*ments*."

"That happens with every bill as it passes back and forth between the two houses," I pointed out. "Everyone has to do a little give and take. We knew it wouldn't come back the same way it went over. Some negotiating has to be done."

"Negotiating?" He gave a dark laugh. "Is that what you call it? By the time it came to a vote on the Senate floor, there was so much pork added to it you could wrap the White House up in bacon and deep fat fry it like a Thanksgiving turkey." He indicated for me to proceed him down the short escalator.

"Granted, I wasn't thrilled with the ten million Texas package," I conceded as we rode down. "But, overall the bill retained its integrity. It would have helped the lower income families."

"The Texas package was the least of my concerns. Did you know Florida stuck on a fifty million grant to research chickens?"

"Wild fowl, migratory birds."

"Ducks, geese, chickens!" He coughed and pressed a hand against his chest. "What does it matter?"

One of the trams that carried passengers through the tunnel to the Russell building cruised around the curve and out of sight. The other tram sat empty with an OUT OF ORDER sign on its side.

"I believe it had something to do with research on aging."

"Fifty million! For fowl! Let's walk."

I squinted at Harper. Beads of sweat covered his upper lip and his coloring seemed to have paled. "Are you sure you don't want to wait for the tram?" I asked.

"My doc says I need to get more exercise." He lumbered past the tram stop to the walking path. "I'd have been willing to vote for it until the Uptown Trio gutted the incentives."

"I agree the incentives were a blow. But, when your support departed, you took your own trio along, Tottengott, Goldman, and Tucker. Surely the incentives were a minor blip that could have been righted through section seven, part c. I won't even mention the position you put me in with the Alliance or the damage it's done to my reputation and possibly my career."

"Pfft. Your reputation is fine," he said. "You can't tell me the National Healthcare Advocacy Alliance is going to fire you over this. You're too well connected, and I'm sure they didn't like the changes either."

They didn't, but I wasn't about to let him get away that easily.

"Besides," he continued, "Tottengott, Goldman, and Tucker make their own decisions. You can't place their votes at my doorstep."

I gave him an arch glare. Harper had been in the Senate for over twenty-five years and was considered the leader of the few moderate republicans—a dying breed—left in the Legislature. Gloria Tottengott, Stephen Goldman, and Rhonda Tucker tended to stick together on votes, and often followed Harper's lead.

He flapped his hand. "Bah. You can direct that look elsewhere. I'm working on something even better. Something that will make S46 pale in comparison. Something that will put the fat cats in their place."

"Really? Tell me. How can I help?"

"You'll know when I'm good and ready for you to know. You lobbyists are all the same. Couldn't keep a secret if your life depended on it, and right now I'm working the back channels. I decided it's time to call in some chips . . . maybe all of them." His breath came out in pants and he stumbled.

"Senator!" I reached out to steady him.

He pulled a roll of Tums out of his coat pocket, but his

hands were so unsteady that he fumbled to open the package.

"Here, let me help you." I used my thumbnail to slit the wrapper, and two antacid tablets fell into his palm.

He pressed his fist against his chest as he chewed. "Must have been the pastrami sandwich I had for lunch."

It was close to six. Lunch had been hours ago, and I didn't like the greenish tinge of his coloring. "Are you going to be okay? Do you want me to get help?" We'd reached the curve, the midpoint between the two buildings. The tram at the far end was empty of passengers and the operator.

"I'll be fine." He puffed past me.

"I'm not sure, Senator." I glanced over my shoulder to see if anyone was coming from the Capitol side. "I think I should—"

His right hand slapped against the wall, his knees buckled, and he pitched forward. I'll never forget the dull, smacking *thud* that reverberated through the tunnel as his skull hit the polished cement floor. In the movies, dramatic events often transpire in slow motion. Not so in real life. The collapse happened in nanoseconds.

"*Senator!*" I crouched down and heaved him onto his back. A bruise on his forehead was already purpling from where it impacted. "Holy shit! Senator Harper!" I shook his shoulder.

No response.

"Help! I need help!" My voice echoed against the glass separating the tram track and concrete block walls.

Adrenaline flooded through my system. "Okay, okay, Cardinal. Think. What do I do?" His chest wasn't rising; I pressed two shaking fingers against his neck. I couldn't feel a pulse. I checked it against my own neck to make sure I'd placed them in the proper location. Sure enough, my own blood pressure beat at a fast clip.

Now what?

I drew in a deep breath. "CPR. Remember eleventh grade

health," I mumbled. "First, shake the person to see if there is a response. Already done. No response. Second, identify a bystander. Point and tell them to call 911." I looked left and right. Not a soul in sight. I lifted my gaze to the ceiling and found a tell-tale globe encasing a camera monitor.

"Hey!" I waved my hands back and forth. "He needs help!"

Then, I proceeded to dump the entire contents of my purse on the floor. The cell phone was the last item to slide out, and I snatched it up like a life line. To my dismay, pressing the power button brought no joy. The screen remained black, and I almost cried in frustration. Once again, I hadn't charged my phone.

"*Damnit!*" I tossed the useless mobile back into my purse.

"Okay, the ABCs of CPR—airway, breathing, chest compressions—two breaths to thirty compressions." A vision of the senator chomping Tums flashed in my mind's eye. I loosened his tie, pulled his head back, and checked his throat. The airway looked clean. I ran my finger in there to make sure, before I pinched his nose and blew. His chest rose.

I got on my knees above the senator's prone figure and put my hands in the proper place, or what I hoped was the proper location, for chest compressions. Never having done it on a real person, I wasn't positive. Harper's body felt softer and squishier beneath my hands than Mannie, the hard-plastic manikin they had us use in school. Stacked one over the other, I began the downward thrusts.

One, two, three, four, five, six, seven.

As I approached thirty, a memory of a *Time* magazine article came to mind. The American Heart Association had changed the ABCs. They recommended untrained bystanders perform straight chest compressions when faced with a heart attack.

Is this a heart attack? Looks like a heart attack to me.

And I most definitely fell into the "untrained" category, so I didn't stop to provide mouth-to-mouth.

"Come on, Harper! Today is not a good day to die. You understand me? *Help! Anyone? Hello? Fire! Rape! Where the hell is everyone!*" I called. The passageway, usually a busy corridor, remained empty of police or staffers. "I'll never live this down if you die on me. Goddamn it, you old goat. Breathe!"

I continued to pound away on his chest when it occurred to me the senator might have a cell phone, and I paused my ministrations to check his pockets.

"Bingo!"

I pulled a black phone out of his coat and pressed the power button. The screen lit up with a lovely sailboat scene behind a numbered keypad. The senator, having been given some good advice, locked his phone with a PIN.

"Shit." I was about to toss it aside when it occurred to me that emergency calls could be made from a locked phone. Never having done it before, I swiped my finger in a circle, and, to my relief, a button popped up from the bottom—Emergency Call. I tapped and waited.

Nothing. "What is going on?" I pressed the emergency icon again before realizing the problem.

No service.

"Are you *freakin'* kidding me here!" I let out a feral yell, tossed it aside, and returned to my chest compressions. *One, two, three, four, five.*

Finally, after what seemed like an eternity, I heard the beat of running footsteps and glanced up to find a Capitol police officer coming from the Russell building.

He skidded to a stop at the senator's feet.

"It's about *time!*" I snapped "Where have you been? I've been calling for help *forever.*"

"What happened?"

"I think he had a heart attack. I don't know, he grabbed the wall, then fell to the floor and hit his head. You need to call for a paramedic." I continued CPR as we spoke.

"Daryl . . ." He spoke into the walkie talkie on his shoulder. "We have a situation. We need paramedics down here immediately. There's a white male. Unresponsive. Possible cardiac arrest."

"His name is Senator George Harper."

"I'm sorry, what did you say?" the police officer asked me.

"This is Senator George Harper."

"We have a senator down. I repeat, we have a senator in cardiac arrest. Get medics in here immediately."

"How long will that take?"

"Not long."

Hurried footsteps, and more feet wearing shiny black police officer shoes came into my line of vision. Conversations went on around me, but I remained focused on my patient.

"Jesus. Isn't that—"

"Senator Harper."

"Christ."

"Jodi, go seal off the Capitol end. No one but police or paramedics. DaShane, you wait on the Russell end. No cell phones. No photos for the press. Understood?"

"Yes, sir."

The shoes retreated. My hands became clammy with sweat and my shoulders began to tire. "C'mon. Wake up, Senator. C'mon, man." Up and down I pumped in a steady rhythmic pace.

The rattling clatter of the gurney rebounded through the passage over the sound of pounding feet.

"We've got it now. I need you to move back." A young blond paramedic gently pulled at my shoulders, and I scooted backward on my bottom, relieved to have the professionals take over.

He started compressions while his partner, a dark-haired,

Hispanic female took Harper's vitals. "Pupils unresponsive. No pulse. Looks like he sustained an injury to the head," she said in a calm, clear voice.

"I think he had a heart attack," I choked out.

The pair of EMTs barely acknowledged my comment as they worked over Harper, spewing rapid-fire medical jargon back and forth to each other.

"Charging the defibrillator." As the woman unpacked the mobile machine, the man at my feet unbuttoned the senator's shirt, moving his tie to the side.

"Uh-oh."

"What?" The female paramedic put the machine on the floor next to her colleague.

"Looks like he's got a pacemaker."

She felt the area just below his collarbone. "Yes, indeed."

"My God, I had no idea he had a pacemaker." I pushed the hair back from my face. "Should I not have performed CPR?"

"You're fine," the man said dismissively. "What's the protocol? I've never dealt with a pacemaker. Can we shock him?"

"If it had a defib it would already have shocked him. What happened when he passed out?" She looked up at the police officer.

He shrugged and pointed. All eyes turned to me.

"He was kind of sweaty and clammy and was breathing heavily, but . . . but he *insisted* on walking. Then his coloring paled and . . . he kind of turned green. I thought he was going to be ill. Then he, just . . . fell forward. I'm sorry . . . I didn't react fast enough to catch him." I looked down at my shaking hands. "His head hit the floor."

Their attention returned to the patient. "Maybe it's gone bad," the woman said. "I've seen it happen. You'll want to place the pads here and here. Make sure they are at least an inch away from the OED. Charging. Stand back."

The little machine gave off a whine and the senator's body convulsed. The blond checked for a pulse and shook his head. "Again?"

"Charging. Got it. Stand back."

Again, the senator's body jumped.

"No pulse," the blond said.

They repeated the step one more time, to no avail.

"Continue compressions. Get him on the stretcher, I'll bag him, and we'll get out of here," the woman directed.

The pair maneuvered him onto an orange backboard and, with the help of the surrounding officers, lifted him onto the gurney. I scrambled to shove the strewn bits and pieces of my possessions back into my handbag before chasing the crowd of first responders down the hall into the Russell building. I followed them as far as the elevator, but there was only room enough for the stretcher and the two paramedics still working on him. The rest of us remained on the other side of the elevator. The doors closed, and all went silent.

Chapter Two

"Someone should call his wife. I don't have her number. They have a place in Georgetown, but I'm not sure if she's here in D.C. or back home in Michigan. Does anyone know where they're taking him? I can call his office and get her number. Her name is Elise . . . Elise"—my voice hitched—"Harper. Someone should notify his staff. They'll want to know."

"Here, honey, take this." The petite African-American police officer standing next to me held out a tissue.

I didn't know when the tears had started. During the mad rush to the elevators, I suspected.

"It'll be okay," the officer continued. "Why don't you come with me? We need to get your statement."

She put her arm around my shoulder and guided me through the stone halls of the Russell building to an office with a pair of industrial metal desks and computers.

"I'm sorry, I don't know why I'm crying." I blew into the Kleenex. "And look, my hands are shaking. I feel cold. Is it cold in here?"

"It's the adrenaline. You're starting to come down off the high. Here." She hung a long black raincoat over my shoulders.

"Thanks" —I noticed her nametag— "Officer Leander."

"Would you like a cup of coffee?"

I nodded. "Cream and sugar, please."

She left me alone and I took the moment of privacy to get a

grip. I wiped away the tears and searched through the mess in my purse for a compact. The mirror showed bright red eyes, matching my nose and cheeks, and I dabbed beige powder over my face. A movement in the mirror had me quickly tossing it back in my purse.

"I'm awfully sorry about . . ." But when I turned, it wasn't the cop I'd expected, it was a different one—male, average height, light brown hair, tough-looking. One hand was in his pocket, the other behind his back. I stood to face him. "I beg your pardon, I thought you were Officer Leander."

"Where'd she go?" His buggy, pale blue stare unnerved me.

"To get a cup of coffee." To my relief, the squeak of her shoes heralded the officer's return.

"Excuse me." She brushed past her colleague and held out a disposable cup. "Here you go."

"Thanks." I wrapped my hands around it, welcoming its heat.

"What can I do for you, Officer . . . er . . . Jablonski?" Leander asked.

"Just came in to see if I could help." His eyes darted between Leander and me.

"You're new here, right?"

"Yes, ma'am, started last week."

"It's best if you return to your post."

"Yes, ma'am."

Officer Leander turned away, but I continued to watch as Jablonski hesitated. Something about this guy wasn't sitting right. He kept staring at me, and not in what I'd consider a nice manner.

"Is there something else I can help you with, Jablonski?"

His gaze snapped to Leander. "No, ma'am. I'll be going."

"Please, shut the door behind you."

I waited for the door to close completely before resuming

my seat. "Am I in trouble, Officer Leander?"

"Call me Jodi, and why would you say that?"

"That other cop didn't seem to like me very much."

"Jablonski? Forget him. He's new. He looks at everyone that way. I noticed it myself when we met last week." Her nails clicked against the keys on the computer as she spoke.

"Has someone contacted Harper's family?" I asked.

"We are taking care of it. Now, why don't you start with your name, and then you can tell me exactly what happened."

"My name is Karina Cardinal. I work for National Healthcare Advocacy Alliance." I recounted my interaction with Senator Harper, starting from our encounter on the elevator. When I got to the part about his collapse, I paused.

"Then what happened?" She drew her eyes away from the computer screen.

"I called for help and, honestly, I can't understand what took so long. Why didn't anyone see us in the cameras, or hear my calls? It echoes down there. One of the guards at the desks to the hallway entry should have heard something."

"A couple of knuckleheads thought it would be funny to put on Guy Fawkes masks and run around knocking down flags in the hallway. The guards responded to the hubbub."

"Both of them?"

She shifted uncomfortably in her seat. "Then what happened?"

"And what about the tram operator? What happened to him?"

"That's a good question." She wrote down a note on a yellow legal pad. "I'll have to look into that. I know we've been having electrical problems with both those trams in the past few weeks."

"Maybe he went to find maintenance when he couldn't find the guards?"

"Let's finish this up," she said abruptly.

I thought I'd hit a nerve, asking questions she was probably asking herself. I sipped the strong coffee and resumed the story up until the point where we all met up at the elevator. "And you know the rest. I really had no idea he had a pacemaker."

"How could you?"

"I mean, I don't recall reading it in the papers or anything like that. They must have done a good job keeping it under wraps three years ago, when he last ran for office."

"Maybe they put it in recently."

"True." I chewed my lip. "Do you think I shouldn't have performed the chest compressions? I mean, I—I just didn't know what else to do."

She shrugged. "You heard the paramedic. He said it was okay, and they were doing it on the way out."

"Lord, I hope so."

"Don't worry about it. I'm sure everything will be fine once they get him to the hospital. I'm going to print this out. You'll need to review and sign it. Put your current address and phone number at the bottom."

Half an hour later, I directed the cab driver to my office and stared sightlessly out the window as the sedan crossed the Potomac River into Virginia. We stopped at a light on the George Washington Parkway, and I frowned up at the brick building on my right—my old office building, a medical association for physician assistants. I'd been happy working there, and they'd been happy with me . . . until I got involved in returning a piece of stolen art. That debacle cost me a broken engagement and eventually my job. The chief operating officer, Joanne, hadn't been too pleased with my side job—representing my soon-to-be father-in-law, who was neck deep in the fiasco. Or rather, she didn't like the reporters on our front lawn, or the FBI agent that made his way into our lobby because of it. She never fired me, but things between Joanne and I became rather cold after that affair. I found myself shut out of important meetings. Some of my duties were passed on to a younger, less experienced staff member.

Reading the writing on the wall, I accepted an interview with NHAA, a healthcare coalition advocacy group, who had been politely courting me for years. I supposed I shouldn't complain. The money was better. However, I missed the more relaxed atmosphere of the association and the comradery with my colleague, Latesha, who had come to my aid at a time when I didn't know who to turn to. A week ago, I started encouraging Latesha to consider applying for an open position at NHAA. As a single mom, I knew she could use the added income, and frankly, I could use a friend. There was no one at my new job in whom I could confide tonight's tragedy, though, come morning, I'd have to tell my boss, Hasina.

The light turned green and the cab crawled forward with traffic. My new office wasn't too much further, and we soon pulled into the parking lot. "It's the silver Camry with the baseball-sized dent in the bumper. Stop, this is it. Thanks."

The best thing about my new job—its convenience to my condo. Only five to ten minutes away, depending upon traffic. Bits and pieces of the night's events replayed through my mind during the drive. It was a relief to get home to my two-bedroom condo—a lucky investment I made six years ago when one of my mom's friends passed away. Her estranged children, who lived in Africa, wanted nothing more than to unload it quickly. The place had never been updated—the kitchen had sported avocado appliances, the bathrooms were pink tile, and the living spaces had wall-to-wall shag carpet. They accepted my low-ball offer, and I finished updating it last year.

After hanging my coat in the hall closet, I dumped half my purse contents onto the kitchen island; the items musically jingled and clanked onto the granite. Two phones slid out together. I must have grabbed the senator's when I gathered my odds and ends from the tunnel floor.

Shaking my head, I eyed the mess. *When did I become so disorganized?* At Christmas, Mom gave me an organizer that moved easily from purse to purse, full of little pockets, zippers, and clips. After tonight's escapade, I determined it was time to take it out of the plastic bag and actually put it to use. No more searching for keys, lipsticks, cell, or wallet in the depths of my handbags. I plugged my phone into the charging station and went in search of the gift.

As I sorted my belongings into pockets, I flipped on the television. The nightly news station broke in with the story. A local Capitol Hill correspondent gave the highlights. "This evening Senator Harper, a Michigan Republican, collapsed at the Capitol. Medics rushed him to Georgetown University Hospital, where he was pronounced dead from cardiac arrest. We will have more on this breaking story when we return."

Even though I knew what the reporter said was true, the reality wasn't computing.

Poor Elise.

"That's it. I need a glass of wine." If any day called for a glass of wine, it was today.

At nine thirty, on the dot, my cell rang with a welcome caller. "I'm so glad you called," I said, answering the phone.

"What's wrong?" Mike asked.

My relationship with Michael Finnegan went back to college, undoubtedly the reason he distinguished my distress with a single sentence.

"Did you hear about Senator Harper?"

"No, tell me."

I went on to describe the events.

"Why didn't you call?"

"It's your first day, I didn't want to bother you in case you were in a session. You said you'd call at nine thirty . . . so I waited." Our dating status, a recent development, was an evolving creature. Mike, an FBI agent working for the cybercrimes division in D.C., was currently at an undisclosed training facility. Or at least, that's what he told me when he announced he'd be out of town for the week. Ostensibly, his flight left at six this morning. He could have been anywhere, Toledo, Texas, or he could've driven down I-95 to the FBI training facility at Quantico. Such was the life of dating an FBI agent.

"I don't have regular access to my phone," he told me. "If something comes up, it's best to text, and I'll get back to you as soon as I'm available."

"No worries. I'm not sure I was ready to talk, but now it's kind of a relief to tell someone what happened."

"You haven't told anyone else?"

"Besides giving my statement to the Capitol Police . . . no. I thought they'd be able to revive him once they got to the hospital. I think I'm still in shock . . . I mean, he died right in front of me." I paced the floor. "I'm having trouble wrapping my head around it. There he was, puffing along, telling me how the House messed up S46—which they did—and how he was working on something better, then *bam!* Down he went. And I didn't even catch him. What kind of person doesn't reach out to catch a falling man? Hm? I'm going to hell, aren't I?" I paused, staring out my sliding glass door into the darkness. The lock snapped beneath my fingers, and I pulled the door open. A humid breeze brushed my cheeks and the smell of approaching rain hung heavy in the March air.

"Did he fall toward you?"

"No, but I should have seen it coming. He'd been wheezing. I should have insisted we take the damn tram. I should have—"

"Whoa, K.C., you need to stop with the shoulda, woulda, coulda routine. It's not like you knew he was going to keel over. Did you?"

"Of course not." I pinched the bridge of my nose.

"It sounds to me like you did the best you could. Besides, Harper weighs twice as much as you do, he would have taken you down with him."

"You're not wrong about that," I mumbled.

"It likely wouldn't have made a difference if you did catch him. Did you ever think it was just his time to go? We've come so far with medical advancement, but death is still inevitable. Today . . . was Harper's day to go."

"Were you always so matter-of-fact in college, or is this the FBI training?"

He snorted. "Maybe a bit of both."

I chewed my lip. "I suppose you're right. I can't control everything."

"Which drives you nuts."

"You know me too well."

"Get some rest. Things will look better in the light of day. Trust me."

I sighed, "You're right."

"I'll call you tomorrow, say . . . eight?"

"That'll be fine. Talk to you then."

"Night."

Lights in the neighboring apartment complex blinked out as early risers went to bed. Car headlamps twinkled in the distance. A vehicle with a pulsing bass pulled into a parking space, then silenced as one of my neighbors exited. Life carried on around me as if nothing had happened, and as far as they were concerned, nothing had.

A raindrop hit my cheek, and I wiped away the moisture.

Mike is right, today was Harper's day to go.

****

Shivering, I snuggled further beneath the blankets. No light shone through the slats of the blinds, and I rolled over to check the time. 2:48. I punched the pillow and readjusted my position, but a chill continued to nip at my nose. March weather in Virginia brought wild temperature swings, and the day had been so mild I'd turned off the heat before going to bed. A cold front must have followed the rainstorm. With a grunt, I pushed aside the covers and opened the door.

Brr, the temperature is even colder in the hall.

I flicked on a lamp and adjusted the thermostat. The creak and whoosh of the old heat pump reassured me, but a cold draft tickled my bare toes and, in my periphery, the drapes billowed.

What the hell?

I pushed them aside. No wonder the apartment was freezing. I must not have closed the sliding door properly. It shut with a soft click, and I scuttled back to bed, pulling the comforter up to my chin.

Unfortunately, the short period of wakefulness turned into an hour of my brain's rehashing of the day's awful events before I fell back asleep.

Chapter Three

In the morning, I stopped by Hasina's office to inform her that I'd seen Harper's death. She kindly offered me the day off, but I declined, reluctant to spend more time alone with my thoughts. Instead, I requested her confidentiality. I wasn't willing to spend the morning fielding a steady stream of office coworkers "stopping by" to offer their sympathies. Still, a few poked their head into my office, asking if I'd heard the news. I sent them away with a simple nod and a "yes, terrible news."

Rodrigo, on the other hand, was a different story. I looked up from my computer to find the Puerto Rican looming in my doorway.

"So, I hear old Harper bought the farm last night. Did you give him a piece of your mind before he kicked the bucket?" He closed my door and slid into the wooden guest chair.

Rodrigo's parents moved to Maryland when he was a baby, which is why he had no Spanish accent. He grew up in a low-income neighborhood and was the only sibling out of four kids in his family to have obtained a college degree. He'd worked social media outlets and phones to whip up public support for S46, and he'd taken Harper's defection much worse than I, which didn't surprise me, considering the benefit it would have brought to poorer families.

Nine years ago, Rodrigo's father, a construction worker, fell off a roof, sustaining a back injury. He went down the opioid rabbit hole to mitigate the pain, and when his insurance wouldn't pay for decent addiction rehab, he turned to heroin. Three days after Rodrigo graduated college, his father died from a bad batch of Fentanyl-laced heroin. Two years later, his mother was diagnosed with lung cancer and passed away within six months. It took the kids years, fighting with the insurance company and the hospital, to come to an agreement and retire her medical bills. It was no wonder Rodrigo took Harper's reversal as a personal affront. My coworker told me none of this. Hasina had, and it's the reason she asked me to reach out to Harper.

"That's not funny, Rodrigo. I was with him when it happened."

He snorted in disbelief. It took a minute for him to realize I wasn't joking, and his mouth dropped.

"It was very traumatic, as a matter of fact. He had a heart attack and I performed CPR."

"Better you than me." He crossed his perfectly creased pant legs and fastidiously picked at a piece of lint. "*I* would have stepped over him."

I eyed his pink shirt with white cuffs, Italian silk tie, designer vest, and slacks. "I believe it. I had to get down on my knees to help him. I sweated through my silk blouse, ruining it."

Rodrigo scrunched his nose.

"I understand you disliked him," I said. "However, I warn you, if you've come here to be mean about Senator Harper, you can save it. He had legitimate reasons for voting against the amended bill, and I'll not have you speaking ill of a dead man in my office." I ended my little speech with a steely glare.

Rodrigo blanched. "Touché. I'll put my claws away. I'm sorry, Karina. It must have been terrible for you."

I didn't deign to answer, instead returning to the email I'd been working on when he arrived.

"Want to talk about it?"

My fingers didn't stop their dance across the keyboard. "No. And I would appreciate it if *you* don't tell anyone about it either. I'm not interested in having a parade of morbid curiosity seekers trotting through my door. Now, I'd like to drop it, if you don't mind."

He shifted, uncrossed his legs, and cleared his throat. "Hasina wants to see the S46's post-mortem report, and our recommendations for future strategies, on her desk by close of business Monday."

I clicked send and stretched my arms above my head. "I started it yesterday. I'll forward a draft so you can add your materials."

"What about our recommendations?"

"What do you think?"

"I think it's an uphill battle, but we made great strides this time. The House is up for election this year. If we get a few of those seats to turn blue, we might have a good chance in the fall."

I gave a distracted nod. "You know, just before he collapsed, Harper was telling me about a new bill he was working on."

"You mean a new healthcare bill."

"I assume so. He said it was better than S46," I mused.

"Did he get into specifics?"

"No, he was really cagey when I offered to help." I rotated my chair to face the window. "He said something about cashing in his chips."

"Who's his legislative aide on healthcare?"

"Christy Manheim."

"You should set up a meeting. See what you can find out."

"I plan to."

"Do it today."

"Rodrigo!" I spun around to face him.

"What?" He put his hands up.

"Her office is still reeling from the senator's death." I tapped my chin. "It's not the right time."

That evening, I received an email from Senator Harper's Chief of Staff inviting me to a memorial service on Friday morning. There was no indication what the funeral plans would be, but I assumed Elise would inter his remains somewhere in Michigan. The service was being held at the National Cathedral by invitation only. I blocked off the time in my calendar, printed the invite, and tucked it into one of the convenient new pockets inside my purse. The bottom of the email recommended arriving early, due to heavy security and tight parking, which basically meant Secret Service would be on hand with their metal detectors and wands.

I wondered who, of the Washington elite, would be showing up to mourn the senator. I also wondered who the Michigan governor would appoint to replace him.

Chapter Four

Wednesday afternoon, the winds whipped my hair and trench coat in all directions as I walked the two blocks to Table Talk, a restaurant I frequented often enough for the staff to call me by name. The scent of scrambled eggs, bacon, and syrup swirled around me as I fought to keep the door from being ripped out of my hands by a gust. *So much for March going out like a lamb.*

Latesha waved me over to the table, and I bypassed the unmanned hostess station to join her.

"It's good to see you." I tossed my coat and handbag onto an empty chair and hugged my friend. She smelled of fresh baby powder and coffee. "You look fabulous in that yellow suit. You're so lucky, with your dark skin, you can pull off that color. I'd look like a washed-out Big Bird if I tried something like that."

"True, but I can't wear a lot of colors you white girls wear. That scarf really brings out the green in your eyes, by the way. I ordered an Arnold Palmer tea for you."

"Thanks." I slid into the chair and took a sip of the sweet/tart tea. "I'm assuming you heard about Senator Harper."

She nodded. "Who hasn't? I understand there's a memorial service on Friday at the Cathedral."

"Did you get an invitation?"

"Nope." She cupped her coffee mug. "Nobody at our office

did. Anyone at yours?"

"Yes."

Latesha's brows rose. "Really? Which muckety-muck got an invite?"

I fiddled with the straw. "I did."

"Get out!" She slapped a hand on the table.

"Nope. Came via email yesterday."

"Girl, who'd you sleep with to get one?"

I gave a weak smile. "I figured everyone in the biz got one until I started asking around. Maybe they're waiting for the RSVPs to roll in before they send out a second round."

She whistled. "Who sent it to you?"

"Sandy, his Chief of Staff."

"Do you think you got one because of your recent work on S46?"

Before I could formulate an answer, we were interrupted by the waitress. "How are my two favorite ladies?" the petite, white-haired woman asked.

"Hi, Ruby," Latesha said in greeting.

"I'm good. And you?" I asked.

"Got my health, a good job, and money in my pocket. Can't complain." Ruby's upbeat response garnered grins from both of us. "What can I get ya?" She whipped out her pad.

After we placed our orders, Ruby bustled back to the kitchen. I leaned forward and indicated Latesha do the same.

"I think I got the invite because I was there when Harper collapsed," I said in muted tones.

"What do you mean, 'you were there?' You were at his office when it happened?"

"No, we were walking the tunnel from the Capitol to the Russell building, talking about S46. He was kind of worked up and then . . . *bam!* He collapsed."

Her dark eyes widened, accentuating the whites. "You mean

he fell down onto that hard cement floor? Right in front of you?"

"Right in front of me."

"Mary, Jesus, and Jo-ho-sa-phat! What did you do?"

"First, I tried calling 911, but my phone was dead and his didn't have service down there. So I yelled up and down the tunnel. Then I started CPR. He hit his head when he fell. It was awful."

"Lordy-bee. How long before the paramedics arrived?"

"It seemed like for-ev-er. The security officer said there'd been some sort of incident, which is why it took them so long to respond. The EMTs had to shock him when they arrived."

She sat back and let out a low whistle. "So, you think he died on the way to the hospital?"

I glanced around and curled my finger. Latesha leaned in again. "I think he was dead when he hit the floor. I had no response even with CPR. He didn't respond to the juice the EMTs hit him with. Nothing."

She nodded. "The news said it was cardiac arrest."

"Yeah . . . I didn't know he had a bad ticker. Did you?"

"No, I did not."

"He had a pacemaker. Did you know that?"

Her brow furrowed. "I can't remember it coming out during his last election."

"Neither did I. The EMTs found it." I arranged my knife and fork and placed the napkin in my lap. "It's kind of weird. I didn't think you could go into cardiac arrest with a pacemaker. Wouldn't it have fixed the rhythm or something?"

"You would think." She shrugged. "Why don't you reach out to Ted Beachler? He's a cardiovascular physician assistant, right? Maybe he can explain it."

I spun my glass in circles as I debated her suggestion. "I think you're right. I'll give him a call and see if he can explain how this happened. One of the EMTs said something about the pacemaker going bad."

"You'd better call Ted. Otherwise, these questions are going to drive you nuts."

"Can you blame me?" I pinched my lips together. "Wouldn't you want to know?"

She had the temerity to laugh. "Not really. None of my business. But I know you, Karina Cardinal. You've got a voracious curiosity, you'll just keep pecking away. Don't you give me that squinty-eyed glare." Her finger waggled in front of my nose. "It's part of what makes you an excellent researcher when it comes to the issues. You never miss a thing, whether good or bad. Always helps when it comes to defending against the opposition's arguments. So you'd better give Ted a call and set your mind at ease. Now" —she pushed back her chair— "I need to visit the ladies' room before lunch arrives."

Latesha wasn't wrong. It had been my own insatiable nosiness that discovered a hidden painting in my former fiancé's father's home—*wow, that's a mouthful*—and my research prowess that identified it as a stolen painting from the Isabella Stewart Gardner Museum in Boston. My subsequent actions ended an engagement and put my life, along with Martin Dunne's entire family, in danger. The fact that Martin had hired a private security company to follow me around was the only thing that kept me from being carved up by a mafia thug.

My mobile chimed with an incoming text, drawing my thoughts away from the disturbing incident. It was Mike.

> *I'm headed home on the next flight out. Want to get together for a late dinner?*
> *Wish I could. I've got a fundraiser tonight. Why are you coming home early?*

It took Mike a moment to respond.

Caught a new case. How about lunch tomorrow?

I checked my calendar.

No can do. Working lunch with the team. Dinner tomorrow?

Fine. Your place or mine?

Do you have food at your place?

I'll meet at yours. 7?

See you then.

My fingers hovered above the keyboard. Should I type the L-word? Neither one of us had said it. We'd known each other since college, been great friends, and I did care for him. Was I *in love* with him?

"What's that secretive smile all about? Who are you texting?" Latesha wiggled her brows as she slid into her seat.

Flustered, I quickly typed,

Have a safe flight.

I was such a chicken.

"It's nothing—just Mike. He's coming home early from training. We're arranging our schedules."

"Mm-hm. So, when do I get to meet this FBI agent of yours?"

"Oh . . . I don't know. Soon, I guess." I slipped the cell back into my purse.

"Well, I hope he doesn't turn out to be a creep like that last guy."

"I don't know that I'd call Patrick a creep."

"He put a secret tracking app on your phone. Didn't he?"

"Well, yes, but . . . "

"But, nothing. That ranks a ten on the creep-o-meter."

"Yeah, you're right. He's a creep."

"You're well rid of that character. Even if he did give you a boulder-sized engagement ring."

I rolled my eyes. I never liked that old-fashioned ring. It was a family heirloom, and I returned it when we broke up. "You know he still texts."

"Get out. What does he say?"

"Oh, just asks how I'm doing. If I'm okay. That sort of thing."

"Did you tell him you changed jobs? Are dating someone new?"

"No."

"Ladies, here are your omelets." Ruby placed two steaming omelets with hash browns in front of us. "Can I get you anything else?"

"Ketchup."

"Hot sauce." Latesha and I spoke at once.

"Here you go." She pulled the condiments out of her apron and hurried off to help another customer.

"So, you'll have to tell me who's in attendance on Friday. Do you think the President will be there?"

I shook ketchup onto the hash browns. "My money's on the VP."

"You think? They *are* the same party." Latesha coated her eggs in Tabasco.

"Yes, but there was no love lost between them. Also, I don't see him cancelling his trade talks with China to come home for Harper."

She tsked. "You're probably right. Wonder who you'll end up sitting next to."

"I'll probably be relegated to the back row . . . behind a pillar, with the rest of the peons." I bit down on the fluffy egg.

"Get there early. So you can take pictures, in case any famous people show up."

"I imagine it'll be filled with other reps and senators, and Washington heavy hitters."

She gave a dismissive snort. "Not them. I mean, famous people. Like Hollywood actors."

"What about news anchors? There's bound to be one or two."

She paused, a forkful of eggs halfway to her mouth. "Depends. Not the local ones. Focus on national ones, like David Muir. He's a fine-looking one."

Her demands made me laugh. "Yes, ma'am."

"Now for heaven's sakes, let's talk about something a little less depressing."

"Okay. . . . There's an opening at NHAA you'd be perfect for."

"Girl . . . " She waved her fork at me.

"C'mon, everyone's doing it. . . . "

Even though Latesha brushed aside my efforts to recruit her into NHAA, I emailed the job description and human resources contact information to her that afternoon. Our lunch only made me realize how much I missed seeing her on a daily basis. For some reason, an unexplainable sense of dread had been tugging at me since the senator's death, and Latesha's down-to-earth personality helped subdue some of that anxiety.

Chapter Five

The *rat-ta-tat-tat* of Mike's signature knock at the door was a welcome sound. He looked tall and handsome in his unbuttoned Navy overcoat and red scarf, his short, dark hair tousled by the wind.

"Something smells good." He flashed a dimpled half-smile at me that would be impish on a little boy, but only served to make him sexier. I never told him that little smile had been making my belly flutter since we met in college; I'd learned to ignore it for years.

"Get in here, you." I grabbed him by the lapel, pulling him over the threshold. The door slammed as I wrapped my arms around his neck and pressed my lips against his. Though taken by surprise, it was but a moment before he returned the kiss. Pressing me against the wall, he tangled his fingers into my hair at the nape of my neck and explored my mouth with his probing tongue. The ring of my landline finally drew us apart.

"Welcome home," I managed to puff out.

"Thanks. Do you need to get that?" He pressed his forehead against mine.

"Nah, they can talk to my voicemail."

"What's in the oven? It smells delicious."

"Salmon steaks."

"I suppose they can't wait?"

"Not unless you prefer burned fish."

"I think they call that blackened."

"Blackened, schmackened, if I don't get it out, it'll be burned and not very tasty."

We'd been taking things slow and had yet to "seal the deal," as they say. I think the two of us were still a bit afraid to ruin a fabulous friendship that we'd developed back in college. When we started dating, a myriad of questions pulled at me. What if I disappointed him in bed? Was I ready to have my friend see me naked? What if he sucked in bed? What if . . . fill in the blank. One thing I didn't want to do was lose my friendship with Mike by jumping into something we weren't ready for. I could imagine Latesha asking me, "Why don't you discuss these issues?" Imaginary-in-my-head Latesha was right. We should. We should have the grown-up conversation.

Taking that into consideration, I'd determined to shift this thing between us into the next gear. Mike's early return only sought to move my timeline forward a few days. Optimistic about the outcome, I'd shaved, put on some pretty panties, and dabbed a little perfume in all the right spots. But I wasn't going to have it ruined by setting dinner on fire. We had time.

Reluctantly, he stepped back and sniffed my hair as I passed.

"Hang up your coat," I directed. "Would you like a glass of wine? I've opened a white."

"Yes, please. And a tall glass of water too."

I pulled the salmon out of the oven.

Mike strolled into the kitchen area. He'd removed his suit jacket and tie and rolled up his sleeves. "Anything I can do to help?"

I stared at those muscular forearms . . . sprinkled with dark hair . . . and those long, agile fingers. I knew I was attracted to him. If the steamy kisses we'd shared were any indication, he was certainly attracted to me. Why was I so worried about going the distance?

"K.C.?"

"Right, here's your water. The wine is over there, breathing. Glasses are in the corner cabinet. Can you pour? I'll be right back, I've got to hit the head."

By the time I returned, he'd poured the wine and was tossing the salad. My moment in the bathroom had allowed me to get my head on straight.

I finished plating the meal. "So how did the training go?" I asked as Mike and I climbed onto stools at the kitchen island.

"Unfinished."

"Does that mean you'll have to go back?"

"At some point."

"That's too bad." We ate in silence. The fish was delicious—flaky yet succulent—and the rice fluffed to perfection.

"This is delicious. Thanks for cooking." He forked a pile of salad leaves.

"No problem. I thought you'd appreciate a homecooked meal." I finished off the rice. "So . . . what's this big case you were called back for?"

He returned his uneaten greens to the plate and stared at them.

"I know, I know, you can't talk about it. Just tell me"—I gently elbowed him—"is it something I'll hear about on the news one day?"

His jaw flexed, and he reached for the wine, taking a gulp before turning hard eyes on me. This was a look I'd witnessed a few times. Only once before had he leveled it at me. I figured he developed it during his time as a Capitol Hill police officer or maybe during his FBI training. Either way, it wasn't a look I cared for; I found it intimidating . . . as I'm sure he meant it to be.

"Hey, don't get mad. I'm just kidding around. Relax. Sheesh." I scooped up a mouthful of fish and shoveled it in.

He let out a heavy sigh. "It's going to come out soon enough. I'm surprised they've been able to keep a lid on it so far."

I swallowed. "What's going to come out?"

"Senator Harper didn't die of an innocent heart attack."

The fork clattered across my plate. "What do you mean—he didn't die of a heart attack? *Of course, he did.* I was *there.* I even spoke with one of my cardio PAs. He said on rare occasions, the pacemaker malfunctions. In Harper's case, his heart must have gone out of whack, and the pacemaker wasn't working properly to slow it down, put it back into a proper rhythm . . . "

Those hard eyes softened into the sweet mocha I preferred. He shook his head sympathetically.

"What? I was *there!*" I pounded my fist on the counter with each word.

Mike pushed off the stool and paced away, running a hand through his hair.

"What is it?" My stomach turned into a hard knot; my earlier ardor deflated like one of Brady's footballs. "Mike? Tell me . . . please."

"I shouldn't . . . but not doing so is like leaving a lamb to slaughter. And you'll find out soon enough." He turned back to me. "Harper's pacemaker was hacked. Someone purposely put it into overdrive, pumping the heart way too fast for the circulatory system to keep up."

"What do you mean *hacked?* How can you hack a piece of equipment in your body? I don't understand. And what does it have to do with you?"

"Technically, anything with firmware can be subject to hacking. People really have no idea how vulnerable we've become by being so reliant on all this technology."

The clouds of confusion cleared. Mike worked in the cybercrimes department. "They brought you home for this case.

Harper's death." Then it hit me. I was the last person to see Harper alive. "Oh-my-gawd." I think my eyes widened to the size of baseballs. "Am I a suspect?"

Mike's mouth flattened and his jaw flexed again.

"Damn it! Is that why you were so hot to get together with me? What's your role in all this?" I jumped off my stool so quickly it fell to the floor with a resounding whack. "Are the police outside my door right now? Did they send you in to divert me so I can't escape? Are you here to take me in?" The questions sliced between us.

"Whoa, K.C., calm down."

"*Calm down!* Are you nuts? *Never, ever,* in the history of the world, did two words"—I held my fingers in a V formation—"do the exact opposite of what they were meant to do. You, tell me right now"—I pointed those two fingers at him—"Michael Finnegan, *what is going on?* Or, you can march your prevaricating ass out of my door for good. And you can deliver a message to your FBI friends: I had *nothing* to do with Harper's death! *I* tried to save him. If they don't believe me—they can . . . they can . . . talk to my lawyer . . . and . . . and stick it up their pipe stack and smoke on that."

Occasionally, like the volatile Irish ancestors on my mother's side, I talked with my hands when I got excited or upset. It's a habit I tried to curb, however on this occasion, I'll admit, the arms were flying in all directions as my voice continued its rise to train whistle decibels. "*Stop laughing at me. This isn't funny!*"

"Stick it up their pipe stack?"

I folded my arms and delivered a death glare that would quell a stampeding bull.

Mike's smile wilted. "You're right. It isn't funny. Technically, you were the last person to see the senator alive. As far as I know, the police are not lying in wait outside your door. But they will undoubtedly talk with you further."

"Am I a suspect?"

"I wouldn't say you are a suspect. You're what they call a 'person of interest.'"

I righted the stool and sat. "I'm a lawyer, Mike, I know what a person of interest is. Why haven't they come to me already?"

"I don't know."

"Do you think they're trying to build a case against me?"

He clasped his hands behind his back and shrugged.

"What's your role in all this?"

"We're following a number of leads. Since I used to work for the Capitol Police, I'll liaison with them and D.C.P.D. cybercrimes unit."

"Who's in charge? D.C.? FBI? Capitol Police?"

Mike sighed. "It's a joint investigation, but since it's a senator, technically the FBI. . . . "

I waited for Mike to elaborate but was met with continued silence. Pushing my heels, I rotated the seat around to face away from him. "What do you know about the lead detective at D.C.P.D. or Capitol Police?"

"Capitol Police is good, he's a younger investigator but graduated top of his class. Now, D.C.P.D.—" Mike hesitated. "He's a twenty-year veteran on the force. His name is John Shinebocker. He's methodical and calculating."

Mike's distorted reflection refracted off the stainless steel microwave door. "In other words, I'd better get my lawyer when he comes knocking on my door."

"Yes."

"What do they know about our relationship?"

"D.C.? Very little." Mike climbed onto the chair next to mine. "The FBI . . . "

I rolled my eyes and nodded. My part in returning the stolen masterpiece had been haphazard. Though no one admitted to what exactly happened, the FBI wasn't stupid, they knew I'd orchestrated the havey-cavey return on behalf of a reluctant client. No doubt, I remained on the FBI's radar. "I'm surprised you risked coming over. Or was it to assure yourself that I had nothing to do with Harper's bizarre death? I'm not going to find bugs all over my home, am I?"

He gave a stricken look.

"I'm sorry," I said. "That was out of line."

"K.C. . . . I came because . . . "

"I know." I waved him off. I knew, in my heart, Mike cared deeply for me. Hell, maybe he even loved me. He had tried to help with the painting fiasco and, just like now, had put himself in an ethically questionable situation to ensure my safety. "If I let anyone know what you've told me, they'll fire you."

"Maybe bring me up on charges."

"Shit."

"Precisely."

I pushed the plate away, my appetite, along with my libido, long gone. He laid a hand over mine, but I slid it into my lap.

"I'm sorry," he said.

Now I knew why I'd been feeling anxious. It was my intuition forewarning me. Since *I* knew I hadn't murdered the senator, the question that remained uppermost in my mind was—who did? And why?

"Want to tell me what's squirrelling around in that noggin of yours?"

"Mike, while I appreciate the risk you've taken in telling me all this, I think it's best if we don't discuss the case further. At least, not until after the police question me. I don't want either one of us to . . . have to cover up more than we already are."

"K.C.—"

"I'm serious. I know this is the second time you've gone against protocol to warn me. And I appreciate it. I really do . . . "

"Okay, okay. I get it. Why don't you tell me about your fundraiser last night? When are you going to take me to one of them?"

"You're not allowed. It was a political fundraiser," I said absentmindedly.

"Oh? Tell me who was there."

"A shitload of rich people and a bunch of lobbyists."

Mike shifted. "Want me to tell you who I saw on my flight home?"

"Who?"

"Michael J. Fox."

"He testified on the Hill today."

"Oh. Did you see him?"

"I saw the crowd surrounding him," I replied in a deadened voice with a finger at my temple.

Mike pushed his plate back. "I should go."

"Yeah. . . . No. . . . Wait. I'm sorry. It's . . . "

"Hey." He pushed my chin up. "I get it. We'll do this another time."

My heart and head pulled in two directions. As much as I wanted him to stay, I couldn't keep my brain from swirling around this toilet bowl of ramifications. There was no way I'd be able to carry on a normal conversation with Mike.

Yet . . .

He didn't wait for my answer. He put his unfinished meal by the sink and went to the front hall closet. I met him there, pausing his fingers as they buttoned the overcoat with my own.

His forehead leaned against mine. "I hate seeing you mixed up in this."

"Don't worry. I plan to extricate myself from it as soon as humanly possible. Or . . . as soon as the police decide to question me again."

His lips came down on mine. "Take care of yourself, K.C.

Call me if the police show up."

"After I call my lawyer."

"Right."

Chapter Six

MIKE

Mike's work phone rang as he drove out of Karina's parking lot. "Agent Finnigan."

"I got it."

"Both? The phone and her computer?"

"Yes, both. I'm searching the materials now."

"I'm sure there is no way she's involved in this. K.C. calls a USB drive 'that flashy thingy.' The thought of her being a hacker is laughable."

"Are you having second thoughts?"

"No. I want her cleared, ASAP."

"The powers-that-be don't believe she's the hacker."

"Then what?" Mike slowed to a stop at a red light.

"She's an innocent bystander. But no one has ruled out the possibility she's a conspirator. Part of the plan to make sure he died."

"Did you find anything in her bank statements or phone records?"

His colleague paused. "Not yet."

"Because there's nothing to find, *damnit!* What's her motive?"

"He voted against the bill."

Mike slammed his fist against the steering wheel. "That's thinner than fishing line, Amir, and you know it. Lots of congressmen voted against the bill. Why Harper?"

"He flip-flopped. Maybe she took it personally."

"Come on," Mike protested.

"Mike . . ." Amir's deep voice skated over the phone lines. "You're too close to it. I've worked with you four years now, if you didn't know this woman, you'd be all over her. As it is, your training and gut is the reason we're doing this off the books. And I'm going to give you a piece of advice—your feelings for her are compromising your judgement."

"You're wrong. It's *because* I know her. I know she had nothing to do with this."

"If you're right, then nothing will show up on her devices and you can submit the findings to Leon in the morning. Are you sure you got out clean? She didn't suspect anything?"

"It's clean. I did it while she was in the bathroom." A horn blared behind him, and Mike accelerated through the green light. "But I'm telling you, the death threat I sent around earlier today . . . I've got a gut feeling about it."

"And Leon wants you to continue following that lead. But you know you won't have access to this part of the investigation. McGill will keep you in the loop only as much as he needs you to remain close to this woman."

Mike cursed under his breath. "Amir . . . "

"What?"

"Just . . . call me if you find something."

"I will. And seeing as we didn't have a search warrant for this information, we both know it would be inadmissible. But I warned you, when you asked me to do this, that if I found anything, I'd have to tell Leon."

"You owe me," Mike reminded him.

Amir let out a heavy breath. "You sure you want to call in that chip on this?"

"If you find something . . . yes. If not, then you still owe me one."

"Fine. If I find something . . . you get one hour to warn her to get a lawyer."

The line went dead and Mike pulled the Bluetooth out of his ear, tossing it none too gently into the cup holder. He had to consciously unlock his jaw and loosen his grip on the wheel. He felt like a heel. No . . . he felt like a piece of shit. But it was better that he did the dirty work. Otherwise, the FBI would get a search warrant and send in a team to tear up her apartment and her office. He'd been part of a team that did this sort of thing. It wasn't pretty, even worse now that everyone had a phone and could record it. Standing by and watching it done to K.C.—that he couldn't stomach.

Amir wouldn't find anything. Mike would take the lack of evidence to Leon, and she'd be none the wiser.

The reasoning and justifications for invading her privacy didn't make him feel any better.

Chapter Seven

Traffic crawled into the underground parking garage as each vehicle was sniffed by a K9 unit and the undercarriage examined with a mirror. I arrived forty-five minutes early and idled in line for ten before pulling forward.

"I need to see your I.D., invitation, and please pop your trunk, ma'am."

I followed the officer's instructions and waited patiently for the team to inspect my vehicle. It seemed to be taking a while for the guy with my I.D. to return, and I tensed with trepidation. Two vehicles ahead of me had been pulled off to the side and searched by hand. Knowing what I knew, it wouldn't surprise me if D.C. police flagged my name.

"Okay, ma'am, you can move forward." He handed my documents through the window.

"Thanks, officer." The car rolled forward, and I released the breath I'd been holding. Security was amped up. The mirror check didn't surprise me; however, the dogs had been unexpected.

Stepping out of the elevator, I was greeted with another line. A large green tent had been set up for security, and the crowd slowly shuffled along, placing purses, coats, wallets, keys, etc. on the x-ray belt and patiently waiting their turn to walk through the metal detectors. Police and Secret Service presence could be seen everywhere. I hovered close to one of the kerosene heaters, warming my hands. Winter continued to hold the northeast in its tight grip, even though today was the first official day of Spring.

As I stepped out of the tent, a Lincoln Town Car pulled up and Congressman Finley exited. Secret Service directed him up the stairs, bypassing all security measures. The Town Car drove off and a black GMC Denali took its place, likely another VIP circumventing security. I followed the rest of the crowd up the Cathedral's stone steps and again handed my I.D. and invitation over inside the door. I made it through the gauntlet unscathed and was directed by an usher to sit anywhere in the unreserved section. The front third of the seats were roped off with 'Reserved' signs. An usher directed Congressman Finley to a row in the roped area. I found a place halfway down on the left side with a decent view of the pulpit.

The building hummed with quiet discussions among the mourners, while next to me, a pair of young twenty-somethings madly texted on their phones, possibly to each other. I got out my phone in time to see Henderson Carroll strolling down the aisle. Surreptitiously, I snapped a picture of the handsome, silver-haired news commentator as he approached my row. Latesha was going to love this. The photo came out well, and I texted it to her with the message:

Here you go. Henderson Carroll. Is he famous enough?

"Excuse me." Someone tapped my shoulder.

I glanced up to find one of the ushers. "Yes?"

"Are you Karina Cardinal?"

"Yes."

"Come with me, please."

Uh-oh. This is it.

I wondered if the police would stake out the senator's memorial, lying in wait for me. But, really, how tacky. It's not as though they didn't know where I lived. They could have come to my home. I didn't want to make a scene, so gathering my things, I excused my way past the half dozen attendees who'd followed me into the row. However, instead of guiding me up the aisle as I'd expected, the usher continued forward past a dozen rows of reserved seating. We finally stopped at the fourth row from the front.

"But, I don't think . . . " My eyes connected with Senator Harper's Chief of Staff, Sandy Harding.

Her shoulder length, silvery blond hair was styled, per usual, in its classically chic bob, and wearing a black suit, she fit right in with the rest of Washington's mourners. However, the wrinkles around her eyes stood out dramatically due to lack-of-sleep hollows and red rims. She waved and pointed to the empty seat next to her.

"Thank you." I maneuvered past the senator from Kentucky, his wife, and a woman I didn't recognize. "Senator, nice to see you. Excuse me, pardon, excuse me," I muttered, bumping into knees and trying my best not to sink my stilettos onto someone's foot. Finally, I reached my destination and, draping my coat over the back of the seat, met the steel blue gaze of Henderson Carroll. He nodded, I returned his nod, and sank down into the chair.

"Sandy, my condolences. Harper was a good man," I said in muted tones. Sandy had been with Harper since his first election.

"Yes, he was. I understand you were with him when it happened."

My eyes darted side-to-side. So far, my name hadn't gotten into the press regarding the senator's collapse, though I was sure my statement was public record. However, if his death was murder, and the police started questioning me, it wouldn't take long before the bloodhounds were on my tail. I shifted and gave a quick nod.

"What can you tell—"

My head rotated, I gave her a hard stare and mouthed the word, "Later." With a slight tilt of my chin, I indicated the news anchor behind me.

No dummy, Sandy clamped her mouth shut.

"How is Elise taking it?" I arranged the handbag at my feet.

"She's devastated."

No surprise there. "Any ideas who'll take his seat until the next election?"

She shrugged. "I think if Elise showed interest, the governor would appoint her. Otherwise, my guess is the lieutenant governor."

I nodded. The right front row stood empty, waiting for Elise Harper and her family. Two more seats on the left also remained unoccupied. Guests continued to pour into the church, including a few Hollywood darlings active in politics, diplomats, and the current editor of *The Washington Post*. Latesha was right, the D.C. elite were turning out in droves for the event. Flowers covered the high altar, and a large color photo of Senator Harper, in his late twenties and handsomely sporting a Navy uniform, sat on a stand, front and center. A choir, in dark robes, waited quietly in their anterior pews.

Finally, almost twenty minutes past ten, the vice president and his wife arrived, taking the two seats on the left. Then Elise, her two children, their spouses, and three grandchildren came in through a side door. Ponderously, the congregation rose to its feet. Elise wore a black dress, pumps, and a black hat. A widow's veil covered her features, undoubtedly concealing exhausted, red-rimmed eyes. The presiding bishop took the pulpit, signaling the beginning of the service with a congregational hymn.

Half a dozen speakers got up to memorialize the senator, or

to read passages from the Bible. A few shared touching and humorous stories about Harper, but it was his daughter Connie who brought the congregation to tears when she read her father's favorite poem, *The Tyger*, by William Blake. Elise's shoulders shook with grief. Poor Connie could barely finish; her brother came to her aid escorting his weeping sister back to the family.

Over an hour after it began, and a pocketful of tissues later, the memorial came to its conclusion. Music rose to a crescendo, echoing around the flying buttresses and permeating the deepest corners of the magnificent limestone walls. The vice president was escorted by Secret Service out the side door, while Senator Harper's family filed down the long aisle behind the bishop.

Like the rest of the congregation, I began gathering my things. My movements were halted by Sandy's firm hand on my forearm. A silent conversation passed between us. I put my purse back down on the seat, and shared small talk with those around me, speaking inanities—how tragic the death, the beautiful touching service. Sandy introduced Henderson Carroll, and we talked about his upcoming documentary on the conflict in the Middle East. We stepped aside to allow those in our row to slide past and exit onto the aisle. Henderson bid us adieu, and we were finally alone. I followed Sandy's lead, retaking my seat.

She cut straight to the chase. "Tell me what happened."

I recounted an edited version of that awful walk in the tunnels.

"So you believe it was a heart attack."

"I'm no expert, but that's what it looked like to me." I didn't mention the pacemaker, assuming Sandy knew. "Why do you ask?"

"Something's up." She glanced around before lowering her voice. "The police came to the office."

My breath caught. "What did they want?"

"They wanted the senator's agenda for the past three months, the call logs, and asked if there had been any new death threats."

"Do all threats still go to the FBI?"

"Yes."

"Has the senator received anything new lately?"

Her mouth turned into a grim line. "Not this month, but there is this one guy who's been sending threatening emails every few months."

"Death threats?"

She nodded. "He spouts white supremacist garbage. It started when the senator voted against the Muslim immigration ban. I know of at least five other Senate offices that got similar ones."

"Was that all?"

"They questioned all the staff members."

"About what?"

"If they knew of any enemies the senator had."

I couldn't help the snort that slipped out.

Sandy nodded. "I know. Right? It's not as though Harper was dirty, but we *all* know, you don't get to his position without making some enemies. I mean, you don't even have to cross the aisle. There are some Republicans that are probably glad to see Harper gone because he was not conservative enough."

"Did you implicate anyone?"

"And commit career suicide? Heavens, no."

"Did the police want anything else?"

"As a matter of fact, his cell phone. Apparently, he didn't have it on him."

"Oh." I reached for my purse. Then stopped myself. Harper's phone wasn't in there. I'd left it on my kitchen counter. Only . . . I couldn't recall seeing it by my phone charger where I'd left it on Monday. "That's . . . unfortunate."

Sandy must not have noticed my odd behavior because she moved on to another topic. "The medical examiner hasn't released the body yet."

"What? Why not? How do you know?"

"Elise told me. She can't make funeral plans until the ME releases the body."

"What does she want to do once it's released? Will he go back to Michigan? Arlington Cemetery?"

"There's a family plot in Michigan."

"I see." I glanced around to make sure no one was in hearing distance. "Sandy . . . before he passed, Senator Harper told me he was working on a new bill. He said it would be better than S46. Sounded like he was calling in favors. Do you know what that was all about?"

She frowned. "Only a little bit. Christy could tell you more. The senator was playing this one close to his chest, but I believe she was working on language. I know he was talking to folks on the House side."

"Really? Who?"

"I want to say Finley."

"Finley?" I frowned. "Are you sure? Those two have never been friends."

"Not positive. Like I said, Christy knows more about it. Why don't you give her a call? Although, now he's gone . . . I'm not sure what it'll be worth. If it's not already on the floor, it's dead in the water. Right now, I've got to keep the day-to-day operations running. Basically, we are in a holding pattern until someone else is appointed."

"Will you stay?"

"If it's Elise . . . yes. She and I have been friends since I joined Harper's office. She could do it. She's smart and has been helping Harper win ever since he first ran for mayor. If not . . . " She shrugged.

"Where will you go?"

"I don't know. There's always someone on the Hill looking for good staff."

"You've been on the Senate side for what—twenty years?"

"Nineteen."

"There will be opportunities in the private sector. It pays more."

"Maybe."

I patted her arm. "You don't have to make a decision today. If you decide to move into the private sector, give me a call. I'll throw your name around in some circles that might be interested."

"Thanks, Karina. That's kind. In the meantime . . ." She got to her feet and, again, I followed. "I think it's time I headed out. Are you going to the reception at the Congressional Country Club?" She drew on a glove.

"No . . ." I slid an arm into my coat. "I need to get back to the office. I'll reach out to Christy in a few days. See if there's anything I can do to help." We wandered up the empty aisle.

"I'll let her know to expect your call."

"Thanks. Please tell Elise—" A pair of men in dark suits loitered near the entrance to the Cathedral and seemed intent on the two of us. My heart sank.

"Tell Elise?"

My attention returned to Sandy. "Oh, sorry, give Elise my condolences, will you?"

"Of course. Do you recognize those men?"

"No. Do you?"

"The one on the left, balding, glasses. He was one of the detectives who came to the office."

I was afraid of that.

"What was his name? Shinbone? Shabby chic? I can't remember, it was something with a 'Sh.'"

"Take care of yourself, Sandy. I'm going to have a word with the detective and his friend." By now the men were staring exclusively at me. The waiting hadn't been pleasant, but now I could take a proactive role. After all, Sandy had practically told me it was a case of murder.

"Be careful. I didn't care for that Shabby Chic investigator. He rubbed me the wrong way," she said in a low voice and avoided looking at the pair.

"I'll be fine. See you later, Sandy." We hugged, then turning my attention to the pair of cops, I walked directly up to them. "Hello, gentlemen. Were you waiting for me?"

"Why would you ask that?" The younger of the two men shifted. He looked to be in his early thirties, no gray around his temple or fine lines around his eyes. I could tell his barrel chest was a result of the bullet proof vest he wore beneath a black dress shirt.

"Sandy told me you'd been to the office asking questions about the senator . . . his schedule, enemies, death threats. If he died of natural causes, why is a D.C. homicide detective sniffing around his affairs?"

"You ask a lot of questions," the balding detective said, chomping a piece of gum.

"I'm Karina Cardinal, by the way. But, you already knew that . . . didn't you, detective? And you are?"

"Detective Shinebocker." He didn't bother to take the hand I held out.

"Linus Moore, Capitol Police." He shook my hand and with his left removed a business card from his front pocket.

I slipped it into my coat. "What can I do for you, gentlemen?"

Shinebocker snapped his gum. "We'd like you to come down to the station and go over your statement."

I pulled out my cell. "Sure, let me check my schedule. I can come by this afternoon, around four. How would that be?"

Shinebocker uncrossed his arms and he stepped closer, invading my personal space. "How about now?"

"Now is not convenient." I didn't move. Unfortunately for Shinebocker, his intimidation tactic wasn't working in his favor. My stilettos gave me a good three inches on the man. I rolled my lips inward to suppress a smartass grin that would win me no points.

"I'm not asking." Peppermint flavored breath rolled across my face, and he took hold of my bicep. Shinebocker's glasses exaggerated his muddy hazel eyes, and I could see why Sandy had taken him in dislike.

Moore shifted uncomfortably.

"Are you placing me under arrest, Detective?"

"Should I?"

"If you're not placing me under arrest, I suggest you release me. I don't care to be manhandled. If you don't already know, I am a lawyer. I know my rights, and I don't believe the city can afford any sort of scandal... about following protocol... police brutality? Especially one that took place in a House of God." I gave him stare-for-stare.

"Shinebocker," Moore interjected, clearing his throat, "I'm sure we can wait until four."

"Four o'clock. We'll be waiting." He squeezed hard enough to leave bruises and swept out, leaving Moore behind.

I refused to flinch, ignoring the pain. "Since he left so abruptly, perhaps you can tell me which precinct I should come to?"

"Do you have a card? I can email you."

I withdrew the little placard from my purse. "Is there a problem I should know about, Officer Moore?"

"Just don't be late."

"Of course. See you at four."

Chapter Eight

Though I'd kept it together during the interaction with the police, my hands were shaking by the time I made it back to my car. I had to take a few deep breaths to calm myself enough to text my boss. I lied, telling her I was headed over to the reception and probably wouldn't make it into the office today.

City traffic was moderate and I drove aggressively, cutting people off and running a red light; it still took a solid thirty minutes to reach my destination. A sigh of relief escaped me as I entered the comforts of my condo. I didn't bother to take off my coat, dropping my keys and handbag on the hall table as I passed it on the way to the kitchen counter where the phone charger lay.

Sure enough, the senator's phone was nowhere to be seen. I checked around the floor, cabinets, and barstools before expanding my search. For the next half hour, I combed the apartment—searching coat pockets, my purse (multiple times), tables, dressers, dirty laundry, between the couch cushions, front hall closet, and underneath the furniture. My search ended where it began—next to the phone charger.

A distinct memory persisted—the senator's black phone sitting next to my white one as it charged. It was there on Monday night.

"Did I see it on Tuesday?" I said to the empty room.

If I had, I would have dropped it at his office.

"Where the hell did it go?"

I turned in a circle, stopping as my eyes alighted on the large sliding door.

"What night did I wake up to turn on the heat and find the back door open? Monday night?" I drew on a glove and, with two fingers, pulled the glass open. "Do lock picks leave behind evidence? Did I even lock the door that night?"

Being on the fifth floor, I wasn't always vigilant in securing that particular entrance. My sister once suggested putting a broom handle in the track—a good piece of advice I never got around to heeding. An inspection showed a slight scratch along the latch, but I had no way of knowing if it was fresh.

I leaned over the iron railing. The complex decks lined up every other floor, as the apartment layouts varied. I didn't see how someone could free climb from the ground. The apartment complex had six floors. I flipped my body to stare upward. Was it possible to rappel from the rooftop?

Stumbling back into the apartment, I collapsed on the sofa.

"Shit, shit, shit," I mumbled, rocking back and forth. If my currently screaming intuition was correct, someone had broken into my apartment to steal the senator's phone. Someone who knew I'd been at the scene. Someone who knew I must have taken it.

Had I been followed? What was I to do now? If I wasn't a suspect before, I would be now.

My options were limited, and I wasn't sure which one was the best way to keep myself out of jail. There was little doubt 'ole Shitkicker was going to ask about the phone. I could lie and say I knew nothing about it. On the other hand, I simply couldn't remember if I'd mentioned the phone in my statement. Assuming I did, I could feign ignorance and tell them it must have gotten left behind in the tunnel. There was no way in hell the pair would believe my story about it being stolen from my home.

I could call Mike. He'd believe me, but it could put him in a touchy situation. Would his superiors take my word? If someone did rappel onto my deck and break in, it was doubtful they would have been stupid enough to leave behind fingerprints. One question kept rearing its ugly head—why risk breaking into my home, as I slept, to retrieve the phone? What was on that phone?

There was another person I could reach out to. He owed me a favor. . . .

I found the Silverthorne Security card with Josh's handwritten cell number in the glass bowl where I tossed random business cards that I hadn't gotten around to inputting into my phone's contact list.

He answered on the third ring. "Go for Joshua."

"Josh, hi! This is Karina Cardinal . . . remember, from a few months ago?"

"I remember."

"I was wondering if you could help me get in touch with Rick."

"He's out of the country right now."

"Oh . . . I see." I chewed my lip.

"Is there something I can do for you?"

"Um . . . well . . . maybe. Is there some way to tell if a lock has been picked?"

"Depends. Using a bump usually damages the pins, a professional lockpick would leave little sign. Maybe some scratches. Look for shiny metal around the lock."

"Okay." I inspected the scratch again. "Listen, have you ever done any rappelling?"

"Yes, ma'am."

"Off of a building?"

"When the occasion warranted."

Needless to say, his answer didn't surprise me. "What signs would I look for? A grappling hook? Holes in the roof, or—"

"Depends. Why do you ask?"

"Uh, research." I pivoted in circles on my tiny back deck.

"Research for what?"

"I mean, asking for a friend."

"Does this have something to do with what happened in January?"

"I don't believe so."

"Do you think someone rappelled off the roof, onto your balcony, and broke into your apartment?"

"Uh . . . " Josh may have dark blond hair and a linebacker physique, but he sure didn't fit into the handsome but stupid stereotype.

"I'm ten minutes away."

"No, really. I don't want to be a bother. If you just tell me what to look for . . . "

"It's no problem. Today is my day off." He hung up.

Ten minutes later, I buzzed Josh in and stood in the open doorway while he made his way up to the fifth floor. He came around the corner wearing dark jeans, boots, and a brown leather jacket. Pretty much the same style of clothes he'd worn when protecting me. He walked with the confidence of a military man and the freshly cut hairstyle only enhanced the impression.

"Josh, you didn't have to come, but since you're here . . . " I waved him into the apartment. "Thank you."

"You think someone came in through the back?" Having been in the apartment before, he didn't hesitate, walking through the foyer, down the short hallway, and into my living room.

I chewed a thumbnail as he inspected the lock and balcony floorboards.

"When do you think it happened?"

"Monday night."

He did the same thing I did earlier, leaned over to look down, then up. Only Josh took it a step further. I caught my breath as he pulled himself up onto the railing and balanced on one foot to inspect the break line where my balcony roof met the brick siding. With cat-like agility, he dropped down, and came back inside.

"What do you think about the lock?"

"It's hard to tell. That scratch does look new, but . . . "

"What about the rappelling?"

"Let's take a field trip to the roof."

"Do you think someone could do it?"

"Undoubtedly."

Joshua bypassed the elevator in favor of the stairs. He held the door for me, but I paused on the threshold. My heartbeat increased and sweat popped out on my upper lip. Two months ago, I'd been attacked in this stairwell. Granted, on the basement floor—still, the hollow echo of steel and concrete affected me at a primal level.

Josh's brows knit with concern. "I can do this alone. Why don't you wait in the apartment?"

Deep breaths filled and exited my lungs. "It's silly, I know. I mean, I should just get over it."

"Have you taken the stairs since that night?"

I shook my head, wiping sweaty hands against my black skirt.

"You're not ready. Go wait in the apartment. It shouldn't take long."

"Will I ever be ready? Am I making it worse by waiting?"

"Not necessarily." His head tilted. "One day, you'll be ready."

"Okay . . . then, I think . . . I think I'll wait."

He nodded and the door closed behind him with a sharp thump. I paced the length of the apartment a dozen times before he returned.

"Did you see anything?" I asked immediately.

"A bent pipe stack, possible scuff marks, and a belay device."

"What's a belay device?"

"A piece of climbing gear used for rappelling. What did he take?"

I pinched the bridge of my nose. "Senator Harper's phone."

"Harper? The senator who just died?"

"That's the one."

"What do you have to do with it?"

"He basically died in my arms as I tried to give him CPR."

Josh let out a low whistle. "Why'd you have the phone?"

"Mine was dead and I couldn't get cell service with his, so I tossed it on the floor along with everything in my handbag. When the paramedics came, I scooped it up by accident," I said, pacing around the kitchen island.

"What's on that phone?"

"No idea. Obviously, someone thinks something important is on there."

"What's the play here?"

I took three more turns around the island. "I think it's time I called my FBI friend."

"The fellow I met in the hallway?"

"The very one." I dialed Mike's number.

To my surprise, he answered, "K.C.? Is that you?"

"Houston, we have a problem."

"Where are you?"

"Home."

"Are the police there?"

"No. Remember the Silverthorne Security guy from a few

months ago?"

"Yes. . . ."

"He's here. And, well, um, do you think you could come over?"

"Tonight?"

"Now?"

"It's important?"

I glanced to Josh's frowning mien. "Yeah, it is."

"Okay. . . . I need to rearrange a few things on my schedule. I'll text you when I'm on the way."

"Thanks." I hung up. "Can you wait for a bit? I'd like you to show Mike what you found."

"No problem." He crossed his arms, planted his feet shoulder width apart, and looked as though he could remain standing in the middle of my living room all night long if need be.

"Why don't you have a seat? Can I get you a drink? I've got coffee, diet soda, orange juice, water . . . "

He took a seat on my couch. "Coffee, please."

An awkward hour of making small talk with Josh passed before Mike arrived.

Chapter Nine

MIKE

K.C., looking elegant in a long black skirt and tall boots, her chestnut mane tamed into a French twist, waited in the doorway with crossed arms.

"What's going on?" Mike leaned forward to kiss her, but she turned away and it landed awkwardly on her ear.

"This isn't a social call. You'd better come in. It involves some explanation."

He frowned and followed her. The scent of fresh coffee hung heavy in the air, and he would have asked for a cup except Karina said, "You remember Joshua?"

All thoughts of coffee vanished as his eyes alighted on the bulky, ex-Navy SEAL and security specialist he'd met in Karina's hallway one January night, not long after she'd been attacked. She'd suffered bruises and a dislocated shoulder. Her explanations for why it happened, who perpetrated the attack, and who hired Silverthorne Security to protect her had been unsatisfying, to say the least. They'd had a fight because Mike knew she'd been withholding information from him. The return of Joshua's presence didn't bode well, and Mike wasn't thrilled to see him here again.

"Agent Finnegan." Joshua gripped Mike's hand.

"What's going on?"

"Shall we sit?" Karina asked.

They stood in the center of her small living room, Karina between the two men, and neither moved to take a seat.

"Okay, so, you remember when we talked on Monday . . . after the senator . . . you know."

Mike nodded and put his hands on his hips.

"Well, I think I told you that I tried to use the senator's phone, but it was locked and I couldn't get cell reception?"

"Vaguely."

"When I was scooping all my worldly goods back into my purse . . . I scooped up the senator's phone by mistake."

Mike's gaze shifted from Joshua to Karina. "And?"

"And it's missing."

His brows knit. "You mean, you lost it?"

"I mean, it's missing." She drew a breath. "I think someone broke into my apartment Monday night and stole it off my kitchen counter."

"You're joking."

Her lips pursed. "I wish I was."

"So what you're telling me, you think someone picked your lock and broke in?" Mike shook his head in disbelief. "You can't get around that floor bolt without using force. Did you forget to slide it down that night?"

"Not the front door." She shook her head. "I think he came in through my balcony. I . . . found it open in the middle of the night."

"What do you mean, you found it open? Why didn't you tell me about this before now?" he snapped.

She crossed her arms defensively. "Initially, I thought I hadn't closed it all the way when I came in from the balcony that night."

Mike's gaze darted from the back door, to K.C., and back to the ex-Navy man. "What does he have to do with it?"

"I asked Josh to check the roof and see if there was any evidence someone rappelled from the roof onto my back deck."

"Jesus." He rubbed the back of his neck.

K.C. grimaced and pressed a finger against her temple. "Josh, can you please take Mike up to the roof and show him what you found?"

"Follow me." Joshua indicated with a tilt of his head.

"Wait, I . . . I think I should go this time."

Joshua gazed down at her. "You sure?"

"No, but I'll give it a try. Can we take the elevator up to the sixth floor first?"

"No problem."

Mike watched their exchange, puzzled, but didn't comment. Once they filed into the elevator, he turned to her. "How was the memorial service?"

"Sad. I sat next to Sandy, Harper's Chief of Staff. She told me D.C. police came to the senator's office yesterday asking questions and requesting his schedule. Sandy thinks there's been foul play. The ME hasn't released his body to the family."

Nobody responded, but he understood K.C.'s message. She wanted to let him know that she had another source of information regarding the senator's death. Its delivery was innocent enough in front of Joshua. The guilt he felt for deceiving her last night remained a little cloud hanging over his head, but so far Amir had found nothing.

They exited and followed Joshua to the stairwell, where he opened the door for K.C. Mike came to a halt as she stopped short, and he waited for her to enter.

"You go first, Joshua." She gripped the door frame, and when she looked back, her face had paled and a sheen of sweat covered it. "Can you cover the rear?"

Mike's frown deepened; obviously she hadn't taken the stairs since that night in January. "Right behind you, K.C."

Breathing deep, she counted backward from ten. "Okay, let's do this."

Joshua climbed a few steps and glanced back.

She remained standing in the doorway, staring up at the concrete and steel incline. Mike saw her mouth the words, *"One, two, three."*

Suddenly, she took off, barreling past a shocked Joshua as her heels pounded up the stairs. Mike bolted after her, shoving past Navy boy in time to see her grip the metal door handle and heave with all her might to stumble into the blessed sunshine. A tepid breeze drifted across Mike's cheeks as he exited, and found K.C. bent at the waist, hands on knees, panting like she'd sprinted a marathon.

"You all right?" He stroked her back.

Her head bounced up and down.

"It'll be easier next time," Joshua commented drily, walking past the pair.

"Sure, sure." She drew in a final breath and straightened. "Okay, where are we headed?"

Joshua led the way to the northwestern side of the building and stood in front of a set of three pipe stacks.

"I figure he tied on to this center steel pipe, it's thicker than the other two. You'll find indents where the rope rubbed off some of the grime. And see that black metal piece on the ground right there, with the loop? It's part of a broken belay device. Considering the location, the intruder probably dropped it bagging up his gear. I didn't touch it in case you can get a print off it. And if you look down here . . . " He headed toward the side of the building.

K.C. took stance a cautionary ten feet back from the ledge. Joshua waved her closer, but she shook her head. "I'm fine where I am."

Mike rubbed K.C.'s arm as he passed.

"I'd wager those are scuff marks."

The FBI agent leaned over the ledge to see the black marks Joshua indicated. Mike had never suffered from a fear of heights, but it was still disconcerting to lean over and look down the six floors. The knee-high brick wall didn't exactly provide a sense of safety. It would be far too easy to lean forward, get off balance and . . .

"Climbing shoes are made high in carbon," an unruffled Joshua explained, "to provide a bit of stick to help ascend. But they tend to leave behind scuffs."

Mike went down on one knee, gripped the low brick wall, and leaned further out. "How fast do you think he could have done it?"

"Assuming she didn't lock the back door? Five minutes. If he had to pick the lock, add another minute or two." Joshua calmly described the break-in as if reading a soup recipe.

Mike's eyes darted around the rooftop, assessing the situation. "And, assuming he knew where the phone was."

"She left it on the counter." Joshua shrugged. "He got lucky."

He nodded. "How long to ascend?"

"I could make it up from her balcony in under two minutes. You can probably get rope fibers off the roof line on her balcony. Though I don't know that they'll tell you anything. Climbing rope can be bought online or at a sporting goods store."

"Why risk it? She could have woken up at any moment. There would have been other opportunities to grab the phone when she wasn't home."

For a moment, Joshua didn't answer. When he spoke, it was in a dispassionate voice that sent chills down Mike's spine. "Maybe he didn't want to risk her passing it to the police. And . . . he was probably prepared to deal with the possibility that she'd wake."

Mike glanced over at K.C. to see how she received the news. Her face, no longer red from her mad dash up the stairs, paled, and she rubbed her arms as if chilled.

Mike stared fiercely at her. "I have to call this in. If what you say is true . . ."

Her Adam's apple bobbed as she gulped and nodded.

"Come on, let's go back to your apartment."

Both the men stared at K.C. She seemed to go a little green around the gills.

"You look like you're about to vomit," Mike observed.

"I might."

"Better to do it up here than in the elevator." Joshua had the temerity to grin.

She made a rude gesture and stomped her way back to the emergency exit.

Chapter Ten

Josh had been right, it was easier on descent. But that may have been because I was far more freaked out by the trained assassin who broke into my apartment to steal the senator's phone than memories of an old attack.

Josh, claiming an appointment, put on his coat to leave, and I walked with him to the door.

"So you're abandoning me?" I tried to say it in a teasing manner, but in my current mood, the joke fell flat.

"Cardinal . . . " He shook his head. "I don't know what you've gotten yourself into . . . but it's . . . "

"I know." I rubbed my temples.

"If you need security, call me."

"Sure, sure."

"I'm serious." His blue eyes pierced me. "Don't wait until it's too late."

"Uh . . . thanks. But, I'm not sure I can afford you."

"We owe you one." He started to walk away, then paused. "You keep your eye on the FBI when they arrive. Your boyfriend there might be concerned about your interests, but you can be damn sure his boss isn't. You should consider getting a lawyer."

I weighed Josh's words as I made another pot of coffee. Was he right? Whose side was Mike on? Even if he believed me . . . would his FBI boss? Was I being foolish and naïve to believe I could handle this myself?

Mike made his call, and thirty minutes later, my apartment was crawling with G-men. Mike introduced them as they arrived, but it had been a blur. There was the Asian forensic guy dusting for prints—of which I doubted there would be any—and a short, thickset guy was out on my balcony tweezing rope fibers from the roof. Finally, a redhead with trendy, black glasses basically snooped through my apartment with a beeping piece of equipment. I followed him around like a faithful dog. Frankly, I felt more violated by the FBI than my secret intruder . . . except for the fact that I doubted the FBI planned to put a bullet in my head if they didn't find what they wanted.

About fifteen minutes after the first crowd arrived, Amir entered. His was the one name that stuck because of his handsome, dark Arabic look and the disturbing, penetrating stare he leveled at me upon arrival. He carried a heavy-duty laptop and requested to see my phone and computer.

"Why?" I asked.

"I need to . . . check to see if a tracking app or malware has been uploaded."

I was beginning to think Josh had been right about the lawyer when my doorbell rang . . . again. "I'll be with you in a minute. Right now, I have to find out what's behind door number two," I mumbled, pulling it open.

I should really remember to check the peephole first.

Standing on the other side was my kindly, but eccentric, neighbor, Mrs. Thundermuffin. Her normally white hair had been recently dyed varying shades of purple, from lavender at the scalp to a deep amethyst at the tips. She wore a sparkly red leather pants suit with fringe dangling off the arms that would have made Dolly Parton proud. It fit her tiny frame as though she'd been sewn into it. Although, the costume seemed incomplete without a cowboy hat.

"Hello, Mrs. Thundermuffin. What can I do for you?" I pulled the door partially closed and stood tall in the opening to block her view.

She rose to her tiptoes trying to peer around me. "Karina, dear, I've been hearing all sorts of noises and seen men in suits bringing up black cases. Do you know what that's all about?"

No way was I going to tell the complex's biggest gossip what the FBI was doing in my apartment. In the inimitable words of Dr. Seuss, I thought up a lie and thought it up quick. "Yes, I'm . . . I'm considering installing . . . surround sound."

Her eyes widened. "Really? Did the board approve that?"

"It's in the initial stages. I haven't made my decision, and it comes with sound proofing." I winked and whispered, "But it all depends on the cost." A crash of broken glass met my ears. My shoulders stiffened. "I'd better find out what's going on. It was good seeing you, Mrs. Thundermuffin. Love the new hairstyle," I said, closing the door before she could ask more questions.

Mike and Red were in the guest bathroom picking up pieces of a glass container I used to store cotton balls.

"Sorry," the young agent sheepishly murmured.

"The FBI can reimburse you for that," Mike grunted.

I sighed, "Forget it. What exactly did you think might be in my guest bathroom?"

"He's checking for bugs."

"You mean like electronic monitoring? Really? Do you think that's necessary? I thought you and Josh determined my intruder did a quick in-and-out job. Do you think he took the time to plant a bunch of bugs around my apartment?"

Mike ran a hand through his short, dark, naturally wavy hair. "We want to be thorough."

"Fine. Just tell me how much longer you think this will take."

"Another hour? I'm not sure. We're waiting for the agent in charge to arrive."

I glanced at my watch, three-fifteen. There was no way I'd make it to my meeting with 'ole shiny head and Moore. "Red, you mind if I speak to Agent Finnegan for a minute?"

He dumped the last of the large glass pieces into the wastebasket and shuffled past me.

"Have you contacted the D.C. cops?" I asked Mike.

"No. We're not ready to read them in."

I mashed my lips together. "I'm afraid you're going to have to do it sooner, rather than later."

"Why would that be?" he said in measured tones.

"I'm supposed to go over my statement with them at four." Mike's mouth pinched, and his brows turned down as I spoke. "There's no way I'll make it if you're still here for the next hour. I need to call them and tell them why I won't be there."

"Who were you supposed to meet with?" he asked.

"Detective Shinebocker and a Capitol Police officer, Moore."

"Were you planning to take counsel with you?"

"Uh . . . it was on my to-do list."

Mike's frown deepened. "I'll call Shinebocker. You'd best call a lawyer."

My lawyer, Jessica Williams, a stylish and beautiful African-American with the height to rival any man over six feet, arrived within ten minutes.

"Either you ran every red light or you had a police escort to get here so quickly," I said, ushering her into ground zero.

"Neither, I was in the neighborhood." She plunked her designer handbag on the kitchen island. "How long have they been here?"

"About an hour."

She clicked her tongue in disapproval. "You should have

called sooner."

Chastised, I glanced away. "Sorry."

"You, there." She pointed to Amir, who was at the dining room table with my laptop. "What are you doing?"

"Checking her computer for malware."

"Unless you have a warrant, you need to stop. Now. Immediately! Unplug that cable."

"Just a minute, I'm trans—" He didn't finish his sentence as Jessica pulled the USB cord that had been attached between the two computers.

"You don't have a warrant, and anything you've accessed from my client's computer will be inadmissible. Understand."

"She gave us permission." Amir stood.

"I did *not* give *you* permission. I asked why you needed it, and then was distracted before I said yes or no. As a matter of fact, the computer was on the far side of the bed, in my room."

"Everybody—*excuse me, agents!*" Jessica snapped her fingers. "Stop what you're doing. And someone please tell me who's the senior agent here."

All eyes turned to Mike. He and Asian forensic guy, who'd just returned from a trip to the roof, were in my kitchen talking about the evidence he'd bagged up there.

"That would be me. Agent Mike Finnegan. You may not remember, we met once."

"Yes, I remember. Please have your agents sit at the dining room table while I have a brief discussion with my client."

"K.C. invited us in to investigate."

Mike's familiarity with me had Jessica's gaze flicking between the two of us. "And I'm advising my client to put a hold on that invitation for a few minutes. It's either the table or the hall. Your choice," she said in her no-nonsense way.

Mike's face flushed, whether with embarrassment or anger, I didn't know.

Amir sank down. Red cleared his throat and sat across from Amir. The rest followed suit, with Mike bringing up the rear.

Sorry, I mouthed.

"D.C.P.D. is on the way," Mike murmured as he passed by. The chair creaked as he folded his frame into it.

"Don't move," Jessica ordered, scooping up my computer. I trailed her into my bedroom. She glanced around, strode past the bed, into the walk-in closet, and directed me to close the door behind us.

"This will have to do. Now, give me the quickest version of what's going on."

I told her about Senator Harper, my discussion with Sandy, and the missing cell phone.

"The phone is bad. If you weren't a suspect, you are now."

"What about the break-in?"

She changed the subject. "What's your relationship with Agent Finnegan?"

I swallowed. "It's complicated."

"You're sleeping with him."

"No . . . we're old friends."

"Friends with benefits?"

"We're dating. It's new." I wrung my hands. "Our relationship is snailing its way into new territory. Honestly, we both want it, but I think we're both a little scared to do it. I suppose we don't want to screw up the friendship. You know what I mean?"

Jessica checked her watch, and I realized I may have shared too much. Clearing my throat, I gave her the short answer, "No, we haven't slept together . . . yet."

"Did he tell you about the investigation?"

Oh, I do not want to implicate Mike. I pinched the bridge of my nose.

"You have a bad habit of covering for the people you care

about. I noticed that on our last case."

This time, I changed the subject. "The D.C. Police are on the way. They wanted to go over the statement I gave after Harper . . . uh . . . after the incident."

She gave me an irritated stare. "When, exactly, were you planning on phoning me? From a jail cell?"

"I was hoping it wouldn't go that far."

"Did you mention the phone in your statement?"

"I—I can't remember. It was a blur. I was traumatized." I squeezed my eyes shut, desperately trying to remember. "Is it better or worse if I mentioned the phone?"

Jessica shook her head. "I don't know. But don't worry, I'm here now." She patted my shoulder. "C'mon, I have to assess what they've done."

The agents were still sitting around the table, whispering amongst themselves. Their murmurs came to an immediate halt when Jessica and I entered the room.

"Gentlemen, what can you tell me about the break-in?" She positioned herself at the head of the table, leaning casually against the back of the chair.

Asian guy and thickset, fire plug guy exchanged side glances and looked to Mike. He gave a swift nod.

Mr. Fireplug leaned forward. "There are signs the lock was tampered with, a fresh scratch. I pulled fibers from the balcony that may be rope fiber, but we won't know until the labs come back. As for fingerprints"—he shook his head—"either he wore gloves or wiped everything down."

"What about the stuff on the roof?" I asked.

"We bagged the belay device and took samples of the scuff marks," Asian guy replied.

"So there *is* evidence of a break-in?" my lawyer prodded.

Nobody spoke.

Jessica planted her palms on the dining table and towered

above the men. "Do I need to file a report with Alexandria P.D. and have them sweep the crime scene?"

Inwardly, I cringed. Two months ago, I'd deceived an Alexandria detective in order to cover up for someone I cared about. Jessica was right, I didn't always use my better judgement when it came to friends and family. The detective never found out that I'd fibbed, but . . . he wasn't stupid. He knew I wasn't telling the whole story. Offhand, I couldn't recall his name; his doppelgänger was Laurence Fishburne, and I'd nicknamed him Morpheus. I doubted Morpheus would be happy or cooperative if he was the detective assigned to my case.

Mike cleared his throat. "We believe there is evidence of a break-in."

"Has anyone checked the camera feeds?" I piped in.

"Amir will acquire and review them."

My doorbell rang.

"I'll get that." This time I remembered the peephole, and I didn't like what stood on the other side. Mrs. Thundermuffin was back and she'd brought a friend—my weird down-the-hall neighbor, Jasper, who housed a small reptile farm in his apartment. I cracked the door open a few inches.

"Jasper, Mrs. Thundermuffin . . . what can I do for you?"

An albino ball python draped around Jasper's neck was slowly sliding its way down his right arm. "Mrs. T said you were getting surround sound. I just got a new sixty-inch flat screen, and I'd be interested in beefing up my system."

"Uh, sure." I watched in fascination as the python moved its head toward Mrs. Thundermuffin's shoulder—the tongue flicking along the red leather.

Mrs. Thundermuffin subtly stepped away. The snake followed.

"I was hoping I could talk to one of your guys about it. And Mrs. T may be interested as well."

"Yes, Jasper here has taken the time to explain the value of an excellent sound system." She sidestepped the inquisitive snake again.

You've got to be kidding me. I gave myself a mental head smack.

"Can we come in?" Jasper asked. Rearranging his reptile friend, he stepped forward.

The snake transferred its interest toward me. "Jasper, you're a nice guy and all, but . . . my apartment isn't pet friendly when it comes to the slithering kind." Jasper stepped back, and I felt only a little guilty about being so abrupt. Meanwhile, the snake's head bobbed upward, giving me the evil eye, as though it understood my insult. "Sorry. This . . . uh . . . isn't really the best time. Why don't I tell them to stop by your apartment when they're done? How about—"

Three men came around the corner, and if I'd had the technology to beam myself to another planet, I would have done it. Leading the charge was Shinebocker, followed by Moore and a handsome black man in a gray suit that I didn't recognize.

"Well, Princess, here we are." Shinebocker chomped his gum as he spoke.

My neighbors stared at the trio with interest.

"Gentlemen." I gave a stiff smile. "Did you ride together so you could take the carpool lane?" Sarcasm came much too naturally as a reaction to Shinebocker.

Immediately, I regretted the snarky comment, because it only sought to fuel Mrs. Thundermuffin's curiosity—I could see her faded, yet shrewd gaze dart back and forth through the group—and 'ole Shiney's face fell into a scowl.

Shinebocker eyed my neighbors up and down. "What's all this? Is the circus in town?" he said in a snide tone that made me want to slug him.

Mrs. Thundermuffin's mouth dropped and she rolled back

on her heels as if she'd been slapped.

"Gentlemen, why don't you come in," I said through clenched teeth as I pushed the door wide.

Shinebocker oafishly shoved past Jasper, knocking the inquisitive snake with his shoulder.

Moore mumbled, "Excuse me," and Jasper moved aside.

The third gentleman nodded genially at my neighbors and strolled into the apartment.

"I'm sorry, you guys, I've got to go. We'll talk later." I closed the door as I spoke, leaning my forehead against the hard wood.

"Karina?" Jessica called.

"Coming."

Chapter Eleven

"Explain to me again why you had the senator's phone." Ole Shiny's head glimmered under the chandelier as his pudgy fingers drummed my dining room table. He'd been at it for at least half an hour, going over my story—why was I there, who else did I see, why did I meet with the senator, what were my intentions, what happened in the tunnel? He machine-gunned the questions at me, and, because I had nothing to hide, I lobbed the answers back at him as quickly as a Billie Jean King returning a serve from Bobby Riggs. I even answered a few, I could tell by Jessica's body language, she would have preferred I didn't.

"As I explained, three times now," I said through gritted teeth, "my own phone was dead. I tried to call 911 on the senator's phone, but I couldn't get reception. When the paramedics arrived, I scooped up all my belongings and his phone as well." Blowing my bangs, I crossed my arms and sat back.

"Gentlemen, I believe my client has been clear in explaining the mix-up with the phone. What you haven't explained to my satisfaction—from your preliminary investigation, my client's home was indeed broken into. Yet, that doesn't seem to concern you."

Amir and Red had left to review the apartment complex's video footage from Monday night. The forensic guys had been sent back to the office to process the evidence by the third man who arrived with Moore and Shinebocker. Mike introduced him as Director Leon McGill, the head honcho running point on the investigation. He and Jessica seemed to know each other, and so far, he'd behaved congenially toward me, leaving the heavy hitting to the detective. McGill's dark espresso complexion showed little response to the accusation Jessica leveled. Moore's frown simply deepened. Mike continued to remain stone-faced, as he had throughout the detective's interrogation, only a slight tic from his clenching jaw revealed any sort of frustration or anger.

Shinebocker opened his mouth to respond, but McGill's dulcet tones cut across anything the detective planned to say. "To the contrary, we are very concerned by this new turn of events." His phone beeped, and he checked the incoming text. "Amir is returning with the footage."

My doorbell rang.

"That's him now." McGill stood. "Shall I?"

"Knock yourself out." I had no interest in dealing with my neighbors again. If it wasn't Amir, I figured this fellow was capable enough to dispatch them post haste. I needn't have worried, Amir entered, and the pair held a whispered conversation in my tiny foyer.

"You know, that reminds me, speaking of footage, I was hoping you could tell me, Officer Moore—"

"That's Investigator Moore," Shinebocker grumbled.

Jessica sniffed at his rudeness.

"My apologies, I didn't know," I said, ignoring Shinebocker.

Moore dismissed my mistake with a grimace and head shake. "No worries, continue, Miss Cardinal."

"Can someone explain to me why it took so long for police to come to my aid after the senator collapsed?" Immediately, I could tell I'd struck a nerve.

Shinebocker turned his hostile gaze to the table. Mike stared hard at Moore, who shifted and crossed his arms.

Jessica glanced up from the legal pad where she'd been scribbling notes and observed the uncomfortable guests.

My intuition hairs stood on end.

Jessica's must have done so too. "That's an excellent question. Karina has said, more than once, she yelled for help and . . . let me see . . . yes, here, I wrote it in my notes, she waved her hands at the camera, requesting help. What on earth took Capitol Police, hell, anyone, so long to respond?"

Moore tugged at his tie and cleared his throat. "There was an incident that took one of the guards away from the desk."

"What kind of incident?" Jessica asked.

Shinebocker made a gurgling sound as the investigator answered, "A couple of teens in Guy Fawkes masks were running through the halls knocking down flags."

"That explains one guard. What about the other?" I prompted.

Moore didn't respond.

Leon and Amir had returned to the dining area, and the director answered, "We believe he was part of it." He pulled out his phone and swiped around before holding it for me to see. "Do you recognize this man?"

My scalp began to tingle. "We met. I think his name . . . something that started with a J. Jacob? No. J . . . Jermanky?"

"Jablonski?" Leon prompted.

I snapped my fingers. "Yes. That's it."

"Where did you meet?" Moore asked.

"He came into the room where Officer Leander took me to take my statement."

"Did he say anything?"

"N-not . . . really."

"K.C." Mike's voice held a warning. "You're quibbling."

"Well, that guy . . . he was unsettling. His bugged-out, pale blue stare." I gave a visible shiver. "His fraternity nick-name would be Creepy Eyes. I was relieved when Leander sent him back to his station."

"So you weren't alone with him?" Leon placed his hand on the back of my chair.

"Not for more than a few seconds. Why?"

"*Jesus*," Mike mumbled and, pushing away from the table, he paced into the kitchen to refill his coffee.

"Who is Jablonski?" Jessica asked, glancing around at the FBI crew, but my gaze remained glued on Mike.

He swallowed a gulp. "He's a goddamn mercenary for hire."

I cringed at his savageness.

Shinebocker inserted himself back into the conversation. "This is an ongoing investigation. Not appropriate for sharing with—"

"FBI is leading this investigation, so it's not your call," Mike responded with unconcealed venom.

I could tell Shinebocker had pushed Mike's limits with his callous interrogation of me, and it appeared his patience with the detective was at an end.

Shinebocker turned to Leon for support, only to be disappointed by his measured response. "I believe . . . Miss Cardinal is providing valuable information to this investigation. The more we know about the events of that night, the better."

Something about our conversation, before Shinebocker interrupted, ping-ponged around in my brain and began molding into cohesiveness. "Hold up . . . do you think Jablonski was trying to retrieve the phone right then?"

"It's possible." Leon took Mike's seat.

Amir sat next to him at the foot of the table. Plunking his laptop down, he opened it and began typing.

Mike's eyes narrowed. "She's lucky to be alive."

Jessica's head whipped around. "Why do you say she's lucky to be alive, Agent Finnegan?"

"That's not true. We don't know what Jablonski's motive was," Leon replied to Mike.

My friend slammed the coffee cup down hard enough to chip the earthenware. "Tell her about the tram operator . . ."

I knew there was a missing puzzle piece.

"Yes! What happened to him? Seriously, where the hell did everyone go while the senator died in my arms?" I cried, pointing at the men opposite me.

"The tram operator was found in a storage room. A large piece of equipment fell off a shelf and knocked him out," Moore answered.

I caught my breath. "He's dead?"

Moore shook his head. "He's got a bad concussion and remembers nothing from that night. Not even why he left his post."

"Don't tell me . . . you thought it was an accident." Jessica flipped to the next page on her legal pad. "But not now."

"The incident is being investigated further," Leon replied with finality.

I turned my attention to Amir. "Did you find anything on the cameras?"

Amir glanced at Leon, who nodded. "Go ahead."

"As a matter of fact—" He flipped the computer around to face the rest of the table. "At 1:19 a.m., we see a man all in black wearing a hoodie, ball cap, and carrying a duffle bag enter the front door behind a pizza delivery man. Pizza man gets on the elevator. Guy in black does not. He waits for the second elevator. He gets off on the fifth floor and we see him turn left, in the direction of your apartment. The complex doesn't have cameras in the hallways, so we can't be sure where he went." Amir paused the video and clicked around the desktop.

"Where do *you* think he went?" I asked.

"If I had to guess, he probably tried to pick the front door lock but couldn't get in because of your slide bolt into the floor."

Another video feed came on screen.

"Six minutes after he gets off the elevator, you can barely see his shoulder in the stairwell camera as he heads toward the roof." Amir clicked another button and the rooftop camera feed popped up. "There is one camera that monitors the roof, it's right by the door. I believe it was disabled using a laser pointer."

We watched the door open, then something bright flashed and the screen went gray.

"Is that it?" Leon asked.

"Eighteen minutes later, we catch him in the stairwell."

The intruder moved at a fast pace, skipping stairs as he went.

The last feed showed the basement door opening and a barely glimpsed portion of his body. He must have plastered himself against the brick to keep from being seen.

My brows knit as I replayed the videos in my mind. "I don't get it."

"What don't you get, K.C?" Mike laid a protective hand on my shoulder.

"Clearly, he had the capability of knocking out all the cameras with his laser. Why only knock out the roof? Why not all of them?"

"Monitoring. Knock out one feed and hope it's overlooked or assumed a malfunction. Kill all the feeds and increase the risk of a police dispatch," Amir replied.

"Okay, but why knock out *that* one?"

"That camera shows a good portion of the roof, and we would have been able to see his movements."

Jessica's head bounced up and down as she scribbled on her

notepad.

Mike shoved his hands in his pockets. "Did we get any shots of his face?"

Amir's mouth flattened. "I'll review it back at the office, but it doesn't look good."

"Is it an open or closed circuit?" McGill asked.

"Closed."

"What does that mean? Open or closed circuit?" I asked.

Amir gave a look that tech savvy people give when speaking to the technically challenged. "Closed circuit television, or CCTV, transmits its feed to a specific location on a limited number of monitors."

"So, it's hard to hack?" Jessica pointed her pen at Amir. "That's why he knocked it out with the laser?"

"Not necessarily. Everything's hackable. With a closed circuit, the hacker would have to be onsite or have an inside man, like the Capitol Hill hack," Mike explained.

Jessica jumped on that statement before I could. "What Capitol Hill hack?"

"Christ! Why don't you go ahead and deputize these two, *Agent?*" Shiney sneered.

My gaze darted around the table. Leon glowered at Mike, who grimaced. Amir busied himself with the computer, and Moore became fascinated with his wedding ring, spinning it around his finger.

"I'm afraid Agent Finnegan has said too much," Leon replied, grim-faced.

"Gentlemen, really, there's no need for all this secrecy," Jessica cajoled.

I narrowed my eyes at Leon. "Are you telling us the footage of me with the senator in the tunnels has been compromised? You didn't see him collapse, or see me waving at the camera for help?"

Leon licked his lips. "Yes, we saw it. However, someone piggy-backed onto the feed and it's . . . fuzzy."

"Fuzzy?" Shinebocker's animosity and suspicion toward me became abundantly clear. As far as he knew—hell, as far as anyone knew—I was part of the plot. On a fuzzy camera feed, my attempts to save his life could be misconstrued. My stomach sank.

"What do you mean someone piggy-backed onto the feed?" Jessica asked. "Do you mean there was another perpetrator controlling the visual?"

"We believe Jablonski and an off-site hacker watched the entire episode play out," Amir replied.

The coffee I'd copiously consumed churned in my stomach. "You're saying, some sicko watched him die? Got his rocks off observing me try to save him?"

"They wanted to make sure the senator wasn't getting up," Mike said in a hard voice.

"So, what? They would have messed with his pacemaker some more if I'd successfully revived him?" My voice came out low and rough.

"That, or sent Jablonski in to finish the job." All eyes turned to Amir. Nobody spoke. He glanced up from the laptop and realized what he'd said. "Sorry," he said with a shrug, "it's just a theory."

The idea of someone watching me struggle to keep the senator alive—waiting to take steps to make sure he didn't get up—seemed particularly nasty. Evil. The very definition of evil. That queasy feeling I'd experienced on the roof, when Mike asked if I was going to vomit, returned. "And you think I'm one of the conspirators?"

Mike opened his mouth, but Leon's voice cut across before he could answer. "Actually, Ms. Cardinal, I don't. Lack of evidence against you, and this break-in, leads me to believe you were in the wrong place at the wrong time."

"Lack of evidence?" Jessica leaned forward. "Have you been investigating my client?"

"We've been investigating everyone involved with the senator. The list is long," Leon assured her.

A single brow arched high as she scribbled on the notepad. "I hope for your sake, McGill, that all of the investigatory materials were gained legally."

"Of course," replied Leon.

But out of the corner of my eye, I saw Mike tap his forefinger and thumb together. It was a tell of his I'd learned from our college days while playing poker. It's how I knew he was bluffing, and I wondered how deeply the FBI had dug into my background and what kind of gray areas they'd crossed to get the information. It also occurred to me that maybe I should have Joshua return to sweep for bugs and check my phone *after* the FBI left.

The phone.

"Why do you think he risked breaking into my apartment to get the senator's phone?" I twisted in my seat to get a better look at Leon. "What's on it?" This was the second time I'd asked. However, the director hadn't been here the first time. I hoped I could prey on his current geniality to get better answers.

He shrugged. "We can only speculate."

To everyone's surprise, the soft-spoken tones of Investigator Moore asked, "Was the phone making any noise, like an alarm going off, when you picked it up?"

My mind went back to that night. "No-o, it looked normal to me. Why?"

"The senator's pacemaker should have been setting off an alarm on his phone, and on his doctor's phone." Moore's lips twisted. "That didn't happen."

"Wait a minute." Jessica splayed her fingers across the table.

"Whoever hacked the pacemaker also hacked the video cameras and the phone?"

Amir closed the computer. "We believe Jablonski might have been using a jammer to block incoming signals."

"So, obtaining the phone was—what? Tying up loose ends?" I mused to no one in particular.

"Conceivably." Leon got to his feet. "I apologize, but I have a meeting to attend. Gentlemen—" He glanced at the D.C. and Capitol detectives. "If you don't have any more questions, I think it's time we let this lady be."

Shinebocker put up a finger and opened his mouth, but Leon quelled him with a single glance. The finger wilted and he mumbled, "No, we're done."

Jessica rose as the men gathered their things. "Just a minute, Agent. What about the safety of my client? She had a break-in. Is she safe to stay here alone?"

Leon surveyed me. "Was anything else taken beside the phone?"

"Not that I know of."

"Then I'd suggest you get something to secure the back door better."

"Secure the door? Is that all you've got?" Jessica harrumphed.

"An alarm system wouldn't be a bad idea."

My lawyer settled an arch look on McGill.

"In addition, I'll have Agent Finnegan reach out to Alexandria P.D. and put in a request to increase patrols in the area," he said genially.

Jessica sniffed, but I had no interest in getting back on my local police radar. "Oh, I'm sure it'll be fine. He got what he wanted. I can't imagine whoever broke in will be back. No need to contact the local cops."

"You're probably right. Nevertheless, we'll contact them."

He held out his hand to my attorney. "Jessica, always a pleasure. Miss Cardinal."

"Call me Karina. Thank you for coming by, Director."

To my surprise, Mike followed the crowd out the door with nothing more than a brief farewell.

As they rounded the corner, I heard Mrs. Thundermuffin's thready voice. "Heigh-ho, gentlemen. And will you be installing the surround sound?"

"I'm afraid not," Leon responded.

I quickly shut my door and prayed she wouldn't come a-knockin' anytime soon.

Jessica stared at me, shaking her head. "What have you gotten into?"

"I have no idea."

She gave a hefty sigh as she loaded her bag. "Well, best lay low and stay out of that D.C. detective's way. He's a real piece of work. It sounds like the FBI has already cleared you, but that Shinebocker fellow has taken a distinct dislike to you. Either he thinks everyone is lying, or he's pissed that the FBI has sidelined him and has decided to take it out on you."

"Why me?"

"It is obvious; Mike cares for you. Those two were like circling dogs. I'm sure your friend only wanted to protect you, but Shinebocker might not believe the FBI did their due diligence investigating you since you have a relationship with one of the agents on the case."

I couldn't argue with her logic. There was a definite pissing match going on between the pair.

"Remember, don't speak to anyone without my presence."

"Listen, Jessica . . ." I shifted from foot-to-foot. "We didn't discuss your fee."

"Don't worry about it. We'll take it out of your referral fee."

"My . . . referral fee?"

She finished packing the last of her belongings and checked her cell phone. "Martin Dunne has put me on retainer."

"Ah. Glad I could increase your clientele."

"Tell me, are you going to be okay? Staying here alone?"

I glanced around the apartment, taking in the fingerprinting dust spread over the counter, on the door, and other various hard surfaces. "Any ideas the best way to clean up this printing dust?"

"First, use a dry cloth to wipe away the powder. Then try Windex or something with ammonia in it to get rid of the rest." Her beautiful, dark gaze studied me. "This has been quite a day for you. Is there someone I can call to come over? I'm not sure I should leave you alone."

I thought about calling my sister and my mom, though I figured both of them would completely freak out and tell me to move in with them. Latesha? She wouldn't freak out, but this was her weekend with the kids. Soccer season had started, and I didn't want to intrude on her time with them. I shook my head.

"You'll be okay?"

Mustering a smile, I said with false confidence, "I'll be fine. It's a lot to process, and all. . . . "

"I have a relationship with Le—I mean, Director McGill. I'll see if I can find out anything more about the case. You work your magic on our handsome Agent Finnegan, and we'll talk again. I think their preliminary investigation, and the fact someone broke into your home, removes you from the suspect list."

"I hope so."

She gave my arm a reassuring pat on the way out the door. "Stay safe."

Chapter Twelve

A persistent knocking woke me at seven on Saturday morning. I wasn't pleased. My brain spent the night circling around the facets of the case like a tornado spins through Kansas, only to come up with no good answers. Right now, seven felt like four a.m. I shuffled to the front door, shoving the tangled mane away from my face. The peephole revealed Mike's smiling countenance. It didn't make me any happier.

"What are you doing here?"

His eyes grew wide and he stepped back. "Well, I—"

"You didn't return my phone calls or texts." I walked away, leaving him to close the door.

"Sorry. I brought you a present."

"Is it coffee?" I continued on my path without a backward glance.

"No, it's not. Hey, where are you going?"

"Back to bed." I closed the bedroom door with a sharp snap.

"Where are your tools?" he called.

"Check the furnace room off the back deck." I faceplanted onto my fluffy pillow, pulled the comforter over my head, and ignored the noise coming from the other side of the bedroom door.

It didn't work.

Twenty minutes later, I tossed the blankets aside and

dragged myself into the bathroom.

Yowza.

The rat's nest was worse than I'd expected, and I'd forgotten to remove yesterday's makeup too. No wonder Mike did the jerk-back move. I wrestled the mane into a ponytail and washed away the evidence of my rough night.

Mike had kindly started a pot of coffee, and I drank half a cup before speaking. "What are you doing?"

A hammer and various drill bits were spread across the living room floor and he was screwing a silver metal piece into the sliding door frame.

"I'm putting a security bar on your back door."

"I was going to take care of that."

A doubtful brow rose.

"Okay, I was just going to shove a broom handle in the track, but it would have worked just fine."

"This is better. I've also emailed you some links to good home security services in the area." He tossed the screwdriver aside. "All your tools are pink."

I grinned to see my bubblegum-colored tools in his long, manly fingers. "Yeah, I know. The grips are built smaller for ladies hands. My dad gave them to me when I moved into my first apartment."

He grunted and picked up a long metal bar.

"I'm sorry I was pissy earlier. I didn't sleep well. And . . . "

"And . . . " He slid the bar into place and picked up a tiny screw.

"Nothing," I mumbled, staring into my coffee cup.

"K.C., what's up?"

I paced away. "You . . . you just left. After all that crap, the interrogation, the FBI brigade in my dining room. Someone broke into my house, and that Shiney guy thinks I've been a party to murder. You didn't answer my calls or texts, and you!

You just left!" Tears burned my eyes. "Oh, hell." I stomped into the bathroom to retrieve a tissue, slamming the door behind me.

It was lack of sleep. Consciously, I realized that's all this fit was about. Yet, it was also something a little deeper, as though my best friend had let me down. Our relationship was getting . . . complicated. I know that's such a cliché. The case. His job. My role in Harper's death. Could things get any more complicated? Still, I wanted to look to him for comfort. We'd had such a great relationship in college. Why couldn't things be that simple again?

The redness from crying and lack of sleep only sought to brighten the green of my eyes. I swiped away the remnants of my ridiculous emotional outburst and pulled the door open to find Mike, right outside, leaning against the door frame, arms crossed.

"I left because I didn't want Shinebocker whispering in my boss's ear. I left because I knew you'd be safe with Jessica, and I figured she'd want to debrief with you—her client—without an FBI agent hanging around. I left because this case is part of my job, and I knew if I stayed and continued to show partiality, my boss would remove me from it, and I can't have that because you are a part of it. And I didn't return your texts or phone calls because I didn't leave the office until after one in the morning, and my phone is locked away while I'm at work, as you well know." He spoke in a calm tone, but the frowning brows, rigid posture, and hard face let me know the tone was a façade.

Getting a closer look, I saw the tightness around his eyes mirrored my own. I laid a hand on his forearm and sighed, "I'm such a brat. Sorry."

The stiffness disappeared and he pulled me to his chest. "Me too. I got caught up in the case. I should have called you at some point."

My ear lay in the crook of his neck; I could smell the

sandalwood scent of his soap. "Do you have any leads?"

"A few." He laid his chin atop my head.

"Am I still a suspect?"

"Not as far as I know."

"But they may keep you out of the loop when it comes to me."

His chin moved against my skull in a brief nod.

"Thank you for installing the security bar. Is it finished?"

"Almost."

"Have you had breakfast?"

The chin waggled no.

"I've got eggs. How about an omelet?"

"I'd love an omelet."

After breakfast, over the dregs of our coffee, we rehashed the case. Mike couldn't say much more about his leads, except that he was following some, so the conversation mostly consisted of me asking questions he couldn't answer.

"What do you think was on the phone?"

Mike followed me to the couch, stretching his legs onto the coffee table, while I curled up against him. "Could be anything or nothing."

"No. Something was on that phone. They sent a guy to break into my apartment to retrieve it. Would a hacker leave some sort of signature from that alarm thingy for his pacemaker?"

"Sounds as if there was a jammer. I doubt the phone was hacked."

"If there was a jammer, how did the hacker get past it to mess up the pacemaker?"

"*That* is an excellent question." Mike played with a lock of my hair.

"I wonder if there was some sort of communication—a text or phone call—that pointed to the killer."

"Maybe."

"Oh, come on, don't tell me all sorts of ideas aren't running through your head too."

He yawned. "It's all speculation, and since it's unlikely we'll ever find the phone, I can't run my investigation on 'what might be.' I have to go with the information I have."

"Do you think the hacker hired Jablonski? Or is he a hired hand too?"

"That"—he yawned again—"is another excellent question."

My mind kept going back to Harper's assertion that he was working on something that would put S46 to shame. What could it be, and why hadn't he shared it with my office? He must have known we'd help him with something that would improve healthcare, reduce costs to the consumer, and lighten the paperwork load for clinicians.

"I wonder what Harper was working on," I mused aloud, but the only sound that met my statement was Mike's steady, deep breathing.

I pulled the afghan across his legs and snuggled closer, drawing on his warmth. Eventually, my brain got off the hamster wheel of questions and slowed enough to fall asleep.

We woke from our late morning nap to the ring of Mike's cell phone calling him back to work. By the evening news, I realized why. The national stations were running with the story that Harper's death was being investigated because law enforcement believed there was foul play. Details were sketchy but the news report made it clear a joint task force investigation was headed up by the FBI.

The FBI's response to the media like a broken record. "The FBI does not comment on ongoing investigations."

Ten minutes later, Latesha rang.

"Hi, Tesha."

"Karina, are you okay? Oh, my heavens, they're saying the

senator was murdered. I thought you said he had a heart attack. You said you were there."

"Yes." I wasn't sure what I could tell Latesha.

"Maybe someone slipped him poison. Was he frothing at the mouth?"

"Not at all."

"Maybe someone gave him a shot that stopped his heart. I've read about that. Makes it look like a heart attack. Or maybe he was a Russian spy and they slipped him polonium."

"I don't know about that. The Russian polonium seems a bit farfetched. Um, listen, Latesha, my mom's calling on the other line. I'd better go."

"I understand. Call me tomorrow."

"Uh-huh." I hung up, turned off my cell, and unplugged the house phone.

On Sunday morning, Mike called—I think to assure himself that I was okay more than anything—because he said nothing new about the investigation, or even much about the press surrounding it. What was clear from my limited conversation with him and from watching the news was that he and the FBI were under a lot of pressure from both Congress and the president to find someone to pin Harper's assassination on ASAP.

None of which assuaged my worries. I wasn't a dummy. No matter what McGill had said, if they couldn't find Jablonski or the hacker soon . . . I might find myself sweating in a gray box of a room, being interrogated for a crime I didn't commit, nor had any clue who did. Being a scapegoat because I foolishly took the senator's phone was not at the top of my list of "Fun Things to do Today."

Even if they cleared me, the press would have a field day ruining my reputation before the FBI released me. As it was, I knew, soon enough the press would get a hold of my statement to Officer Leander, or one of the paramedics, or a Capitol Police officer who saw me in the tunnels. I counted the people who knew—Hasina, Rodrigo, Sandy, Latesha ... too many. Eventually, the press would crack one of them, and *Headline News* would be knocking on my door for an exclusive. I realized, in the coming days, I'd be looking over my shoulder for reporters. Again.

Chapter Thirteen

Monday, I found Hasina waiting in my office. I can't say her visit was unexpected. She wore a kelly-green spring dress with a matching sweater, her long black mane swept up into a French twist. She perused the photos lining the bookcase. They were pictures of me with a variety of senators, congressmen, and two former presidents.

"How old were you when this was taken?" she asked in her faint Indian accent, pointing to a group photo with a former first lady.

"High school. We were finalists in a writing contest about the importance of education for women." I laid my case and handbag on the desk. "I suppose you're wondering about Senator Harper? Have a seat."

Hasina folded herself into the guest chair while I followed suit behind my desk.

"I had a meeting with the FBI on Friday after the funeral. There's not much that I can tell you. As you've heard on the news, they suspect foul play. Something caused the senator to have a heart attack." I had no interest in laying the case before my boss and decided it would be in my best interests to provide the bare minimum. "I told them what I knew, which isn't much." I shrugged.

"And you . . ." Those dark eyes scrutinized me.

I put on a face I called "Interested Neutrality," something

I'd perfected during mock trials at law school. "... Am cooperating with law enforcement. As you can see, I'm not under arrest."

"Do they have any idea who the perpetrators are?"

"No clue. The FBI does not comment on ongoing investigations. But, from what I gathered, they are following some leads."

"Well, now that's out of the way. I wanted to talk to you about the leadership committee meetings coming up at the end of the month. This is the first time you'll be a part of them, and I wanted to let you know what to expect."

Half an hour later, Hasina exited my office. Rodrigo was at my doorway within moments of her leaving. He didn't even bother to knock, instead came in without a by-your-leave, closed the door, and parked himself on my guest chair.

"So now it's murder." His eyebrows waggled as he crossed his legs.

"Apparently."

"Did you know?"

I gave him an unsmiling stare. "No."

"Did the police question you?"

"Yes."

"And ..."

"And ... nothing. I told them what happened. Again. They asked the same questions. Again. That's it," I said in a disinterested voice.

"Well, that's no fun."

"Sorry to disappoint." I turned back to my computer. "And I'd appreciate it if you wouldn't spread the gossip around the office."

"Absolutely. Scout's honor." Rodrigo made a zipping motion across his mouth.

I had my doubts, but short of kidnapping and locking him

in a closet, there was little I could do to make him keep that promise.

"So, did you find out anything more about the bill Harper was trying to put together?" He changed the subject.

"As a matter of fact, I did. I sat next to Sandy Harding at the funeral, and she told me Christy Manheim had been working on it. She also mentioned something about Finley, in the House."

"Finley! No way. That man wouldn't touch a healthcare bill if his grandma's life depended on it."

I tended to agree with Rodrigo's sentiment, but I didn't speak my thoughts aloud.

"Maybe she meant Folliero. When are you meeting Christy?"

"I'm going over at lunch around one."

"Should I go with you?"

I eyed Rodrigo. When it came to approaching certain people, Rodrigo could be an asset. Even though his exterior persona sometimes gave off a flibbertigibbet vibe, he was no empty-headed fool. Long and short, Rodrigo's persuasive ability was different than mine and his manner could be disarming. "I think today, I'll take the confiding girl talk approach with Christy. We can sympathize with each other over Harper's death. Besides, I'm afraid your anger at Harper's flip-flop might show through."

"You're probably right." He stood and brushed the nonexistent wrinkles out of his pants. "Do you want me to reach out to Folliero's office? Nose around, see if I can get a beat on what angle Harper was working?"

"Let me get back to you after I talk with Christy."

"Will do." He turned to leave but paused at the door. "By-the-by, I've got two tickets for opening night of Turandot at the Kennedy Center this Friday. Want to come with me?"

I gaped, taken aback by his invitation. "Um . . . what about

Alfonse?"

He rolled his eyes. "Working. *Friday? I simply can't get away on a Friday, dahling,"* Rodrigo said, imitating his partner's French accent.

Alfonse was the Executive Chef for a Michelin rated restaurant in Adams Morgan. I'd met him in passing. Rodrigo's birthday was my first day, and Alfonse brought over a mouthwatering Mediterranean meal for the entire office to share. Rodrigo called it a guilt meal, since Alfonse couldn't get off work for his birthday. If Alfonse had been my significant other, I'd guilt him into a meal daily and be as big as a hippo. Everyone knew about Alfonse.

There was no denying I enjoyed the theater, and it was a rarity that I got tickets to an opening night. "Let me check the calendar." Friday held a notable absence of evening activity, and I figured Mike would still be up to his neck in this investigation. A night out that didn't include a fundraiser was exactly what I needed. "I'd love to go to the opera with you."

"I'll pencil you in. Wear something snazzy, there's a reception beforehand at the Rooftop Terrace."

"I won't let you down."

****

I cruised down the third-floor hallway at quarter to one and found Christy Manheim exiting Harper's office.

"Christy!" She started when I called her name. "Hi, I finished my last meeting early. Is this still a good time?"

"Sure . . ." She hesitated. "Actually, I'd forgotten we were meeting. I was just going to get lunch."

I got the sneaking suspicion Christy was trying to dodge me. "No problem, I haven't eaten either and I'm starving. I'll join you. Where are you headed?"

"The bistro across the street."

"Lead the way."

Christy ordered the Ginger Teriyaki chicken and I settled on a Garbanzo Bean salad. We were able to snag one of the tiny square tables at the back.

Before I could take a single bite, Christy leaned forward and whispered, "Listen, I know what you want to talk about, and there was simply nothing I could do."

"Uh, Christy, I'm not sure we're on the same conversation train here. What couldn't you do?" I returned in similar low tones.

"Talk Harper out of switching his vote, of course. Isn't that why you're here?"

"No, no." I shook my head. "I already know why the senator changed his vote. He told me. That's all water under the bridge."

"Oh." She sat back, and for the first time since I greeted her, her shoulders relaxed. "Then what did you want to talk about?"

"I sat next to Sandy during the funeral, and she told me you'd been working on a different healthcare bill with the senator." Christy looked blank. "I was under the impression she'd mention it to you. Anyway, I wanted to offer my help."

Christy popped a piece of chicken into her mouth and proceeded to chew, very slowly, as she thought about what I'd said. She swallowed and took a drink before answering. "I suppose, the situation being what it is, and since Sandy told you . . ."

I waited while she dithered, afraid if I said the wrong thing she'd clam up. The fact that she was being so cagey about this practically had me on the edge of my seat to hear what the senator had been cooking up.

She leaned forward again. "You see, the senator was working back channels to gain support for legislation he wanted

to introduce. He said it was important to keep it 'hush-hush'"
—she used finger quotes— "until he could gain enough support
in the Senate and the House."

"Mm-hm."

"He was going to propose a bill to create sweeping changes
to the pharmaceutical industry with price caps and revamping
FDA regulations. He said it would be the first step toward
reining in the excessive drug prices."

"I'm . . . shocked. Isn't the Republican party all about
making government smaller? Something like this would create
huge oversight to enforce."

"Not as much as you'd think."

"I still don't understand. What's the big secret? Democrats
have been proposing something similar for years. Last year, they
proposed allowing Americans to purchase their drugs from
Canada so we can access the discounts Canadians receive
through their government's price regulation. Not much different
than what you're saying Harper had planned. Moreover, he must
have known he'd never get enough of the Republican votes to
make it happen, and the party would crucify him." I took a bite
of crunchy salad.

"I wasn't even sure he could get all the Democrats on board
for something so sweeping."

"So, why take the chance? It's career suicide, not to mention
the money. . . . Wait a minute." The little hamster in my head
slowly started walking on the wheel. "Pfizer closed up their
research and development shops in Michigan. Right?"

"R and D? Yes, about ten years ago."

"You don't have any of the biggies there anymore, do you?"

Slowly, her head moved back and forth.

"Was Harper getting any money from Big Pharma these
days?"

"A number of smaller biotech companies have opened up

shop in the Southeast where Pfizer used to be. There were donations, but nothing substantial compared to what it used to be."

"Was he . . . no, he couldn't. . . ."

"When Pfizer was in Michigan, it gobbled up every smaller company in its path. Now that Pfizer is gone, we've seen almost twelve percent job growth in the sector, mostly from new biotech companies, medical devices, and drugs," Christy told me.

"So . . . what, was he bouncing his ideas off the new company CEOs?"

"More than that. About four months ago, he held a private meeting with five CEOs. Every one of those small companies would like to take a bite out of the Big Pharma sharks and make room for themselves."

"So much so, they'd risk price fixing?"

She shrugged. "The new guys want in on the market."

"I don't know. When was Harper up for re-election? Two or four years?"

"Four."

I nodded. "Let me guess, he wasn't planning to run. So, he was playing the long game? Hoping the Senate would flip Democrat?"

"And the House, but there's a possibility he wouldn't need the flip."

I gave an unladylike snort. "You've got to be joking. There's no way you'll get something like this to pass under a House run by the Republicans."

She took a sip of her diet soda. "You'd be surprised."

I gave her a sideways glance. "Sandy said something about reaching out to Finley."

Christy's lip curled.

"Finley. Not Folliero?"

"Finley." She chewed another piece of chicken.

"I don't believe it."

Again, I had to wait for her to swallow. "Believe it," she said.

"Why? He's from New Jersey. Let me think . . . J & P is based there. I know he's taken money from them. It would be akin to political suicide."

"Did you know he had a grandson who died two years ago?"

I thought a moment. "Vaguely, I remember that. I thought he had some rare form of cancer."

"Hunter Syndrome."

"Huntington's Disease? How awful, that's a death sentence and there's no known cure."

She shook her head. "Hunter Syndrome, it's different. Causes all sorts of awful symptoms, including cognitive impairments. It's due to a protein or enzyme deficiency—I can't remember. Anyway, there's one drug on the market, Elaprase."

"Never heard of it."

"Guess how much it costs?"

I shrugged. "Eighty grand."

"Try five hundred thousand."

I choked on my drink, and wheezed, "Five hundred thousand?"

"Annually. His daughter quit her job to stay at home with the little boy and take care of him. When the boy was six, the father was killed in a car accident and she lost his insurance. She goes back to work part-time and sells everything to continue to pay for the medication because it was working. The house, nice cars, furniture, even her diamond engagement ring. Then, she can't pay anymore. She gets in arrears. The medication stops, the little boy comes down with an infection and . . . " Christy turned her hands up in a helpless gesture.

"Where was Finley during all of this?"

"She's progeny from Finley's first marriage. The divorce was ugly. They were estranged for years. Too much pride. My understanding—by the time she reached out to Finley—it was too late to make a difference. He was there in the final weeks, trying to move heaven and earth to save that little boy, but it was too late." Her face drooped with sorrow. "The boy had just turned ten."

The story brought tears to my eyes. I sipped the cold soda and cleared my throat to cover up the well of sympathy for that poor woman. "Holy moly. That's quite a story. I don't understand why Finley hasn't been using his platform to jump up and down and demand change. I mean, when it hits that close to home, and you have a public microphone at your disposal . . ."

Her lips twisted. "As you said, J & P paid mightily for his last election. *I* think he's been waiting for Senator Golden to retire so he can run for his seat. But, until then, every two years, he's up for election."

"Yeah, that's a lot of fundraising."

"And J & P isn't the only Big Pharma he takes money from."

"You think he's afraid if he rocks the ship too soon, it won't pass and he won't get reelected?"

"Maybe."

"Who makes Elaprase?"

"A UK based company. Get this, their main office in the US . . ."

My brows rose. "Let me guess, based in Jersey."

"You got it."

"Have they donated to Finley's campaign?"

"A hundred thousand last election."

"So, he had the connections. He could have gotten the drug for his grandchild."

"He *did* get it. But the infection had set in too far. The boy ended up in renal failure. There's only so much the body can take."

"That's terrible, how awful for him and his mother. How did you find out all of this?"

"Elise is friends with Finley's current wife. She told Elise, and Elise told the senator."

"I'm still unclear. What was Harper's motivation? He didn't have a kid with Hunter Syndrome."

"You're right." She forked the remains of her dish and pointed it at me. "One of Harper's constituents came to me about the medical bills for her teenage daughter's cancer treatment. Her bill was six hundred and fifty thousand. It might as well have been a million dollars. She's a music teacher, and her husband teaches high school math and coaches the soccer team. They have three kids. She was here in D.C. with her son, chaperoning a Model UN field trip. I was her last-ditch effort to get the bill collectors off her back."

"What about insurance?"

"The cancer facility was out of network, and the insurance company claimed the immunotherapy was 'experimental' and wouldn't cover it."

I rolled my eyes. "That is such crap. Insurance companies are starting to cover immunotherapy everywhere. We all know it's the wave of the future for curing cancer."

"The insurance company covers *some*" —she thrust the fork in the air for emphasis— "types of immunotherapy, just not *this* particular kind. The family was ready to sell their house and move into a two-bedroom apartment to pay the bills."

I bit my lips in frustration. "This is how people end up homeless. It's disgraceful that parents in our country can't take care of sick children without having to sacrifice their home. What happened?"

She gave a rueful smile. "Elise walked in as the woman was leaving. She'd been crying and Elise noticed. Of course, she asked what was going on, and once she heard 'cancer' and 'child' Elise turned into a whirlwind. The senator was called over from the Capitol, and I spent the next weeks working with the senator and Elise to get insurance to pay for about half of it, and the rest of the debt forgiven. I've never been so proud to work for the senator as I was on that day."

"You should be. I've always had respect for Harper, now I've got even more. What about the girl with cancer?"

"Right now, she's cancer-free."

"Sounds like the hospital was the one overcharging."

"They were, but the immunotherapy itself was over half the bill."

"Wow."

"Exactly."

"Do you think this move to create a bill came from the senator or Elise?"

Christy sipped her drink as she considered the question. "The senator. After we worked on the first case, word spread. We were deluged with requests."

"You know the Democrats have been trying to push this type of change through for years. Even some Republicans voted for the last bill. Why not simply join with them on tweaking the 'Purchase Your Pills from Canada' bill? With the votes Harper could rally, it would likely pass in the Senate."

"Yes, but not in the House," Christy reminded me. "Which is why he brought Finley on."

"Okay, Finley can garner more votes in the House. But still, not enough to get something so drastic as government sanctioned drug price modulation passed. That's a pipedream in today's climate."

"Exactly. He figured, the threat of this bill passing in the

Senate would scare Republicans in the House enough, especially with the upcoming elections looking like more of the House will flip to blue, to loosen the reins and compromise by passing the 'Buy Your Pills from Canada' bill. Once that passed, he figured it would only be a matter of time before American pricing became more competitive, and $500K medication would become a thing of the past."

"Are you *sure* Harper was a Republican?"

Christy laughed at my comment. "Absolutely, the senator realized, as any normal human being with a brain would, that there are about half a dozen drug companies here in America running the pharmaceutical industry. They work together to make it harder to create generics so they can spend years longer making big bucks on their drugs. You want to talk about price fixing—the drug companies are already doing it. Just like the oil industry—they've created their own OPEC for drugs."

She wasn't telling me anything I didn't already know. The difference was it was coming out of a Republican staffer—who are generally known to be lenient toward big corporations. Republicans allowed that the market would correct itself by creating its own competition. Which, in an ideal world, was true, but what we'd come to see was that the powerful banded together in order to maintain that power and crush the smaller competition, thus creating a monopoly. Same thing happened in the banking industry and the healthcare insurance industry. There were about five large healthcare insurance carriers that covered seventy-five percent of the population.

"Do you think Finley will move forward without Harper?" I asked.

"I don't know. I tend to doubt it."

I doubted it too. Without a counterpart in the Senate, I couldn't see Finley hanging himself, even if he had a personal interest in getting things changed. "Who were you working with over in Finley's office? Jim, his healthcare aide?"

"No, Finley was keeping this close to his vest. He definitely didn't want word to get out until he'd gained the support he needed and knew that Harper was willing to follow through with his proposal in the Senate. I spoke with Nick Ross, his Chief of Staff. I'm not even sure Jim knew about it."

"I know of Nick Ross, but I don't *know* him," I said. "I'm sure my organization would be interested in working with the congressman on an initiative like this. Do you think I should approach him?"

"I don't even know if he'll acknowledge it. The day after Harper passed, Ross closed me out. Hasn't returned my phone calls or emails. I figured it was his way of shutting this down."

"Wasn't Ross on board?"

She gave a half-shrug. "I'm not sure he was. It's possible he was only working with me because Finley told him to do it."

I sat back in my chair, crossing my arms. Christy checked her watch and began gathering her dirty dishes. I took my cue.

"Thanks for talking with me. I'm sorry this initiative was cut short by the senator's passing. Please let me know if there's anything I can do."

We said our goodbyes, and I walked toward Union Station to catch the Metro back to the office. The day was sunny, but a chilly wind whipped the Columbus Circle flags into a frenzy, and I flipped up the collar of my coat. As I waited to cross the street, I rang up Rodrigo and told him about my discussion with Christy.

"Finley? Hm, that's a real turn of events. Are you going to reach out?"

"I'm not sure. It's not as though Finley and I have been on the same side of the aisle on the legislation I've worked in the past. I don't know how to approach him. Christy said they've shut off communications since the senator died." I dropped a dollar into a panhandler's cup as I strode past, and a reedy "thank you" followed in my wake.

"What about reaching out to Nick Ross?"

"Christy didn't seem to think he was one hundred percent on board with the idea. I'm not sure he's an ally."

"I know him," Rodrigo said.

My footsteps paused. "You do? How?"

"You're new, so you don't know this about me, but three years ago, I weighed seventy pounds more than I do now. To jumpstart my weight loss, I joined one of those fitness boot camps. Nick Ross was in my class."

"So, you're friends?"

"Well . . . not exactly. We were *friendly* during boot camp. He'd just moved to D.C. from Finley's home office to be his Legislative Director. He wanted to run the Marine Corps Marathon and took the boot camp for his training."

"Did he know who you worked for?"

"No. We didn't talk shop. I only found out who he was when I did some of my own research."

"Have you run into him since?"

"Yes, once. He didn't recognize me, I'd lost so much weight. Even after I explained where we met, he was clueless. To give him credit, he's not the only one who didn't recognize me after I lost all those pounds."

"Let me think about this," I said. "Maybe we can arrange to run into him."

"I'll call Finley's scheduling secretary and see what I can find out."

"Good idea. I'm headed underground to the Metro. I'll meet you at the office soon."

Twenty minutes later, I breezed through the glass doors. Rodrigo waited for me in the building's lobby.

"What did you find out?" I asked, pushing the elevator

button.

"There's an event on Wednesday. Finley is a guest speaker. Nick might be there for it."

"Can you get us in?"

"Probably, but—"

"Do what you can." We stepped into the mirror and steel elevator.

"The meeting is out in Reston."

"No problem, I'll drive."

"Karina, it's a right-wing Christian evangelical event, I'm not sure we'll fit in."

I brushed off his concerns. "We'll be fine. You're Catholic, right?"

"Lapsed. Let me rephrase, I'm not sure *I'll* fit in."

My gaze swept him from top to bottom. The pink shirt and purple striped tie looked good with his darker Puerto Rican skin tones and the shiny gray suit fit him to tailored perfection. I had no doubt a pair of pink and purple socks were hidden beneath his pant legs. I understood his clothing choices, though perfect for metrosexual New York City styles, bordered a fine line in bland-beige-land of D.C. fashion, and might stand out at a conservative Christian gathering.

"Just wear your black suit with a white shirt and a plain tie. I've seen you play it straight before. Oh, and don't forget to wear black socks." I pointed at his gray oxfords.

He pulled a face.

"Listen, I realize you would prefer to take a pass, but I need your introduction to Nick Ross," I cajoled.

He gave me a skeptical look. "Are you sure this isn't a wild goose chase? We've got a forum to prepare for and a committee meeting in a few weeks."

The elevator doors swooshed open and, always a gentleman, Rodrigo indicated I should proceed him, but I didn't go far. We remained near the elevators, out of sight from the glass doors that led into the NHAA office, and continued our conversation in low tones.

"My point exactly," I told him. "What if we can come to the next committee meeting with a new initiative in our pockets, headed up by none other than the Honorable Richard Finley. My God, what a coup!"

"Are you going to tell Hasina?"

"Sure." *At some point.* "Now go get those tickets."

"I'll see what I can do."

We entered the office, and as I watched my fashionable colleague continue to his cube, there remained only a slight twinge of guilt on my conscience. Granted, I hadn't lied to Rodrigo, it would be quite an accomplishment if we could bring Harper's plan to the Alliance through Finley. It also might wipe away some of the stink of failure from our S46 flop. Not to mention, maybe getting a little posthumous recognition for Harper. What I hadn't told him—my Spidey senses were tingling. If it did nothing more than put the hairs on the back of my neck to rest, I needed to have a direct conversation with the esteemed congressman.

Chapter Fourteen

Tuesday went by with only a short conversational "check-in" from Mike. It was clear, more from what he didn't say than what he did, that he was hotly following a lead and had little time for me. I wasn't offended, because if he'd actually come over I might have been drawn into a confession about my Spidey tingle, and I wasn't really in the mood to have Mike look at me with either pitying eyes, or worse, his infuriating I'll-humor-you-smirk he could deliver that was akin to a dog style head-pat.

Wednesday arrived in typical March fashion—with rainy skies. Per usual, the drizzle brought on car accidents and slowed traffic in the D.C. metro area. Our ride, which should have taken thirty to forty minutes, took over an hour and had us arriving late for the luncheon event in Reston.

After a brief conversation with the concierge, Rodrigo and I hustled through the hotel hallways to the Silver Ballroom. The doors were closed, but a young lady wearing the black vest of the hotel staff sat at a table outside the room. A large white sign that read *C2ARM Annual Meeting* sat on a tripod next to the door.

"Hello." I smiled at the brunette while unbuttoning my raincoat. "Traffic was a bear getting here. Is this the Christian event?"

She nodded, and Rodrigo passed her a pair of printed

tickets.

"I heard there was an accident on I-66. Always happens when it rains." She scanned our tickets. "You haven't missed much. We just closed the doors, and they're probably still taking their seats."

"I love your panda earrings! Those are adorable," Rodrigo uttered.

She blushed and fingered the earrings. "Thanks, they were a gift. All the tables with numbers on them are reserved. General admission seating is in the back of the room, no numbers. Feel free to sit at any one of those."

"Thanks," I murmured

Rodrigo held the door open, and I breezed past, stopping short as a most bizarre sight met my eyes.

"What the hell," I muttered under my breath.

"I don't think we're in Kansas anymore, Dorothy," Rodrigo said in appalled undertones.

Approximately thirty round tables were filled with white and silver-haired men and women. If I had to guess, I'd say ninety percent were of retirement age, making Rodrigo and I the youngest pair in attendance. But it wasn't the age of the patrons that made the scene so odd, it was that more than half of them wore a variety of crowns or tiaras above their brow. A few fancy gold crowns encrusted with multi-colored stones, reminiscent of Charlemagne's time, graced the heads of some gentlemen, while others wore cheap plastic pieces similar to those my sister and I wore for dress-up as kids. Moreover, the men were dressed in their Sunday-best suits, while the women wore colorful flowy gowns. Rodrigo fit in fine with his black and white ensemble, but my conservative gray pantsuit stood out of place compared to the hippy flower-power frocks.

"What's with the Disney Princess crowns?" Rodrigo's wide-eyed gaze darted from one table to the next.

"Rodrigo, I thought you said this was a right-wing Christian event," I murmured through my toothy smile.

"That's what Finley's scheduler told me."

A distinct sinking feeling settled in my gut. "Do you think she was having you on? I don't see him anywhere."

"Me neither."

By this time our statue-like presence was starting to garner stares from nearby tables. "C'mon." I tugged on his sleeve. "I see some empty seats at the table to our right." The table drew me, not only due to the available seating, but also because the occupants had hair color other than white or gray.

Rodrigo and I nodded and smiled at the two couples seated at a table for eight. I guessed the median age of the foursome to be in their late-fifties and surmised the hair color came out of a bottle. Before we could offer verbal greetings, the squeal of a microphone reverberated through the room, making everyone cringe.

"Good afternoon, ladies and gentlemen." A white-haired gentleman at the podium tugged at the microphone, which ended up falling off its perch and landed with a loud thud.

The lectern was mounted at the center of the long head table and that was where I finally spied our quarry—the only person on stage *not* wearing a crown atop his white-haired head. Nudging Rodrigo with my elbow, I tilted my head toward the front. He glanced up from the knife he was wiping with his purple linen napkin. The knife clanked as he set it absently on top of his soup spoon.

With some help from a hotel staff member, the octogenarian emcee got the mic adjusted properly and continued his speech. "I'd like to welcome you to the third annual meeting of Christians for Second Amendment Rights Management. My name is Buzz Pinhold, Founder and President of this fine organization." He spoke with a lilting Kentucky accent.

Rodrigo gasped, and my jaw fell open. For the first time, I zeroed in on the sign taped to the front of the podium. Though I was too far away to read the words that circled the logo, I could clearly make out a purple cross overlaid with the black silhouette of an assault weapon. And, upon further inspection of Buzz's crown, I realized he wore a circlet of upright rifle bullets. While Rodrigo silently clawed at my knee, I glanced around the room and realized one more thing separated the two of us from the rest of this group—we weren't card carrying NRA members. Which probably meant we were the only ones not packing heat.

Buzz carried on, recognizing the rest of the board members sitting at the head table and ending with the special guest and award recipient, Representative Finley, who, by this time, maintained a look of feigned interest. He raised his hand in acknowledgement of Buzz's introduction. Buzz then introduced another yahoo wearing a gold crown inlaid with red plastic rubies as Harold Shmeissenfenster, C2ARM's Award's Chair.

Harold's measured southern intonation droned on about the importance of second amendment rights, and how they played into his Christian values. He then proceeded to quote unfamiliar biblical scripture. When he cited a psalm foreign to me, Rodrigo made a queer choking noise, and I began to wonder if Harold had "creatively reinterpreted" his bible to coincide with his beliefs.

Eventually, he wrapped it up with, "It is now my honor to present this year's C2ARM Humanitarian plaque to Congressman Finley for his family values that reflect our Christian way of life, and for his continued support to keep assault rifles from being banned, thus maintaining the integrity of our sanctified Second Amendment Rights."

I gulped back the repugnance that rose in my throat. By this time, Finley's coloring had paled and he fidgeted uncomfortably in his seat. I had a sneaking suspicion the congressman hadn't realized the significance of the award, or the strange organization conferring it upon him. If I had to guess, one of his staffers was going to get an ass-chewing for not properly vetting the event. Glancing around the room, I noticed no one had their ever-present phones out snapping photos of the prestigious event. I found my answer sitting on the table. A gray Yondr bag rested next to the woman on my left.

I'd read about Yondr cases in the *Wall Street Journal,* and this was the second event I'd attended using the system. Before entering, phones were dropped into lockable cases to create a technology-free experience. Individuals kept control of the case, and on the way out there would be stations to unlock the phone and recycle the case. More and more schools and organizations were beginning to Yondr phones to keep them off social media and the proceedings out of the press. With our late arrival and Rodrigo's compliments, the brunette taking our tickets must have forgotten to jail our phones in a Yondr bag.

Since all eyes were turned toward the podium, I surreptitiously snapped a picture of Finley accepting the award, and a few photos of the general assembly, then set my phone to silent, lest it ring and give me away.

Finley's truncated acceptance speech consisted of a short and sweet, "Thank you."

Harold's face showed surprise, probably expecting something more from our esteemed congressman. Nonplussed, Finley returned to his seat. Not to worry, Harold shook it off with aplomb, making a joke about short speeches from politicians, and announced that lunch would now be served. Hotel staff, waiting in the wings, bustled around the room, distributing the first course.

The woman on my left smiled and introduced herself as Cecily. "Is this your first time at a C2ARM event?" she asked.

"Yes, it is." Her silver tiara reminded me of one buried somewhere in my closet, a relic from my twenty-first birthday pub crawl. Stymied for conversation, I blurted out the first thing that came to mind. "That's a nice tiara you're wearing."

Her pink, lacquered nails reached up to adjust it. "Thank you, I received it during a blessing ceremony last year."

"It's . . . nice," I bumbled. Cecily's companion turned to the other couple and started a conversation about a new handgun he'd recently purchased. The conversation was completely out of my league. The most lethal thing I was packing was a small pink stun gun that fit handily in my purse.

To my relief, a waiter's arm reached in front of me and I leaned out of his way as he put down a plate of crisp green salad. "Goodness, this looks lovely," I said to Cecily. "Would you mind passing the salad dressing?"

After handing over the gravy boat of vinaigrette, Cecily must have decided I was a lost cause, because she turned away and joined the handgun conversation. Which was fine, because I wanted to keep an eye on Finley.

Rodrigo tucked into his salad, and under the hum of conversation, I whispered, "Turn off your phone, or they'll force you to lock it in a Yondr bag." I nodded to Cecily's imprisoned cellular.

Rodrigo furtively stuck a hand in his right pocket to do as I suggested.

Our salad plates were removed, and a dubious gravy-covered chicken and mushroom course arrived. Before I could fork my first piece of fowl, a waiter came up to the congressman and whispered in his ear. Finley cumbersomely rose, tucked the plaque under his arm and, after a brief discourse with Buzz and Harold, exited the dais stage right.

I shoved my chair back. "Excuse me, I must go to the ladies."

None of our tablemates acknowledged my leave-taking because their heads were crammed together, admiring Cecily's husband's handgun. So intent on the congressman, I'd missed the introduction to show-and-tell. However, Rodrigo's mute gaze speared me.

"Feel free to continue eating. I'll only be a moment," I assured him.

His face turned to panic as he watched me seize my coat and purse.

I burst out of the ballroom into the wide empty hallway and took off at a fast clip. On the drive over, I'd had Rodrigo contact the hotel to see if Finley had taken a room. He was often known to do so during fundraisers in order to have a private space "to conduct business," code for: get his palms greased. The front desk claimed to have no guest under Finley's name, however it wouldn't be unusual for him to use a nom de guerre or book it under one of his staff members. I jogged around the corner and spotted a large bank of elevators. As I hurried toward them, the congressman came from the opposite side and pressed the button. My arrival coincided with the elevators and I followed Finley into the gaudy orange box.

He pressed twelve, stared down at his phone, and mindlessly asked, "What floor?"

"Twelve." The doors closed. "It's nice to see you again, Congressman Finley."

He drew his gaze away from the phone to give me a puzzled look. "I'm sorry, I don't recall."

"Karina Cardinal. I work for NHAA."

"Oh, right, you were working on the healthcare bill. Shame it didn't pass," he said without an ounce of sympathy.

"Yes, shame," I murmured in a fadeaway voice. "I was just in the C2ARM luncheon and saw you receive their Humanitarian Award. Congratulations." Looking pointedly at his empty hands, I wondered if he'd ditched the plaque in the closest trash receptacle he could find.

"Did you?" He cleared his throat and tucked the phone in his pants pocket. "Not the type of organization I'd expect you to be a member of."

"Oh, I'm not. I stumbled across it by accident and didn't realize I was in the wrong room until after the speeches started. But I found them so thought-provoking, I simply had to stay."

"Glad you enjoyed it."

"As a matter of fact, I was able to get a picture of you accepting the award."

He paled. "But . . . it . . . it was a technology-free event. There weren't supposed to be any—"

"Electronics?" I finished his sentence. "Yes, I noticed the Yondrs on my way out. I guess since I arrived late, they forgot to have me lock it up." My grin bordered on evil. "Shall I share the news? Send around a tweet? I think your constituency would be interested to hear about such a *distinguished* honor."

He licked his lips, adjusted his glasses, and pierced me with his shrewd, blue gaze. "What is it you want?"

"Twenty minutes of your time."

"I can have my scheduler—"

"Let's bypass all the formalities, shall we?" I checked my watch. "I'm free now. What about you?"

The elevator doors opened, and we were met by a slender man of average height, his crew cut hair sprinkled with grays, and his face sharpened by hawk-like features. "Congressman, I did as you asked . . ." I followed Finley off the elevator, and the man's voice faltered.

"Nick, I'd like to introduce you to Karina Cardinal, she works for NHAA. Miss Cardinal, my Chief of Staff, Nick Ross."

"Mr. Ross."

"Miss Cardinal." His grip was strong and firm and the veins

around his wrist bulged as we shook hands.

"I've agreed to give her a few minutes of my time."

Nick frowned. "You're stretched for time; the NTSB conference call has already started."

"Contact Sheila and let them know I won't be on it today and push my next meeting."

"Very well, sir."

"Miss Cardinal, I have a suite. If you'd like to join me there, I can give you your twenty minutes."

"Lead the way."

The room was your average hotel suite. It consisted of a neutral beige couch, two navy blue slipper-style side chairs surrounding a coffee table, and a television. The window curtains were open wide, and a standing lamp lent a soft glow to the rain-darkened room. A door to the separate bedroom was partially open. The coffee table in the suite was scattered with papers, a laptop, and Nick's half-eaten lunch. My stomach rumbled. The small salad had not been very filling, and the scent of Nick's steak and potato meal almost had me wishing I'd had time to eat the gelatinous-covered chicken. Almost.

Finley went directly to the wet bar and, reeling off the options, offered me a drink from the minifridge. I accepted a diet cola, and the congressman poured himself a club soda. Meanwhile, Nick sorted the papers on the table, shoved them into an attaché case, put the computer on top of the case, and his lunch on top of that. Balancing the items, and without another word, he retreated into the bedroom. The door barely made a sound as he closed it.

I took one of the slipper chairs while the congressman man-spread across the couch, adjusting the yellow, striped tie across his rotund belly. "I suppose you want to discuss the recent legislation I voted against. I'll tell you, there were a number items I agreed with. However—"

"Actually, that's not what I want to talk with you about."

"Then . . . how can I help you?"

"First, I wanted to say how sorry I am about what happened to your grandson."

The genial look he'd plastered across his face fell. "I don't know—"

"Come now, Congressman, you don't need to play coy. I spoke to Harper. As a matter of fact, we talked about the pharmaceutical legislation you were discussing, right before he died. I don't know if you're aware, but I was with him when he passed." I figured I'd get a better reaction if I claimed Harper gave me the information rather than a staff member. It did. For every sentence I spoke, Finley produced a variety of facial expressions ranging from disbelief, to surprise, to disconcertment.

He shifted uncomfortably and tugged on the tie. "He told you?"

"Yes. As a matter of fact, NHAA would be very interested in working with you on this initiative. However, before he died, the senator wasn't able to tell me how many votes *you* thought you'd be able to get."

"The idea is moot." Finley shrugged. "Harper's death saw to that. He was supposed to supply Tottengott, Goldman, and Tucker along with half a dozen other hard liners. Without him . . ."

"What if we got a Democrat to sponsor the bill? Or maybe, I'll work on Tottengott, Goldman, and Tucker and get one of them to sponsor on the Senate side."

"Forget it. It'll never work. The pharmaceuticals are very close to the Republican party, got them wrapped around their finger." He sipped his drink.

Shocked by his confession, I watched his Adam's apple dip as he swallowed, and decided to try a different tactic. "But what about your grandson? Doesn't that make you angry?"

"Of course, it makes me angry." His face reddened, and he slammed his glass onto the coffee table hard enough for the clear liquid to splash over the side.

"Then let's *do* something. You and me. If *you* can deliver the House, I'll do everything in *my* power to deliver the Senate. Let's call it the Harper Pharmaceutical Bill." I leaned forward, slamming my fist onto my palm. "Do you want to see the same thing that happened to your grandson and your daughter happen to other families? We need to take back the power and give it to the people. Why are we the only developed nation with this problem? Hm? Does that make you proud, Congressman?" My voice rose, and Finley jerked back. "No? Then stop taking the handout. Stand up to the oppressors!" I ended the speech with my fist in the air. I'll admit, I got a little carried away on my soapbox. If I hadn't been wearing heels, I might have jumped up on the coffee table.

Nick stuck his head through the bedroom door. "Everything all right?"

The congressman's expression could only be described as thoughtfully bemused. "We're fine."

Nick retreated. I sipped my diet soda as Finley scrutinized me, rubbing his chin. "You're very passionate. I suspect it's your passion that makes you good at your job."

"Aren't you?"

He gazed past me. "I was . . . once."

"If you can't be passionate about your children . . . what can you be passionate about, Congressman?"

"Nick!"

The stern features of his chief of staff popped out again. "Sir."

"Join us, will you?"

Nick came to stand next to the couch. I began to wonder if

I'd pressed him too far and was about to be ignobly thrown out on my keister.

"That legislation you were working on with Harper's people . . ."

"The pharmaceutical one?"

"That's it. I want you to reach out to them. Start working on the language."

"But—" Nick's eyes slid back and forth between his boss and me.

"What?" the congressman barked.

"Without Harper . . . " Nick eyed his boss warily. When Finley didn't respond, he cleared his throat and continued, "I was communicating with Christy Manheim. I'm not sure how much longer she'll be in the office."

"At least until the governor appoints someone. Let's move it forward. Have something to me by Monday." Finley got to his feet. "Will that make you happy, Miss Cardinal?"

I took my cue and stood as well, donning my raincoat. "It's not about *my* happiness, Congressman. It's about the health and happiness of the children in this nation." I couldn't resist one last punch.

"Leave your card with Nick, and we'll be in touch."

I fished one out of my purse and handed it over. Nick accepted it without a glance and stuffed it in his pants pocket.

"Thank you for your time, Congressman." We shook hands and Nick escorted me to the door. As I exited, my purse handle caught on the lever-style knob, bringing me to an abrupt halt. Turning to unhook it, I found those hawk-like features scowling down at me. He wiped the glower off faster than a hare escaping a trap, but I'd seen it and it left behind a feeling of foreboding. Christy had been correct, Nick was not on board with the agenda. I'd have to figure a way around him.

I checked my messages on the way to the elevator. There

were a dozen texts and two voicemails from Rodrigo. He wasn't happy with me and expressed his frustration using some choice words.

> *I cannot BELIEVE you left me here with these wack-a-loons. You better get back here soon.*

A few minutes later, he'd sent another.

> *It's been a while. Where are you? Tacky Tiara lady is asking.*

He'd waited barely two minutes before texting again.

> *WTF? Where are you? And WTF is in this chicken dish? It's disgusting, dripping with brown slime. This is so NOT gravy.*

Another only a few minutes later, and then a rash of them one after the other

> *Finley's gone. Did you follow him? Are you with him now? Tell me where, I'll join you.*
>
> *OMG, I think I just ate a gravy covered roach. Mushrooms should NOT be crunchy.*
>
> *That's it. I'm done. I'm leaving this gun-loving, crown-wearing quack party. Meet me in the lobby.*
>
> *I've been in the lobby for 10 minutes now. Where are you?*
>
> *I am SO going to get you for this defection.*

His final message was sent less than a minute ago.

> *I need to get this gravy covered cockroach taste out of my mouth. You can find me in the bar.*

I didn't blame him; it'd been a dirty trick I pulled, leaving him behind, although I figured he'd make his own escape sooner than he did. However, even Rodrigo's annoyed texts couldn't kill the excitement buzzing through me. It was time for a celebratory drink. I texted him.

On my way to the bar. Drinks on me.

Chapter Fifteen

The euphoria lasted less than forty-eight hours. One week after I attended Harper's memorial service, I awoke to the news that Congressman John Finley was dead. All the major channels plastered it across their morning talk shows. Just past midnight, his Lincoln Town Car was hit by a freight train in Northern Virginia. He and his driver had not survived the impact. Investigators had yet to make an official statement, which led to an array of speculation by talk show news anchors and so-called experts as to how such a tragedy could happen.

Coffee forgotten, I sank down onto the couch. My hand blindly searched the cushion for the remote, and finding it, I cranked up the volume as Channel 7's Sam Cactus introduced onsite reporter, Linda Lorelei. Police cars and flashing lights lit up the background as she delivered her report, but no footage of the train or smashed up car appeared on screen. I paused the newscast and searched the area surrounding Linda to see if I could get some clue that would identify the location of the accident. Train tracks in Virginia ran southwest out toward Manassas, or directly south paralleling the Route 1 corridor and Potomac River. Over the reporter's shoulder I could make out a warehouse and the last three letters of a company name—ERS. I pushed play and waited to see if the camera would shift to pick up more of the name. Linda took a moment to turn and describe the scene behind her and—boom—TOLVERS flashed across the camera's line of sight.

In an instant, I had my computer open. It emitted a low whirring as it booted up. A Google search revealed Tolvers Trucking Company and, zooming in on the map, I found it located south of D.C. in between Route 1 and the north-south train tracks.

The broadcast moved to a split screen between Sam and Linda. Sam asked, "Linda, do we know what the congressman was doing there?"

"No, we do not. The statement from the congressman's office simply said their thoughts and prayers were with the family during this dreadful time and asked that the public give the family privacy to mourn."

Sam posed an excellent question, considering the congressman rented an apartment a few blocks from his office; it seemed an odd place for him to be at midnight.

Morbid curiosity had me searching social media sites. A few minutes on Twitter, and I found what I'd been looking for—wreckage. The body of Finley's Town Car was a crumpled mess of steel, practically unidentifiable. Damage to the car was far worse than the high-speed accident that killed Princess Diana back in the 90s. One picture revealed a collapsed roof, doors crushed, all the glass blown out. The train must have been traveling at a fast clip; another photo revealed yards of debris from the initial impact to where the train finally stopped. Surprisingly, it didn't derail. The front engine showed minimal damage, and Linda said the engineer had been taken to the hospital for minor injuries. Train 1, Car 0.

The cell phone ringing startled me out of my contemplative daze. When I saw Rodrigo's number, I sent it to voicemail and dialed Mike instead.

"Agent Finnegan," he barked.

"Didn't get your coffee this morning?"

His voice noticeably softened. "Sorry, thought I picked up my work phone. I've been up to my eyeballs in this investigation, which is why I haven't called."

"That's what I figured, and it's not the reason for my calling now. Did you hear about Finley?"

"Yes."

"Is the FBI investigating?"

"They're on scene along with local law enforcement, NTSB, and Federal Railroad Association investigators."

"It's awful." I muted the television. "How could something like this happen?"

"You'd be surprised. Almost two thousand collisions happen yearly."

"Jeez. I had no idea train-car collisions were that rampant. How come we don't hear about them?"

"You do when it's local, like today, or when it kills a large number of people—"

"Or when it involves someone famous?"

"Precisely."

"Wow, first Harper, now Finley," I mused.

My last volley received no audible response.

"Mike . . . do you think the two are connected?"

"At this point, I couldn't even begin to speculate. My work phone is ringing again. I've got to run. Let's plan dinner for tonight. I'll call you." He hung up before I could utter another word.

Since I hadn't gotten around to drinking my now cold coffee, it took a moment for Mike's words to penetrate my boggled brain. He'd said, "at this point." Did that mean there *could* be a point in which the two would intersect?

Ugh! I pressed the heels of my hands against my temples. I needed a fresh cup of java and some sustenance if I planned to scramble down that rabbit hole. Which is exactly what it would turn into—a maze of unanswerable questions. At least, unanswerable for me. I'm sure detectives and agents could get what they needed in a matter of minutes.

I dispensed the skinned-over liquid down the drain, poured a fresh cup, and drank half of it before returning Rodrigo's call.

"Have you heard?" he asked, bypassing the usual civilities.

"About Finley?"

"Yes." His breath blew across the lines. "Thank the lord we didn't tell anyone at the office. Just one more lost cause we'd have to explain. There is no way this goes anywhere now that Finley's gone."

"I suppose you're right." I played with the rim of my mug. "Does any of this seem strange to you?"

"It all seems strange. But, if you mean the congressman getting hit by a train. Yes. It seems weird. I thought that only happened in the movies."

"I did too, until my FBI friend informed me that over two thousand train-car crashes happen every year."

"You're kidding!"

"Apparently not."

I stuck a slice of whole wheat bread in the toaster and pushed the lever. I never understood how people could do the low-carb diets. Oh, I'd read all the latest studies on how gluten was the enemy, and through genetic modifications we'd ruined wheat. However, bread, pizza, crackers, toast points, and brie had all gotten me through some rough times. I supposed it was my vice; I simply couldn't give up bread. "Are you coming into the office this morning, or do you have other meetings?" I asked.

"I've got offsite meetings this morning, but I'll be in after lunch. Are we still on for the opera tonight?"

It's a good thing he mentioned it. I'd forgotten. "Sure." I made a mental note to text Mike and let him know I couldn't make dinner tonight.

"Don't forget a cocktail dress. See you this afternoon."

I took a long, hot shower. No matter how much water beat down on my cranium, it couldn't pound out the feeling of apprehension that stayed with me throughout the day. It probably didn't help that I kept returning to the ghastly photos on Twitter.

Mike called midday. "I'm sorry, I have to cancel our dinner."

"No problem. I meant to text you, I can't go either. I'm going to the opera, to see Turandot, with Rodrigo tonight."

"Who's Rodrigo?" he asked sharply.

Was that a touch of jealousy I heard in his voice? "My gay coworker. I told you about him."

"Oh . . . right." That definitely sounded like relief. "Why didn't you tell me about the opera this morning?"

"Frankly, you barely gave me a moment to get a word in edgewise. And this past week, you've been relatively incommunicado."

He sighed. "I know. These cases are sucking me dry."

"Cases?"

Ignoring my question, he carried on as though I hadn't spoken. "I'll make it up to you. How about I pick you up for brunch on Saturday morning? Say, eleven?"

"You talked me into it. See you Saturday."

****

The cocktail party atop the Kennedy Center wasn't actually inside the lovely Rooftop Restaurant. It was in a generic box of a room next to it. Waiters with glasses of cheap wine and beer wove through the crowd while buffet tables in two corners provided a selection of finger foods. High top tables were scattered through the room.

Rodrigo, looking snazzy in a brown vest, navy slacks, and

blue shirt with French cuffs, had been able to elbow some space for us at one of the tables. With a Michelob in one hand, he nibbled his way through a variety of cheeses on his plate with the other, while I—in a black dress I usually referred to as "Old Faithful"— drank something resembling a Chardonnay and crunched on a celery stick.

"How did you get invited to this, again? The sign outside indicated this is a reception for the performers' friends and families. Do you know someone?"

Rodrigo snorted. "No, but I have a friend who works in the box office. He put me on the list. Usually these things can be light on attendance, so nobody notices a few extra people. However" —he eyed the room— "tonight it looks as though everyone's friends and family showed up."

He wasn't kidding. The room was wall-to-wall people, and they were dressed to the nines. The ladies wore cocktail and long formal dresses with their best jewelry. Conversation from all sides overwhelmed the piped in music, and the poor waiters barely made it ten feet into the room before being mobbed and their trays emptied. All the bodies made the temperature rise.

"Everyone is very fancy tonight," I commented.

"What?"

"Everyone seems to have pulled out the family jewels tonight."

"It's a charity event. The ticket sales are going toward Autism Awareness."

Someone jostled my arm, and I would have been covered in wine if it had been full. "I think I'm done here," I said in Rodrigo's ear. "I'm going to hit the little girl's room. Meet me in the hallway when you're finished."

He tipped his beer glass in acknowledgement, and I zigzagged my way to the exit. It was a breath of fresh air when I stepped into the hallway. I wasn't sure where the restrooms were on this level, so I took my chances with the right. My instincts were correct, a sign directed me, but as I turned the corner, I was brought up short by a long line of ladies.

Not being a good line-stander, and knowing the building had multiple bathrooms, I headed in the opposite direction and meandered the hallways in search of a ladies' room without a line. I finally stumbled across one on the opposite side of the building next to an alcove with an old-fashioned circular couch surrounded by pillars and antique mirrors. I'd always loved those types of round couches and decided I needed a selfie reclining on it. However, since it'd taken me so long to find the restrooms, my needs were now urgent. The photo op would have to wait. To my relief, the bathroom was empty, and I had my pick of the four stalls.

As I exited, voices of an arguing couple derailed my selfie plans. I waffled, trying to determine if I should retreat into the bathroom to wait them out or walk away and return later with Rodrigo. I'd just decided it had taken me so long to find the restroom that I'd better find Rodrigo, when I heard something that stopped me in my tracks.

"Nicolas, I promise you, I haven't spoken to anyone since his death."

"I never should have said a word. You can't be trusted!" a man's voice spat. That voice sounded vaguely familiar.

"How can you say that?" the woman said.

I shifted to see if I could see around the pillar and get a gander at the pair. Luck was with me. The antique glass must have been a two-way mirror. The man had his back to me, but the woman . . . she wore a brown cocktail dress that matched her long, sable-colored hair. Her heart-shaped face was dominated by a pair of square, black-rimmed glasses that were popular nowadays. But that face . . . I knew that face, and I wracked my brain to put a name to it.

"You talked to someone? One of your cronies? They would have been very interested in the turn of events. Wouldn't they?"

"Lower your voice, please, I don't like what you're insinuating," she said through stiff lips. Her eyes darted around the small enclosed space, then she whispered something I couldn't hear.

The man responded in a quieter manner, so I only caught a few words: "things under control," and "changing political climate . . . never be able to hold them off."

I shifted position to hear the conversation better.

"I don't understand. I thought it was an accident," the woman responded.

"Then explain to me, *Karen*—" He hissed her name. "Why do I have three voicemail messages from an FBI Agent?"

When he said her name, the puzzle pieces snapped in place. The woman was Karen Ferngull, Deputy Secretary of Health and Human Services.

"I—I'm sure I don't know," Karen stammered.

"We're done here." He turned, and I had to press a hand to my mouth. I knew I'd heard that voice before—Nicolas, a.k.a Nick Ross, Congressman Finley's right-hand man.

Karen caught his sleeve. "Nicky, wait. Give me a chance. Meet me at our usual spot tomorrow. Noon?"

"I don't think you understand, Karen, it's over. Ties severed." He yanked his coat from her fingers and straightened out the cuff. "One last piece of advice: Your friends are playing a dangerous game. I hope you've insulated yourself."

I rotated, pressing myself behind the pillar, and prayed Nick wouldn't notice me as he strode past—my position looked exactly like it was, that of an eavesdropper, and there would be no way to talk my way out of it. I needn't have worried, he didn't give a backward glance. Peeking back at Karen, I found she'd removed her glasses, her shoulders drooped despondently, and the look in her eyes could only be described as . . . longing. She collapsed on the sofa, her profile toward me, and I took the opportunity to make an immediate departure, all thoughts of my silly selfie having vanished.

Hustling back toward the reception room, I practically mowed Rodrigo down as I powered around a corner.

"Whoa!" He grabbed my shoulders to keep me from knocking him down. "Slow down, speedy. What's your hurry, and where have you been? I thought you went to the bathroom. I've been waiting outside for ten minutes."

"Sorry, I wasn't watching where I was going. I found a different restroom without a line."

"The doors should be opening soon, if they aren't already. Let's head downstairs before the masses realize the food is all gone and start flooding out."

Judging by the increased din in the hall and bodies spewing from the entryway like a tidal wave, I reckoned word had already gotten out about the lack of food. Nevertheless, I allowed Rodrigo to lead me to the crowded elevators, remaining silent on the short trip down to the main level. When the doors opened, I pulled Rodrigo in the opposite direction of the throng. "Do we have to go in immediately?"

He checked his phone. "I guess not, we still have twenty-five minutes before it's due to start. And they rarely start on time opening night. Why?"

"I could use some fresh air. Let's take a walk." I curled my hand through his elbow and led him through the heavy glass doors onto the River Terrace. The terrace was a large expanse of Italian Carrera marble with arresting views of the Potomac River; Rosslyn, Virginia skyline, and the infamous Watergate complex, depending on which direction you chose to stand. The nighttime air was relatively mild, and handfuls of folks dotted the balustrade as the setting sun striped the clouds in a rainbow of pinks, reds, and oranges. I chose a place along the handrail away from the other patrons and contemplated the Potomac River. My own mind was the exact opposite of the slow-moving waters and would be better characterized by the crashing turmoil of Niagara Falls. The meeting I'd just witnessed between Karen and Nick swirled in my mind.

"Are you going to tell me what that pensive look is all about?" Rodrigo interrupted my thoughts.

I gazed down the rail at a canoodling couple. The woman's lips were moving, but the rushing traffic below drowned out whatever she had to say. Blowing out a breath, I answered Rodrigo with a question of my own. "What do you know about Nick Ross and Karen Ferngull?"

His mouth made a moue. "How did you hear about them?"

"I just witnessed a rather heated discussion between them on my way back from the bathroom."

"Hm . . . sounds like trouble in paradise."

"Paradise? I thought Karen was married."

"She is."

"So, you're saying she and Nick Ross are having an affair?" That would explain her forlorn look and their hushed tones.

His lips twisted. "I figure Nick and Karen met while he was working at Finley's home office in New Jersey. Karen was working for J & P Pharmaceuticals then. They probably met at a fundraiser or something. J & P has sunk millions of lobbying dollars into Republican party pockets. When she moved to D.C., her husband remained behind at their mega-mansion in Jersey. He's into real estate or something."

"So she moved to D.C. not long after Ross?"

He squinted in thought. "I guess that's about right."

"How did you know they're having an affair?"

"One memory sticks in my head as clear as crystal," he explained, tapping a finger to his temple. "On the last day of boot camp class, Nick walked three blocks away from the gym—I remember because I'd trailed behind him on the way to my own car, still huffing from the workout—he got into a waiting white BMW. Once he closed the door, I saw him lean over and kiss her."

"How close were you? How do you know it wasn't just a peck on the cheek between friends?" I scoffed.

"No, it was a lover's kiss." He folded his arms. "There was definite tongue action. *And* . . . as she drove down the street, I watched her swat his hand away from her breast as he copped a feel."

So, when Nick told Karen he was severing ties, he meant their affair. Their conversation outside the bathroom ran through my head again, taking on a different connotation.

"Now you go."

"What?" I refocused on Rodrigo. "Oh. Well . . . I think I just witnessed their breakup."

"Really?" He leaned in closer. "Did she end it or did he? Don't tell me, her husband found out."

"Not that I know of. Nick made implications that she'd revealed information, but she said she hadn't talked to anyone since *his* death, whoever *he* is. And then, just before he walked away, he said that he hoped she had protected herself."

Rodrigo nodded and clicked his tongue. "Pillow talk. Gets people in trouble all the time. That was a relationship ready to blow up in their faces at any moment. Finley would have been furious if he'd found out Nick was sleeping with her."

"I imagine so. Now, they're kind of working on the opposite side of the tracks, so to speak, with her working for the administration and him on the legislative side of things."

Rodrigo's mouth formed an O, and I realized what I'd said.

"You know I didn't . . . I mean . . . oh, hell, you know I wasn't referring to the accident."

But it was too late, my reference to the tracks had Rodrigo connecting dots. "You don't think that Karen had anything to do with Finley's death . . . do you?"

I gave him a fierce look. "I don't see how. I mean, how could she have orchestrated a train wreck?"

"Wait a minute, let me think for a minute."

I didn't like watching thoughts run through Rodrigo's brain that had briefly squirreled in my own head.

"Whose death? Whose death was she referring to? Harper? Finley? Nick Ross . . ." He snapped his fingers. "It's Finley."

"What?"

"She messed with his car. Got it to stop on the tracks."

I shook my head. "How did she get the car to stop on the tracks at the exact moment the train was coming around the corner? How would anyone know he was going to be there . . . at that time? Even if you cut the brakes, you can't determine exactly where they'll go bad and stop the car."

"You're right, *she* didn't do it. *They* did it. They messed with the braking system."

"They? Who's *they*? You know that sounds crazy," I said dismissively.

Yet . . . Harper's pacemaker had been hacked, though Rodrigo didn't know. It'd already been proven that a car's system could be hacked. I remember reading an article a few months ago on this exact issue. Security specialists had been warning carmakers that all the fancy, keyless technology left vehicular computers open to hacking through security holes. At the 2010 Enigma Security Conference, a University of California professor demonstrated the vulnerabilities by hacking into a Chevy Impala and disabling the braking system. If you could disable a pacemaker, brakes on a car were a no-brainer. I could see where someone could simply stop a car right where you wanted it to.

I shook away the thought. "Again, who's *they*? And what's the motive?"

"Wait, just wait." He rapped his knuckles against the metal railing, paced away, pivoted, and returned. "I think I know who 'they' are. Who would it damage if we could get this bill passed?" He held out his hands, prompting the obvious.

My lashes dropped to half-mast and I replied drily, "You know who, Big Pharma."

"*J & P! It's Karen and J & P!*" he said gleefully.

"Rodrigo, Karen doesn't work for J & P any more. She works for the president. And who at J & P would be stupid enough to conspire against a senator and congressman?"

"No, listen, Karen probably still has tons of J & P stock. You and I both know, just the whiff of a price-fixing bill moving through Congress could tank their stock."

"So, she, no—they—did it for money? That's just *ridiculous*." I yelled the last word as a plane flew overhead on its approach into National Airport. It passed by and I lowered my voice. "I think you're blowing a simple breakup way out of proportion here. Maybe this has to do with her husband. Maybe he found out and Nick was angry about it because if her husband makes a stink, Nick could lose his job. Let's go inside."

Rodrigo must have noticed my gaze darting back and forth to the other patrons, for he didn't argue as we swept onto the red carpets of the Grand Foyer. The general buzz of conversation hummed around us, bouncing off the extravagant crystal chandeliers as voices floated up into the rafters of the sixty-foot ceilings.

"Their conversation is definitely suspect. We should ask around. See if we can find out more. Maybe I can reach out to Nick Ross," Rodrigo mused.

Regret settled in. "Listen," I murmured in an urgent undertone, "we don't know what any of this means. I only caught bits of Karen and Nick's conversation. Whatever theory you're rolling around in that head of yours is sounding a little crackbrained. All the reports are saying the train wreck is a simple accident. *I'm* not Nancy Drew, and *you're* not Sherlock Holmes. Get it?"

"What do you suggest we do?"

"Nothing."

"Nothing? *Nothing?* How can we stand by and do nothing?" Those dark brows rose high on his forehead. "What did Nick's final words mean?" he whispered fiercely.

"Maybe it just meant that Karen better have kept their affair a secret or her job could be in jeopardy. Or her actions could reflect poorly on the president. Besides, this is ridiculous, there is simply *no* motive. There wasn't even a bill, or a whiff of a bill. Those two old men were still farting around. Even if there was a bill, there's no way it would have passed in a Republican Congress. I can think of a dozen congressmen alone who wouldn't have allowed it to get out of committee. I don't care what votes Finley 'thought' he could get, it's all speculation. There's no way someone's going to murder a congressman *and* senator on a *what-if.* Pharma would've stepped up donations, lobbied hard, and killed it before it got legs to stand on."

"Okay, maybe a Ferngull/J & P conspiracy is a little farfetched. But there's something here. I can feel it in my bones." He made a fist. "We have to tell someone. The police or FBI. It's a lead. Right?"

I didn't know what *it* was, but I could tell Rodrigo wasn't going to let *it* go. "Fine," I sighed. "I will tell my FBI contact what I heard. Okay? Then it's in their hands, the professionals, you know?"

"Promise?"

"Yes, of course. I plan to see him this weekend. I'll let him know."

"You'll tell me what he says?"

"Yes."

"On Monday?"

I rolled my eyes. "Yes. Sheesh. Now hand the lady our tickets."

I thought that would be the end of it. However, fate is a funny thing. The usher guided us to our seats and a man, already seated, rose to let us pass.

"Miss Cardinal?"

You guessed it. My eyes met those cold, hooded features. "Nick Ross!" The surprise in my voice was genuine. "You're here!"

His brows drew down, enhancing the bird-of-prey look, and Rodrigo poked my back.

"I—I mean," —I drew in a breath and tried again— "I'm surprised to see you . . . with the accident . . . and all."

"It's a charity event, didn't feel I could miss it."

"I'm sorry to hear about Congressman Finley. You have my condolences."

"Thank you."

"I believe you've met my colleague, Rodrigo Alvarez."

"Yes . . . of course. It's . . . good to see you again." They shook hands, and I could tell by Nick's blank look that he had no clue who Rodrigo was.

"Let me add my own sympathies. Congressman Finley was a good, hardworking servant of the people. He will be greatly missed." Rodrigo was certainly a skilled bullshitter. I'm not sure how he didn't choke over those words, when so many times in the past, he had cursed Finley's "pig-headed" stance on legislation.

"Thank you, your kindness is appreciated during this difficult time."

"Of course, what a tragic accident. Be sure to let us know if there's anything we can do." Rodrigo produced a contrite expression that put my teeth on edge.

Nick turned to me. "It looks like we won't be working together after all."

"Shame," I purred, keeping a straight face. "I was looking forward to collaborating with you."

Another couple waited impatiently behind us, and I moved past Nick as the five-minute bell binged and the lights dimmed. We took our seats, and I uttered out the side of my mouth, "Not a *word.*"

Chapter Sixteen

Rodrigo must have agreed, because we didn't speak again until intermission. When the houselights came up, the two of us followed the rest of the crowd out to the Grand Foyer to stretch our legs and get a desperately needed drink. Luckily, our Orchestra seats were in a good spot and the music so moving, I'd been able to put Finley, the train wreck, and Nick Ross out of my mind and enjoy Puccini's libretto. However, while Rodrigo stood in line for drinks, I milled about and found myself drawn toward a coterie of men gathered around . . . you guessed it, Nick Ross.

I pulled out my phone and, with the nonchalance of a Siamese cat, sauntered in the vicinity the group, stationing myself behind of one of the taller men. Luckily, they were speaking loudly enough that I didn't have to hover too close. My back to the group, I donned a fierce expression while tapping my phone screen as though answering a complex text or responding to an email. In reality, I played Candy Crush.

As I suspected, the conversation revolved around the congressman's accident.

"What I want to know," piped in a voice with a Boston accent, "is what on earth was the congressman doing out there. I mean, don't get me wrong, isn't that kind of a ghetto area of Virginia?"

"Those tracks aren't far from the Potomac. I believe there

are million-dollar houses along there, and a marina too. Meryl and Shayna Westingshire have a second home down around there," said the man at my back.

"Still doesn't explain why Finley was down there. Nick, don't you know?" Boston voice asked.

" . . . nothing on the official schedule . . ." was all I caught of Nick's faint reply. He excused himself and left the group.

A snort drew my attention away from the colored candies at my fingertips, and I glanced up to find Elise Harper standing a dozen feet in front of me with a plastic glass of chardonnay in one hand and a black Gucci purse in the other. She wore a black dress with a black and red harlequin scarf around her neck.

"Elise?" The shock I felt at seeing her out in public so soon after her husband's death couldn't be feigned.

She glowered past me at the men who were now dispersing and wandering off in ones and twos. "I can tell you what he was doing there." She took a swig of wine.

I approached her. "Mrs. Harper, I don't know if you remember me, I'm Karina Cardinal. We met at the Women in Business fundraiser a few months ago."

Her bloodshot gaze shifted to size me up. "I remember. You came to the funeral. You sat with Sandy."

"Yes, I did. I didn't get to tell you in person, but I had a great deal of respect for your husband. He was a good man, and I'm so sorry for your loss."

Her eyes narrowed. "George spoke about you, he once called you spirited. Shrewd, but spirited."

I swallowed, unsure how to answer. "I'm surprised to see you here, I thought you'd be home in Michigan."

"A good friend had tickets, and Autism Awareness is an important cause to me. She thought it might cheer me up," she said drily.

"You're looking . . ."

"Like hell?" Her voice came out gritty and hard.

Makeup hid most of the tell-tale signs, but even the best foundation couldn't conceal the sagging mouth and dark undereye half-moons. ". . . Tired. How are you holding up? You said you came with a friend." I searched the milling crowd for someone to whom Elise might belong. "Perhaps I can help you..."

"Hanging on by a thread." Another gulp of wine went down, and I noticed her neutral nail polish was badly chipped. "There are things *I* must tie up here in D.C., including my husband's murder, before moving permanently back to Michigan."

I flinched at her terseness and scrambled to think of a response. "I'm . . . sorry to hear you'll be leaving the area. I thought . . . you might consider taking your husband's seat until the election."

She delivered a wry look. "No, I'm done with politics and the public life. I'm sick and tired of the press thinking my private life is their next story. Speaking of a story, have I got one for them. You heard those gossiping milkmaids?" She indicated with her wine where the now dispersed gathering of men had been. "*I* can tell you what Finley was doing in Virginia."

"Really? What?"

"High stakes betting."

"Poker?" That's not at all what I'd expected to hear.

"Poker, blackjack, sports games, take your pick. They'd bet on anything and everything. About a dozen Capitol Hill insiders get together monthly to bet on a basketball or football game and play cards. And I'm not talking for chicken stakes."

"What do you mean?"

"You ever wonder why Senator Wyatt stopped driving that classic Mustang and switched to a hybrid?"

"I assumed he garaged the Mustang and decided to go eco-friendly."

"Ha!" She guzzled the rest of the wine. "He lost it. To the honorable Congressman Grant Odom."

"Did—did your husband ever play with them?"

"Once. Wyatt invited him to a game a few years ago. George wasn't much of a gambler and he couldn't stomach the questionable company and high stakes. Or the overabundance of liquor."

"So, he'd been down to . . . what? Is it a home or a boat in Virginia?"

Elise gave an elegant shrug. "No idea. The game moved around. They even had a secret password to get in. It was all very speakeasy . . . and childish, if you ask me."

"Finley was a regular?"

"According to George." She tutted, "Stupid ass probably lost the farm and decided to end it all on the tracks."

"You think his driver agreed to that?" I said, unable to hide the tone of reproach.

That hard gaze rested on me. "No . . . you're right. Taking an innocent life along with his own wasn't his style. The news is probably right. It was just an accident. But if they get a hold of the reason he was down there to begin with . . ." She released a slow whistling sigh. "The press will have a field day. Poor Bitsy Finley. Can you imagine?"

Thinking back on some of my own interactions with the press, it wasn't hard to see how they'd blow something like this up into a mountain of a scandal. "Who was in charge of finding the venues?"

"They took turns. It's another reason George wasn't interested. The one he attended was at an estate in McLean. He said it was owned by one of Wyatt's campaign contributors. He felt the entire thing was shady."

The chimes sounded to let us know the opera would soon

resume.

"That's my cue." Elise tossed her plastic glass in a nearby trash can.

"Mrs. Harper . . . Elise." I placed a hand on her forearm. "I . . . I was with your husband when he collapsed. . . ."

Her gaze sharpened to a needle point as it bore down upon me. "Yes, the police told me."

I'd figured the cops had told her. Removing my hand, I questioned if going down this road was a mistake. "He . . . he spoke your name . . . at the end. He was thinking of you."

Those bloodshot eyes shimmered, and she inclined her chin. "Thank you . . . for that." Then she gripped my arm, her fingers, stronger than I expected, curled like the talons of an eagle. "Be careful, Karina. Don't let them beat you down. Keep up that passion and spirit my husband spoke of. D.C. is a dangerous, old boys club. Watch yourself." She sniffed and, releasing me as abruptly as she'd latched on, strode away.

My heart pounded, considering her words.

"You look like you could use this," Rodrigo said by way of introduction, and held a half-glass of red wine in front of my nose. "I couldn't find you, so I helped myself."

Gripping the thin plastic, I gulped down the cheap wine, much like Elise had just done. "Thanks."

"Is it true?"

My brows rose questioningly.

"Harper's last words?" he clarified.

I shook my head. "No."

"Then why say it?"

"I thought . . . I thought I was comforting a grieving widow."

"I'm surprised she's here." He watched her walk up the curving staircase to the box level.

"Me too. She seems to think Finley was at a private poker

game."

"The infamous floating craps game?"

"Floating craps game? I don't think she mentioned craps."

"Like from *Guys and Dolls*." Rodrigo rolled his eyes at my blank look. "Your musical theater knowledge is sadly lacking. The roaming Capitol Hill poker game? Rumor has it there are some pretty big folks playing."

"How do you know this? How have *I* never heard of it?"

"I listen to the gossip. You're too high class for that."

"Right." *More like, out of the loop.* "Anybody from the White House administration play?"

Rodrigo's eyes narrowed. "Not that I know of. Solely Capitol Hill. But . . ."

"But?"

"Maybe you're right, and Finley's death has nothing to do with Harper. What Elise told you about the poker game—it's dirty. Could be motive. Maybe Finley won a ton of cash and someone wasn't pleased. A new player who doesn't like losing? Maybe his car was pushed onto the tracks at just the . . . right? . . . or wrong time?"

Rodrigo's speculation about the poker game wasn't completely off base. However, it would be the very devil to prove it.

"That's what you need to tell your FBI friend, and . . ." He looked past my shoulder.

"And?"

"No time. The ushers are closing up. Come on, I don't want to miss anything."

We hotfooted it to the nearest door and slipped in as one of the red-vested ushers pulled up the doorstopper. The lights dimmed, and we shuffled past the other attendees. Nick Ross's seat remained empty through the final act, and Rodrigo never got back to explaining his thoughts about the poker game.

Chapter Seventeen

MIKE

"I thought we were going out for brunch. Is that what you're wearing?" Mike stood in K.C.'s doorway, wearing black jeans, a blue button down, and gray sport coat. She, on the other hand, wore a pair of faded leggings and a ratty UVA sweatshirt that, if he recalled correctly, went back to her freshman year.

"Come in. I decided to cook. We're having brunch at home. I have a quiche Florentine in the oven and I'm just about to put on the French toast. Would you like a Mimosa? Iced tea? Coffee?"

"I'll have the tea. It smells delicious." He trailed her into the kitchen. "But you didn't have to do this. I was happy to take you out."

"Oh, I know."

"How has your week been?" He stood in the middle of the kitchen.

She went to squeeze past to get the pitcher of tea out of the fridge. She smelled of vanilla and her coconut shampoo; she always smelled so good to him. Without thought, he caught hold and pulled her in for a kiss. She seemed surprised at first, but soon melted into his embrace and actively joined in. He pressed her against the pantry cabinet and considered tossing her up on the counter—to cross that line they'd been dancing around. He ran his hands down to her hips and squeezed.

BUZZ!

Mike practically dropped her on the floor as he turned in a

crouch position to defend against the incessant buzzing.

"It's just the oven timer. The quiche is ready," she panted, pressing fingers against her reddened cheeks as she pushed past him to silence the noise. "You seem a little on edge. What's going on?"

He straightened. "Nothing in particular. But with you? I never know."

"Ha, ha. Very funny." She laid the steaming quiche on the stove top. "The tea is in a glass pitcher in the fridge. Help yourself. I need to get the French toast started."

Mike poured himself a drink while K.C. dipped bread slices into the egg batter and laid them on a hot griddle. "So, how is the Harper case going?" she asked.

"Well, I think we're following a good lead."

"What's that look? You've got more than a lead. Have you got the guy?"

"The FBI does not comment on ongoing investigations," Mike replied from rote.

It was true, he had a lead and a damn good one at that. He'd tracked a series of death threats the senator had received to a hacker who went by the screen name NKBarbie. The hacker's affiliations included a handful of white supremacist groups on the dark web, and the FBI profiler who'd drawn up the dossier on this guy believed the NK in his hacker identity stood for Nikolaus "Klaus" Barbie. Barbie was a Nazi SS officer also known as the "Butcher of Lyon", a moniker earned for having tortured numerous French prisoners during WWII. Seemed appropriate for a white supremacist whack-job to take a famous Nazi as his avatar.

The hacker's threats had been widespread after a vote on an immigration bill that passed eight months ago. All of the Democratic party members received the same generic death threat that they'd tracked back to NKBarbie. However, he seemed to believe that any Republican who voted for the bill was a traitor to party and country, and the death threats to the Republican members of Congress in favor of the immigration bill were quite personal. He'd even told Harper to drop dead. NKBarbie had been credited with at least three different government hacks that clearly showed he had the skills to pull off Senator Harper's pacemaker hack and could have hired Jablonski through the darknet. The question that remained was whether NKBarbie was the mastermind behind the hit, or if there was a bigger fish running the op.

Yesterday, Mike reached out to a hacker informant he'd used in the past. The informant, a.k.a. LadyBlue, confessed she'd worked with NKBarbie in the past. Mike revealed to LadyBlue what the FBI believed NKBarbie's role in Harper's death had been and asked for her help. She said she'd have to think about it. So now Mike played a waiting game. Having dealt with informants in the past, he'd come to learn which ones needed a push and constant handholding, and which ones simply needed the facts and room to come to their own decision. LadyBlue was an independent thinker. There were moral lines she wouldn't cross, and Mike was banking on the fact that she'd see the murder of a senator as one of those lines. It didn't make the waiting any less torturous, but Mike was a patient guy and knew that sometimes you had to wait for a timid bird to come to you. If she didn't reach out by Monday, he'd contact her again.

"Whoa! It's like a tickertape parade happening in that brain of yours. Don't forget, I can read you. You're on to something. What is it? You can tell me. I promise I can keep a secret."

His brows drew down, along with his mouth. "Yes, I'm *well* aware of your secret-keeping abilities. It provides me no end of heartburn."

"Hey!" She wielded the spatula at him. "I told you about the break-in.”

"Yes." He folded his arms. "But what *aren't* you telling me?"

"As a matter of fact, one of the reasons we're eating here is because I have a whole bunch of stuff to tell you. I've got some leads for you."

"Why doesn't that ease my worries?"

"I have no idea." She flipped the bread. "Can you go ahead and cut the quiche?"

A few minutes later, they pulled their chairs up to the dining room table, where K.C. had set out placemats and silverware.

"Tell me your news," Mike said as he cut into his French toast.

"First, what can you tell me about the train wreck? Was it simply an accident?"

Mike's fork paused on the way to his mouth. "Why wouldn't it be?"

"Why are you being evasive?"

He popped the French toast into his mouth. The bread melted on his tongue as he chewed the sweet goodness. "Do I taste almonds?"

"Yes, I put almond extract in the batter. You're quibbling."

"Oh, no, counselor, not quibbling." He wiped his mouth to cover the grin.

She wasn't biting. "*Was* the train wreck an accident?" she said slowly, as if speaking to a toddler.

"There has not yet been an official decision."

"In other words, the FBI is looking into it further?"

"The vehicle—what's left of it—is being investigated by the FBI. NTSB and the FRA are investigating the train and the railroad crossing gates, which were *not* down as they should have been when the train came through."

"Does that happen often?"

"Occasionally. More than it should. Now it's your turn. I

can tell you're bursting with news."

K.C. proceeded for the next half hour to fill him in on her interactions with Finley at the C2ARM event. "I'm telling you these folks were a little . . . cuckoo." She swirled a finger next to her ear. "Have you heard of them? Does the FBI have a file on them?"

"The crowns sound familiar. I believe we've got dossiers on the group and some of their leaders."

"Well, that's good." She continued her story, next covering Nick Ross and Karen Ferngull's alleged affair and the breakup she'd heard at the Kennedy Center, and finished with Elise's revelations about the Capitol Hill floating poker game.

"While certainly titillating, I don't see how their affair connects to Harper's death. Nor am I impressed with your colleague's implausible conspiracy theory."

"I know. I told him the same thing. It's thin as phyllo dough. But I'm telling you, something smells fishy. This floating Capitol Hill poker game . . ." K.C. sighed and pressed a pair of fingers to her temple. "I spent the hours between two and four in the morning processing all of the information I've learned in the past few days. And while every piece has a perfectly logical and innocent explanation, something doesn't sit right with me. It's a math problem, yet *every* time I try to tally it all up, the abacus falls apart. I'm missing a piece of the puzzle. What am I missing? *Think*," she hissed, tapping those fingers harder against her forehead

Mike had continued to eat while K.C. told her story, listening with interest enough to humor her. When she mentioned her middle of the night insomnia, he'd looked closer, beyond the layer of makeup, and identified the puffiness beneath her lashes and the overall tension in her shoulders where he knew she carried her stress. He felt bad he couldn't tell her about NKBarbie, but he could do his best to put her mind at ease.

He pushed to his feet.

"Where are you going?"

Her eyes followed as, without a word, he came around the table and laid his hands on her shoulders and started massaging, his thumbs kneading the tissue at the base of her neck and spine. She moaned, letting her head drop forward.

"First, you need to relax and eat. It looks like you've lost five pounds since I saw you last Saturday, and you've taken all of three bites out of your meal. Second, even though I can't tell you what's going on in Harper's investigation, what I *can* tell you is that the lead I'm working is *very* promising. Off the record—"

"I'm not a reporter."

"Then let's say 'speaking hypothetically,' we believe we've identified the hacker. It's now a matter of locating him. There are literally dozens of agents, not to mention D.C. detectives, working on this."

"I know that." She tilted her head, allowing him to dig into a thick knot below her left shoulder blade.

"Now," he asked, "I've known you for how many years?"

"Urgh, please don't make me do math right now." She let out a groan of pleasure. "Ohhh, you got it. Right there, harder, dig deep. Uhhhh, yeah. Let's just say since college."

"Fine. Since college, I've learned a few things about you. You're very loyal to your friends and family. It's part of the reason you got yourself involved in that museum mess a few months ago."

"I have no idea what you're speaking about."

He rolled his eyes at her continued denial. "The other is, you tend to take the weight of the world onto your shoulders." He pressed a thumb into another knot. "Both figuratively and literally. And, somehow, you've taken it into your head that it's your job to find Harper's killer, likely due to the fact that he . . .

well, let's not mince words, he died in your arms. Which, by the way, I've been meaning to give you the number of a psychiatrist who works with FBI agents. But, we'll get back to that. As I was saying, you're trying desperately to find a killer whom you haven't the skills nor the tools to find. Neither is it your job to do so. Moreover, for some reason I cannot fathom, you've taken on Finley's death as well, trying to connect the two through . . . what? This mobile poker game? Or was it because they were *talking* about proposing a new bill together? I'm confused. Where did you say the connection came in?"

"Gee, when you say it like that, I realize either, A. I'm way off in left field. Or, B. You're just being an ass. However, since you're an ass who's massaging the past two weeks of stress out of my body, I'll let it slide and admit that you're probably right. Harper and Finley's death don't have anything to do with each other. If" —she pushed his hands off her shoulders and turned in her chair to face him— "if *you* accept that there is a possibility that there is something dirty about this poker game."

"I will consent to the following: the poker game is certainly dirty. There's no gambling in Virginia. But, as you know, the FBI tends to turn a blind eye to private games in people's basements. There are far more pressing concerns than chasing down a bunch of spoiled, wealthy senators and congressmen who want to put their prize Cadillac in the pot."

"It was a Mustang. A classic 1965 convertible GT."

He cleared his throat. "K.C., I think you are off base here. You're seeing conspiracies around every corner. Like I said, with the senator's death and the break-in—"

"Don't forget being a prime suspect for the murder, myself, *Agent* Finnegan." The sarcasm oozed off her tongue.

"Now you're getting defensive."

"Of course, I am. This is exactly why I worried about telling you all of this. That you wouldn't take me seriously, pat my head, and tell me to 'leave it to the professionals.'"

"K.C." Mike's voice held a strong note of warning.

"Don't 'K.C.' me. Just like with that damn painting, I *know* in my gut."

"What painting? I thought you didn't know anything about a painting."

K.C. reddened and glanced away. "There is something fishy going on."

He let it go. "Tell me what exactly is fishy."

"Well, what about what Nick said to Karen about her friends playing a dangerous game, and he hoped she'd insulated herself? If that doesn't sound . . . suspicious, I don't know what does."

Mike froze. "When did he say that?"

"I *told* you. When I was eavesdropping on their conversation."

"No, you didn't tell me that. You told me they broke off the affair. What were Nick's exact words?"

"What I just said—her friends were playing a dangerous game. He hoped she'd insulated herself."

"What friends?"

"He didn't elaborate, and I wasn't in a position to ask for clarification. But Elise said Harper played poker at some lobbyist's home. Maybe they were playing at Karen's home . . . and . . . maybe something went wrong. Finley lost something big. Maybe to Karen herself."

Mike rubbed his chin and paced away.

"Ha!" K.C. pointed. "See, *now* you're thinking that it *is* kind of suspicious."

"It's certainly . . . odd."

"Sus-pish-us." She crossed her arms and gave him a squinty-eyed glare that actually made her look really cute.

Mike bit his lips to keep from breaking into a grin which he knew would piss her off. "Okay," he capitulated, "I'll make you a deal. I will use some of my contacts—i.e. FBI resources—to look into this Capitol Hill poker game." She opened her mouth, but Mike cut off whatever she was about to say. "*And* I will check out Nick Ross and Karen Ferngull. As government workers, we'll have files on both."

"And if you find any red flags?"

"It'll be followed up."

"Fine." K.C. turned back to her food, making a show of rearranging her napkin. "And don't forget to check on that C2ARM group. Maybe they found out he ditched their plaque in the circular file and got offended."

"I wasn't finished."

Her fork and knife paused above the plate. She rotated her head with raised brows.

"I want you and your work friend to lay off this independent investigation you've been running. *If*, as you say, there is something behind all of this, you may be putting yourselves in danger."

"More danger than having a mobster attack me in the stairwell, or a merc for hire break into my home in the middle of the night?" she said with wide-eyed smartassness.

Mike blanched, and he ground out, "That's not funny, K.C."

Her face fell into contriteness. "No, it's not."

"I need your word."

"Fine. If you promise to look into it. Then I will stop . . ."

"Snooping?"

She tsked. "Investigating."

Good lord, this woman was persistent. "When you're not a professional, we call that snooping."

Her mouth pinched up. "When you act like an ass, we call that, 'unlikely to get laid.'"

His face lifted. "Really? Today?"

"Not today. *Ass.*"

"Hm. I wonder . . ."

The squinty eyes were back, but Mike simply stared her down. Subtly, he licked his lips and gently ran a finger down her arm.

Her mouth twitched. "Do you think it ethical to sleep with a murder suspect?"

"You're not a suspect."

"Are you *sure* about that?"

He cleared his throat. Although he wasn't investigating her, he hadn't gotten a definitive answer from McGill when he asked about Karina's status in the case. McGill had left it at "person of interest" and suggested Mike keep an eye on her. "Make sure she doesn't leave the country," he'd said. After that, Mike stopped asking and pursued NKBarbie with a single-minded determination.

He plopped down into his seat at the table and ran a hand through his hair. "I suppose we should wait until this case has been cleared up."

"Actually . . ."

He looked up with hopeful anticipation.

"Never mind. I guess you're right. We should wait until my name is completely cleared. God forbid the papers get a hold of the story. What tabloid fodder—I can see the headlines now: *FBI Agent Sleeps with Senator's Murderer.*" She made a grand gesture, as if the headline was emblazoned across a marquee. "Which, by the way . . ." Her gaze snapped back to him. "I've been wondering why the vultures haven't been at my doorstep since you announced Harper's death was murder. Why didn't one of them dig up my name?"

"None of the records are public until the case is closed."

"So, after the arrest, or after the trial do they become public?"

"After trial."

"Whew. That's a load off my mind. It'll be old news by then."

"I suppose."

"Hm, I don't know. You're looking pretty hot today . . . maybe . . ." She looked down at her ratty sweatshirt and brushed at an old stain. "On the other hand, I can see why you're not tripping over your own two feet to carry me off into the bedroom." She brushed aside a stray hair, tilted her head in just that way, and grinned at him.

His work phone buzzed with a text message. "Sorry, I've got to take this."

K.C. shrugged as he left the table to check his encrypted Blackberry. The text came from LadyBlue.

> *I'm in. NKBarbie will be at Blackhats in the Big Easy Con in New Orleans next week. I've arranged a meetup. He's confirmed he'll be there. I leave on Tuesday. The meet is set for Wednesday. Use this number to reach me.*

Mike couldn't believe his luck. Not only was LadyBlue in, she'd set NKBarbie up for them. Wednesday. They'd have to start getting things together to arrange the sting. There was already a contingent of FBI folks planning to attend the hacker con. If he hadn't been on this case, he would've been there too. As it was, he'd already transferred his conference registration to another agent.

Mike replied to LadyBlue.

> *Yes, we can make it happen. Will contact you soon with the details.*

He turned to find K.C. ignoring him and tucking into her meal. He hated to cut their date short. They were getting so little time together these days. Once this case was over . . . he made a silent promise.

"You're not going to like this. I have to go. Work." He held up the phone.

Slowly, she chewed and swallowed. "Now?"

"I'm afraid so," he said with regret. "I'll be going out of town for a while."

"Where? Can you tell me?"

He debated for a moment. "Louisiana. I can't tell you anything else."

"This is it, isn't it? The lead you've been following? It's panned out? Ooh, I can tell by the shine in your eyes. You're excited. Well, don't worry about me. Go get 'em, Tex."

"Tex?"

"Would you prefer pard-ner? Sheriff? Super Agent?"

"I prefer Mike."

"Go get 'em, Mike! *Yehaw!*" As she spoke, she jumped onto her chair, circling her hand overhead, looping an invisible lasso.

It was so darn cute and comical, Mike couldn't help the silent laughter that shook his shoulders. This was the spontaneous, fun K.C. he remembered from their college days. Like the time she'd taken the dare to sing "There's No Business Like Show Business", à la Ethel Merman, on the table at Taco Bell, at two in the morning, in exchange for a burrito. She'd been out of cash and had post-study-group munchies. It was good to see the kookiness come out as if it'd been lurking beneath the surface of the highly polished D.C. lobbyist. Especially considering the recent stress she'd been under.

"When did you suddenly come from Texas?" He gripped her at the waist, helping her off the chair. Without shoes on, her nose came right to his chin.

"Dunno. It seemed appropriate. You know, to pump you up, like football coaches and military leaders do before combat. I'm *trying* to be supportive here."

"Thanks, I appreciate it. Now is the time for you to kiss the hero before sending him off into battle."

And she did just that, leaving him with a kiss that would send even the most hardened of heroes into the fray with renewed energy and confidence.

Chapter Eighteen

Just as I put the last dish in the washer, my phone rang. Rodrigo's smiling face stared back at me. I guess he couldn't wait for a report until Monday.

"Hello, Rodrigo."

"Did I catch you at a bad time?"

I pressed the start button, and the dishwasher began its gentle hum. "Not particularly."

"What are you doing this afternoon?"

I'd cleaned the apartment yesterday afternoon, and since I'd originally planned to spend the weekend with Mike, his abrupt departure left me at a loose end. There was always work but . . . bright sunlight slashed across my living room floor. A robin landed on the balcony railing and began to sing. This morning, the weatherman predicted a mild day in the upper sixties. It appeared spring had finally arrived.

"Karina?"

"I think I'm going to get a mani-pedi today. Why?"

"Uh . . . well . . . I was wondering if you wanted to drive down to Potomac Mills to go shopping?"

Potomac Mills is an outlet mall in Virginia, just off I-95, in one of the worst traffic spots of the north/south corridor. Even on Sunday, you could spend half an hour or more sitting in crawling traffic. However, it wasn't the traffic concerns that had me stumped. The fact that Rodrigo would call me out of the blue to go shopping seemed odd. I didn't feel like we had a shopping together sort of relationship. We were work colleagues. Shopping was an activity I did with girlfriends, or my sister.

"You want to go shopping? With me?"

"There's an IKEA down there. I need some storage bins, and I want to look at their bookcases."

"Oh, furniture. Actually, I'm interested to see what kind of closet organizers they've got. What time were you planning to go down?"

"Whenever you're available. Alfonse already left for work. He has to prep for the Sunday brunch buffet."

"I can go anytime." I knew Rodrigo lived in the city with Alfonse. "Do you want me to meet you somewhere closer to the highway?"

"You're in Alexandria, near the GW Parkway, right?"

"Yes, my apartment complex is just off the Parkway."

"Text me the address. I'll pick you up, and we can take the Parkway south to avoid 95 traffic."

"Okay. Text me when you get into the parking lot. I'll come down."

Thirty minutes later, Rodrigo and I motored south along the George Washington Parkway past the wildlife preserve and Belle Haven Park in his Subaru Forrester. He'd opened the sunroof and the radio blasted out a turbulent Bach concerto. Beyond the initial greetings when I got in the car, we didn't speak. I enjoyed watching the beautiful scenery of fluffy pink cherry blossoms and blooming white Bradford pears while Rodrigo seemed intent on the music and the road ahead. The concerto came to an end as the entrance to Mount Vernon flashed past, and he turned the music down.

"Did you talk to your FBI friend?"

"As a matter of fact, I did. He said he'd look into it. See if there were any red flags."

Rodrigo gave a grunt. "Anything else?"

I didn't feel the need to tell him about my promise to Mike to keep my nose out of the investigation. "No. Why? Should there be?"

"I wondered if he'd tell you anything about the case."

"The FBI doesn't—"

"—comment on ongoing investigations," Rodrigo finished for me. "I get it." He turned the music back up and we didn't speak again until he took an unexpected left.

"Hello . . . I don't think this is the right way. You have to stay on Route 1 until we hit the Prince William Parkway. It's about another mile down the road."

"We're taking a detour." He slowed as we drove through a neighborhood filled with small, boxlike brick houses that, I guessed, were built in the forties or fifties. Judging by the variety of work trucks, panel vans with attached ladders, and late model cars, it looked like a working-class neighborhood. Many houses had quirky additions jutting out the side. Some were rundown, while others had been completely renovated with second floor additions and new vinyl siding. The new houses stood out among their smaller counterparts. I'd never been in this area before.

"What kind of detour?" I asked as I ogled a red brick rambler with a short white picket fence. Its miniscule front yard was filled with gnomes, Japanese pagodas, tiki torches, and spinning decorations with no rhyme or reason to the layout. It was as if someone had hit a fire sale at the local nursery, bought everything they could fit into the pickup truck, then simply tossed it out the back end, allowing the pieces to remain wherever they landed. "If it's supposed to be scenic, so far, I'm not impressed."

"Just a little further."

We continued past the housing communities into a warehouse district, but it wasn't until I saw the Tolvers Trucking sign and the railroad crossing in the distance that I clued in to our destination.

"You're taking us to the scene of the accident, aren't you? Why?"

"It's on the way," he said with nonchalance.

But I knew better. "Rodrigo—" My voice held a warning note. "What are we doing here?" The entire reason he called *me* to go shopping became as clear as my mom's Waterford crystal glasses.

"Call it morbid curiosity. Don't you want to see where it happened?"

I had seen it. On Twitter. However, since we were here, it couldn't hurt. Rodrigo slowed the car to a creep as we approached the tracks. The railroad crossing signal remained silent, its red and white gate up. A yellow, diamond-shaped road sign warned NO TRAIN HORN. To my dismay, he continued in creep-mode across the two sets of parallel tracks, slowing as much as he could without actually coming to a stop.

We glanced left, then right. There was no blind curve or trees to block the view. The tracks came and went over the road straight as a balance beam.

Finley's car had been hit by a southbound train. Small bits of metal remnants and glass glinted along the sides of the tracks and a lonely yellow streamer of police tape wiggled in the breeze. The rear tires bumped over the second set of tracks and I released the breath I'd been holding. We came to a T intersection where Rodrigo brought the car to a complete stop, and then we stared at each other.

"How did they not see that train coming?" Rodrigo asked the question that I'd been thinking as we'd turtled over the crossing.

"It was dark. The crossing arms never came down, and that sign back there said the train doesn't blow its horn here. Probably something the neighborhood banded together to put a stop to. I mean, look at that house," —I pointed over my shoulder to the left— "it's practically on top of the tracks."

As a matter of fact, an entire row of homes backed up to the tracks. I couldn't imagine having trains in my backyard. Set back from the railroad, on our right, rose a fancy neighborhood of mini-mansion style homes, with two and three car garages, perfectly manicured front lawns, and swimming pools, built around the early 2000s, if I had to guess. In juxtaposition, to our left stood older homes, ramblers, and cape cod styles, developed over decades, not dissimilar from the neighborhood we'd passed through on our way here. One of the houses looked like something directly out of *The Brady Bunch* show.

I continued, "I'm guessing wrong place, wrong time. Maybe Finley's driver had been drinking or was distracted by his phone."

"How do you know the crossing arms never came down?"

My mouth dropped open and I stared at Rodrigo. "How did I? They said it on the news." *Didn't they?* Mike told me. Had they not released that information to the public?

"Hm. I didn't remember hearing about that. Which way?"

"Left," I said at the same time as Rodrigo said, "Right?"

"I think there's a marina down that way." I pointed to the left. "Let's check it out first, then we'll come back here to Richie Richville."

Rodrigo swung the wheel to the left. This part of the neighborhood had been organized in a grid pattern with square blocks. The first street on our right had Rodrigo slamming on the brakes.

"Holy shit." He rotated the wheel. Straight ahead of us, at the end of the block, stood an enormous three-car garage waterfront home. Judging by its exterior, I would guess the house was more than 4000 square feet. I couldn't tell from the front, but I surmised it had a dock and probably a fancy boat off the back.

"How much do you think that's worth?" Rodrigo asked.

"A million two?"

"It's got to be worth more than that. I say two point three." He turned left and cruised the strip of waterfront homes.

A few more looked built within the past decade while others were older and more modest in size. We worked our way out of the neighborhood, back to the main road, and it wasn't much further until we arrived at our destination. A modest sign identified the Tyme-n-Tyde Marina. The chain-link gates were open, and we followed a red pickup truck inside. Two enormous, yellow-beige warehouse-type structures blocked the view to the Potomac River. A couple of large boats were up on stands and the parking lot was almost full.

"Should I park?"

"Sure. It's a nice day, let's check it out." I was unsure what we were looking for, but I enjoyed enviously staring at other people's boats as much as the next guy.

He parked on a grass spot next to the red pickup. A grizzled guy in flip-flops, ballcap, and ratty khaki pants gave a friendly wave, then heaved a cooler out of the back of the truck. I stepped out of the Subaru and figured I fit in with my white T-shirt, denim capris, and red Chuck Taylor sneakers.

"Could you do me a solid and shut the tailgate for me?" the stranger asked.

"No problem." I gave it a shove and slammed it closed.

"Thanks, poppet." He trotted away with his full cooler.

Rodrigo glanced at me and mouthed the word *poppet?* I bit my lip to keep from laughing. My coworker's style harkened to preppy-chic in his red skinny pants, black and red striped polo, and leather loafers with no socks. We followed our Jimmy Buffett lookalike at a leisurely pace. The rev of an engine had me stopping short, and I threw out an arm to halt Rodrigo. An enormous forklift carrying a cabin cruiser wheeled past us. The driver positioned the boat over a slip, then lowered the arm into the water with a gentle splash. Two guys standing on the dock grabbed the bow and stern lines, pulled the boat forward out of the forklift prongs, the arm raised, and the driver backed up. Once out of the way, the dock guys tied the lines to the cleats, then hurried to a neighboring dock to help an incoming boat. Jimmy Buffett yelled something to the forklift operator, and the big red machine maneuvered back into the dark opening from whence it came.

"It's a boatel." I took off my glasses to see better into the cavernous warehouse. Boats racked side-by-side four levels high. The marina, or cove was a better term, housed a bunch of docks for dropping and removing the boats by the forklifts. Across the cove, half a dozen large boats, tied to conjoining docks, bobbed gently in the water. I guessed they ranged from thirty to forty feet. Big, but they were nothing compared to some of the yachts and ships I'd seen at the Alexandria marina—some with their own dinghies or jet-skis attached to the stern. In a side area out of the water, two boats were up on stands, being washed down.

"Can I help you, folks?"

Rodrigo and I turned to find the voice.

"Up here," it replied.

It took a moment for my eyes to adjust to the dimness of the mechanics' garage. A sandy-haired man in jeans and a grease-stained T-shirt stood above us in a bright yellow bowrider with its engine lid up.

"Hi. We've never been here before. I saw the sign for your marina and we decided to swing in."

"You looking for a place to slip your boat?" he asked.

"Uh . . ."

I cut Rodrigo off before he could say anything, "Well, I'm not sure. What's the largest boat you can put into the boatel?"

"Twenty-six feet. With an eight-foot beam."

"Uh-huh." I had no idea what he meant by beam. "What about those docks across the way?" I pointed.

"The largest we can put over there is forty, but they're booked for the season."

"So, you don't really dock the big ones, fifty-, sixty-footers here?"

He shook his head. "Nah, our channel isn't deep or wide enough to handle something like that. You'd get hung up." He pointed to his right where a Navy blue, striped bowrider filled with young kids slowly made its way through the narrow inlet. "You might want to try the Belmont Bay or Hoffmaster's on the Occoquan if you need to slip something that large."

The giant forklift wheeled out another good-sized, black-and-white cabin cruiser. Rodrigo and I watched the process in fascination as *Gone Fishin'* dropped into the water. Once the vehicle backed out of the way, Jimmy Buffett loped down the dock with his cooler and climbed aboard.

I returned my attention to the mechanic. "How late at night do you run the forklifts?"

"In the spring and fall, until six. During the summer, until eight."

I nodded.

"What happens if you come in later than that?" Rodrigo asked.

"You have to dock it yourself. The boys will put it away in the morning."

I glanced around. This little marina was doing a booming business, but instinct was telling me this wasn't where Finley came on Thursday night. Not only because it'd been both rainy and windy that night, also because none of the boats in front of me looked swanky enough to host a secret card game for Capitol Hill congressmen.

"Thanks for your help."

"Anytime." The mechanic ducked back into the engine.

"What are you thinking?" Rodrigo asked as we sauntered back to the car.

"I don't think the card game was held here."

"No? Too pedestrian? I don't know, one of those forty-footers looked big enough to hold the game." He glanced back over his shoulder.

"True. But I spotted four different cameras, and there may be more. Too many to provide the secrecy this clan seems to crave. Also, we had a thunderstorm Thursday night. Nobody wants to be rocking on the water in a thunderstorm."

"The storm," he said, ruefully snapping his fingers. "I'd completely forgotten about that. One more reason they may not have seen the train coming."

"Yes." It occurred to me we already had the answers to what happened. A tragic accident on a rainy night. Were we wasting our time driving around the area?

Back at our T intersection, Rodrigo stopped. "Should we check out Richie Richville?"

"Up to you."

"I want to see some of those swanky homes."

We weren't disappointed. The houses wound around each other in circles and cul-de-sacs, all of them built with an eye toward having at least a tiny glimpse of the river. The backyards were surrounded with see-through, wrought iron fencing that allowed open sight lines to the water. About fifty percent of those yards housed swimming pools. Many of the homes further back from the water had second floor balconies. The homes directly on the waterfront were similar to the first one we'd gawked—four to five thousand square feet, plenty of garage space, and lots of decking to enjoy the view.

"Not too shabby." Rodrigo pointed to an enormous waterfront home at the end of the court with an inground pool and private dock.

"They're all enormous," I sighed. "And every one of them could easily house an upscale poker game. There is no way we'll be able to tell where Finley came from. Even Nick Ross said he didn't know where Finley was headed that night. Nothing was on his official schedule."

Rodrigo leisurely circled the cul-de-sac before bringing us to an abrupt standstill, his gaze glued to the rearview mirror.

"What's up?"

"That's Karen Ferngull's car."

I looked over my shoulder. "Which one, the black SUV in the driveway or the BMW sedan on the street?"

"White BMW."

"You remember the license plate?"

"No."

"Then how do you know it's hers?"

"I just . . . know," he said with the intensity of Dirty Harry.

I snorted. "There are a million white beamers in our area. Heck, I bet every one of these homes has a BMW or Mercedes in the garage. How do you know it's Karen's?"

"That white BMW has D.C. plates."

"Are you sure? I can't tell. Back up."

"I'm not going to back up."

"Why not? And so what if they've got D.C. plates? *You've* got D.C. plates. I see D.C. plates in Alexandria *all* the time."

"Trust me. I saw the D.C. plates. As a matter of fact—" He coasted the car around the corner, parking next to the curb, and turned the engine off. We had a good view through the branches of a magnolia tree of the BMW.

"What are you doing? Going to knock on the doors and ask if Karen Ferngull lives here? Can she come out to play?"

"It's a stakeout," Rodrigo informed me.

"A stakeout? Are you kidding? I thought we came down here to visit IKEA."

"This may be a break in the case."

I had a feeling this stakeout fell under Mike's interpretation of snooping, and I doubt he'd be pleased. "Honestly, Rodrigo, I think the cops and FBI have it all under control. I doubt they need our help. Besides, look at this neighborhood. Someone's going to notice us. How long do you think we can sit here before the cops show up?"

"Scooch down in your seat. Like this."

"Yeah, because that's not at all suspicious." I stared at my carmate as he tried to fit his long legs under the steering wheel. "Oh, for heaven's sakes. Look, that house across the street is for sale. Go get one of the flyers and we'll pretend to be interested in it."

"You're right. That's a brilliant idea." He opened the door and kind of rolled out of the car to retrieve the flyer.

"What's it listed at?"

"Seven eighty-one. Here." He passed me the three-page brochure.

"Very nice." I studied the materials while Rodrigo diligently kept an eye on the white BMW. "It's got five bedrooms, four baths. Four thousand square feet. A huge kitchen, look." I pointed to a photo. "I envy that kitchen. Except for the granite counters, not a fan of that color. Wait, check out the study, it's got a fabulous view of the water. Am loving—"

"Holy shit. It's *her*," Rodrigo hissed and slunk down again.

Sure enough, Karen Ferngull ripped open the car door and slung her purse inside. She followed the handbag, slamming the door. She then proceeded to make a phone call in which a lot of pinched face and hand gestures ensued.

"Whooee, she's pissed about something."

"Did you see which house she came out of? I didn't notice." I asked, craning my neck to get a better view.

"The one across the street with the rocking chairs on the front porch."

The car roared to life, slammed into gear, and peeled out. I watched in horror as Karen whipped around the corner so fast, she almost clipped Rodrigo's back end.

"What the hell! That bitch is cray-cray. Did you see she almost hit my car?"

"I don't think she even noticed. Should we follow her?"

Rodrigo started the car and took off down the street. Karen had already turned onto the main road out of the community, so her car wasn't in sight. However, there weren't too many roads coming into this area, and I had a feeling Karen was headed back to the highway.

"There she is, crossing the tracks. Don't get too close. We don't want to tip her off."

Rodrigo slowed the car to stop at the T intersection and turned left. Our slight hesitation cost us. The railroad crossing lights blinked and the arms descended. A moment later, a freight train barreled through. Rodrigo cursed under his breath and shifted in the seat. By this time, I knew following Karen was a lost cause. It was probably for the best; I imagined we'd just be following her back to D.C. The sign was correct, the engineer didn't blow the horn. It felt very nostalgic to hear the rumbling click-clack of the wheels on the rails as the graffitied freight, blackened coal and dripping oil cars rolled past. I remember on family car trips it was always an exciting adventure, at least for us kids, when we'd have to stop for trains to pass. I counted seventy-five cars in total. Eight vehicles stacked up behind us while we waited.

The gates moved up and Rodrigo gunned it, bumping over the tracks.

"Whoa, Rodrigo, give it up. We'll never catch her."

He slowed down and sighed. "You're right. Where to now?"

I stared at him. "You're kidding, right? IKEA?"

"I almost forgot." He gave a sheepish laugh.

"Well, I, for one, am done playing detective. Take me to the mall, Jeeves. I want to look at closet organizers."

"Yes, Miss Daisy." The car remained silent for a few minutes before Rodrigo picked up the conversation again. "So . . . I think we figured out where Finley went on Thursday. Wonder who owns that house."

Not wanting to encourage his amateur sleuthing, I grunted and turned to stare out my window at the passing neighborhood.

"Why do you think Karen was so pissed?"

"No clue."

"Are you going to tell your FBI friend what we saw?"

I let out a puff of air. "It's not as though we really know anything."

"Come off of it. You think Karen being down here, not a mile from where Finley got hit by a train, is a co-inky-dink?"

"I think there's very little to go on." Mike would probably consider this snooping, so it wasn't in my plans to fill him in. "I also think it's time to stop sleuthing and start shopping."

He ignored my hints. "I wonder how we can find out who lives there."

"Tax records," I said without thinking.

"Really?"

"Yes, one of a few places we can check."

"We can do that when we get back to your apartment."

I'd planned to check on the home's ownership without Rodrigo so I could snoop without witnesses. However, it occurred to me that Rodrigo was turning out to be rather helpful. We'd both witnessed Elise's revelations at the Kennedy Center and now Karen's hasty departure. Even though I'd questioned Rodrigo's ability to keep his mouth shut, I hadn't had any of my coworkers goggling at my door, asking questions about Harper's death. He'd also known about Karen and Nick's affair and skillfully gotten us into that C2ARM event. Even though we hadn't been working together very long, perhaps I wasn't giving my officemate enough credit. I'll admit, flying solo could be a little exhausting. Maybe having a copilot wouldn't be such a bad idea.

"Sounds like a plan. Now, remind me, what are you looking for at IKEA?"

Chapter Nineteen

"What's Troika Star, LLC?" Rodrigo asked as he leaned over my shoulder, pointing at the page of property tax information for the house on the river.

"Don't know. I've never heard of it." After an afternoon of shopping, Rodrigo and I returned to my condo to check out the house in Virginia. A Google search into Troika Star, LLC came up empty. There were lots of organizations with the name Troika in it, but no Troika Star, LLC. "I wonder if it's one of those corporate homes that allows executives to stay in it," I mused.

"Like a corporate benefit?"

"Not dissimilar from the corporate jet, or box seats to a sports game."

"So, how do we figure who owns the LLC? Can your FBI friend help?"

"I'd rather not ask."

"Why not?"

I chewed my lip and confessed, "Well, I sort of promised him I'd stop investigating the case."

My coworker burst into laughter. "And here I am dragging you back into it."

"Yeah, I noticed."

"I'm sorry." He patted my shoulder and dropped into the dining room chair on my left. "No wonder you've been so hesitant. I thought you were hiding things from me. In reality, you simply don't want to be involved anymore."

"Well . . . that's not exactly true. Considering our discoveries this afternoon, I'm still interested. Finding a strange LLC only stokes my curiosity."

"So, you're back in?"

I sighed. "I am."

"Great." He scribbled down Troika Star, LLC on the pad of paper at my elbow. "Since you can't go to your FBI friend, I'll work some of my contacts."

"What sort of contacts?"

"Never you mind. I have contacts." Ripping the sheet of paper, he stood and pulled his windbreaker off the back of the chair.

"I may have someone I can ask. . . ."

"Don't worry. I'm on the case. I'll see you tomorrow at work. Ta, darling." He danced out the door on feet lighter than Gene Kelly.

Once he left, I spent another half an hour searching Google for a thread of information on Troika. It yielded nothing more, and I decided to call the next best thing to the FBI.

"Go for Joshua."

"Hi, Josh, guess who?"

"Karina. Any more break-ins?"

"No. Am I interrupting? Are you on a job?"

"I've got a minute. What can I do for you?"

"I was wondering if your company has research capabilities."

"What do you need?"

"I'm trying to find out more about a company called Troika Star, it's listed as a Limited Liability Company. They own a home on the Potomac, down in Woodbridge."

"I can have someone look into it," Josh said.

"Don't spend too much time on it. I just figured you might have access to databases that I don't."

"We do. And it's no problem."

"Oh, one other thing," I said, "have you ever heard of a mercenary going by the name of Jablonski?"

"No, why?"

"FBI thinks that may have been who broke into my apartment."

"I'll ask around."

"That'd be great. Thanks, Josh."

"No problem."

An hour later, I sat in front of the television, watching the news and eating leftover Chinese, when my doorbell rang. I muted the TV. I wasn't expecting anyone, but it wasn't out of the realm of possibility that it could be one of my neighbors.

It wasn't a neighbor.

The man who stood on the other side of my peephole I'd only seen twice before. The first time, in the stairwell where he saved my life. The second, in a police lineup where I'd lied to the investigating detective. In his forties, he had cheekbones to die for, short-cropped military hair, and today he sported manly scruff around his jaw. The black leather jacket he wore hid lethal muscles and at a guess, a no-less-lethal gun.

"Batman!" He'd told me his name was Rick, no last name. I'd given him the nickname Batman because of the way he swooped in and out of my life. "This is a surprise. Come in." I pulled the door wide.

A half-smirk played around his mouth as he passed me.

"Can I get you something to drink? Have you eaten? I have leftover Chinese; shall I get you a plate?"

"I'm fine, thanks." He remained standing in between my kitchen and family room.

"Why don't you have a seat?" I indicated the stools at the

kitchen island.

"Josh passed your questions along to me."

"I suspected. Though, I'm surprised. I didn't think the research would yield an in-person visit. Much less a visit from the boss. So, what's the deal with Troika Star?" I folded my arms on the countertop.

"It's a shell company owned by another shell company. We're digging further to find out more. But that's not the reason for the visit." He pulled his cell phone out of his back pocket.

"Okay. What's the reason?"

He tapped the screen a few times. "Is this the man you know as Jablonski?"

The man had a goatee and fuller cheeks, but I had no problem seeing past the facial hair. That eerie, ice-blue stare and hooked nose were not easily forgotten. "Yes. He didn't have a beard, and his hair was blonder. Why? Who is he?"

"Naftali Rivkin, former Mossad."

"Israeli intelligence?"

"Exactly."

"Why would a Mossad agent be involved in this?"

"He went rogue six years ago. The Israelis disavowed him and put a price on his head. Supposedly, he turned over information to the Syrians that got two agents killed and burned an entire ring of assets. He's been making money taking jobs on the black market. He's well-trained and deadly."

"So . . . he's a bad man."

"Very bad. And you're on his radar. That's bad too."

"Actually, the FBI feels he got what he needed by stealing the senator's phone. I can't see why I'd be in his line of fire."

His eyes darted around the room. "Did the feds sweep for bugs?"

"Yup."

"Do you mind if I do so?"

"Knock yourself out," I said.

Rick pulled a rectangular, black device, about the size of a cell phone, out of a cargo pants pocket at his knee. Extending the antenna, he started sweeping the room.

"The prevailing theory is he came in through the back door," I offered. "Got the phone and left. Josh'll tell you. I can't see how I'd be a threat to him now."

Rick finished his sweep and tucked the device back into his pocket. "You may be right. Nonetheless . . ." He reached into his jacket's interior pocket and laid a small, black snub-nosed handgun on the counter. It said RUGER along the side. "This is a nine-millimeter. It fits comfortably in a woman's hand and uses a seven-round single stack magazine. Have you ever used one?"

I recoiled from the deadly weapon. "Yes, once. In the stairwell. That didn't go very well."

"Actually, it wasn't too bad. You didn't hit me."

I delivered a deadpan glare.

"So, that's a no to the gun? Would you feel more comfortable carrying a knife?"

"No. I have a lovely little pink stun gun that fits nicely in my purse and won't actually kill anyone. However, I don't think you understand my situation. My cute little stun gun is currently residing in my office desk, because I can't carry any of that stuff on the Hill. Which means that seventy percent of the time, it's left at the office or in my car's glovebox, because I'm constantly going through security checkpoints. Really, it's almost more hassle than it's worth."

He tapped the weapon. "What about keeping this here at home, for self-defense? Bedside table? I can train you how to use it. We've got a gun range at work."

"Tempting, but no."

"Then let's talk home security."

"Speaking of security, how did you get in?" I tilted my head and produced a frown. "I didn't buzz you."

"Followed one of your neighbors. This building is amazingly unsecure. If you're carrying a Dino's pizza box, anyone will let you in."

I bit my lip, knowing I'd held the door for the pizza guy in the past. "True. But at least we've got cameras now. That's a deterrent, right?"

"Maybe to a nickel and dime thug. I suggest you get an alarm system for your apartment."

I thought of the email links Mike sent last week. I'd printed them out, and they were now buried somewhere underneath the magazines on my coffee table. "Funny you should mention it. My FBI friend made the same suggestion. Who do you recommend?"

"I have two companies for your situation." He pulled a folded piece of paper out of another pocket. "Names and phone numbers are on here. They can have you set up in a few hours, and if you mention Silverthorne Security, you'll get a discount."

"Do you think it's really necessary?"

"You tell me. You want another Jablonski incident?"

"Hell no. But, it's not as though I've got nightly intruders."

"I made it into the building," he pointed out.

"Ah, but you wouldn't have made it past the slide bolt, or my new trusty back door bar." I made a sweeping motion—à la *The Price is Right*.

"Trust me." His eyes tightened as he surveyed the room. "If I wanted to get into your apartment, I'd find a way. There are always the windows."

"Cripes. You're freaking me out. Okay, okay." I rubbed my temples. "I'll get myself a security system. Happy?"

"I'll be happy when it's installed." His hand splayed across the gun, and he made it disappear back into his jacket.

"I'll put it on the top of my to-do list Monday morning," I said, slipping the piece of paper in my purse. "Is there anything else?"

"Not at this time. I'll have someone get back to you about the shell company."

"Oh, one more thing," I said. "Do you know anything about a secret Capitol Hill poker game?"

"I've heard tell." His eyes slid away from mine.

I crossed my arms and waited.

"What kind of information are you looking for?" he asked at last.

"What do you know about it?"

"I'm afraid you'll have to be more specific," he hedged.

"It moves around?"

"Yes."

"Do you know where it was this past Thursday?"

"Nowhere. They don't play on Thursdays. It's the second Wednesday of the month."

"Always?"

"Unless they have a vote or are working on passing a budget bill. Then it moves to the third Wednesday."

Made sense. Wednesday was the one day of the week guaranteed to have the most congressmen in D.C. However, this poker game seemed less and less "secret" if so many people knew about it. And, Rick seemed pretty damn sure on what days they met. "How do you know all this?"

"Trust me, I know."

"Do you provide security?"

He remained mum.

"Did you know Finley's driver?"

He gave a single sharp nod. "Frank Salovar, we'd met."

"Does he drink?"

"Not when he's on the job. Very professional."

"What do you think about the train wreck?"

He shrugged. "It's a tragedy."

Again, I waited for him to elaborate. I waited in vain. To be honest, this was the most I'd ever heard Rick speak. Our other conversations had been short and to the point. Rick was a man of few words—or perhaps a man who watched his words carefully. I'd pegged him as former spec ops, but it was entirely possible Rick had been a spy. After all, they practically grew on trees here in D.C.

"Do you have any more questions for me? If not . . ." He slid off the stool. "Don't forget the alarm system. Monday."

"Why did you come?" I asked. "Why do you care?"

He shrugged. "I owe you."

"The police lineup?"

"For one."

I walked him to the door. "Considering your dashing rescue, I imagine we're even. How are the ribs?"

"All healed." He pounded his side where the injury happened. "Looks like the shoulder's in good condition."

"It is. I keep meaning to find a self-defense class. Can you recommend one?" I asked, opening the door.

"I'll email you."

"Do you need my email?"

"Got it."

Of course, he does.

He slipped around the corner before I could ask him another question.

Two things came out of his visit. First, I still had no idea who owned the house on the water. Second, Rick got me freaked out about Jablonski all over again. That night I placed glass vases in front of all my windows and triple-checked the locks before heading to bed. It was one of the rare occasions I wished for a roommate. I considered inviting my sister Jillian over, but I ruled it out, knowing she'd have to get up too early to get to the middle school where she taught English.

Chapter Twenty

I'd expected Rodrigo to be impatiently waiting at my door when I arrived on Monday. Instead, I had to wait a full fifteen minutes before he graced my office.

"So, something is hinky with this Troika company," he said, picking up our conversation where we'd left it. "Nobody owns it."

I nodded and confirmed, "It's a shell company owned by another shell company. We're trying to pin down the registrant. I have a feeling it's some sort of corporate tax shelter."

Rodrigo's mouth pinched at my revelations and he gave me the stink eye.

"What?" I said defensively. "I've got other connections besides the FBI. They're working on digging deeper."

"I think we should go stake out that house tonight."

I laughed. "No, thank you. What do you think you're going to find? I doubt Karen will be back down there any time soon."

"I'm telling you, this house is the key to Finley's death," he said dramatically with a clenched fist in the air.

"Okay, Sherlock, that's a stretch. I'll admit Finley was probably there. But, whoever owns the house didn't hit him with the train. Don't worry, we'll find out more when we know who owns it. No need for a stakeout. Just patience."

"Fine." He released a big breath and stood. "We'll do it your way. I'm going to get some coffee. You want any?"

"I'm good. Thanks."

An email notification binged. It was from Rick. The subject read SELF-DEFENSE CLASS. Clearly, he was as economical in his writing as his speaking. It provided an address, time, and had tomorrow's date on it. He didn't even have a fancy signature at the bottom. Just his name. Rick.

I responded in kind with one word: CONFIRMED.

Back atcha, Batman.

Afterward, I contacted two security companies and arranged for them to come out and provide quotes at the end of the week. Mike and Rick would be proud. As a matter of fact, I left a message on Mike's cell, letting him know.

****

Tuesday evening, I wove my way through the District into a dodgy warehouse neighborhood in Southeast. My GPS took me to a location that had me temporarily stymied. In front of me rose a large black iron gate, and behind it, a nondescript warehouse. It took me a few minutes to realize there was a callbox. I pressed the well-used, cracked yellow button.

"Yes?"

"I'm Karina Cardinal. Here for the self-defense class." No response. "Rick sent me." I smiled directly into the tiny camera and waved.

"On your left, use one of the visitor spots." The disembodied voice sounded male, but was so distorted, it could have been female.

The big gate jangled as it rolled back, allowing me to drive through. I parked directly in front of the solid black double doors that read Silverthorne Security and slung my purse over my shoulder as I exited the car. Before I'd left my apartment, I'd changed into a pair of yoga pants, sneakers, and a pink T-shirt that read "PAs Do It Better." One of the doors opened, revealing a scarred face I hadn't see in a few months.

"Hello, Jin. Did you miss me?" Jin had been my driver when Silverthorne protected me in January.

The compact Korean delivered a blank stare and motioned me inside. A long, neutral-colored but brightly lit hallway laid in front of us like a big beige ribbon.

"Follow me."

Jin also prescribed to the man-of-few-words motto. Whereas Joshua and I had formed a bond, I always felt Jin looked upon me as one would a pesky younger sibling. He also either didn't like or get my humor, but I swore one day I'd make him laugh.

Three doors down and on our right, he knocked. Rick opened the door, and the smell of gym sweat and pine tree air freshener wafted into the hallway.

"You're late." Rick, already sweaty, wearing a black tank top and green camo cargo pants, waved me in.

"I got lost."

I walked into a large fitness area with a variety of weight machines, free weights, two treadmills, a stair stepper, and a couple of stationary bikes. All the machines surrounded a square area of blue padded mats. It didn't take me long to guess this was the sparring zone. Rick and I were the only ones in the gym.

"I thought this was a class."

"It is."

"Like, with other people."

"Joshua will join us later."

"And . . . I'm the only student?"

"Did you want to bring a friend?"

"I'm not sure. I wasn't expecting to be alone."

"Do you feel uncomfortable, just the two of us?"

I surveyed the handsome guy in front of me with his furrowed brow and hard jaw. I hadn't been afraid of him armed in my apartment. That had been my turf and he'd been dressed. Here, in his gym, his muscles exposed and shining with sweat, he looked . . . tough and dangerous. Having seen him in action, I knew how dangerous he could be.

"Jin is watching from the monitors." He pointed to cameras in each corner of the room. That didn't fill me with confidence. First, I wasn't too sure of Jin's feelings about my safety. Second, I didn't like the idea of him watching me fall on my ass— although it might get him to laugh. "If you like, I can ask Josh to come in now."

"You're not going to beat the shit out of me, like they do in boot camp, are you?"

That half-smirk broke through, and his gaze lightened. "No. If I teach you properly, I'll be the one sporting bruises."

"Where do we start?" I tugged the scrunchie off my wrist and pulled my hair into a ponytail.

He had me warm up on the stationary bike for fifteen minutes before guiding me over to the sparring mats.

"We'll start simple. Make a fist."

I balled up my hand the way the Tae Bo guy did on the DVD. Sometimes I would work out to it when I couldn't get to the gym or yoga class.

"That's good. At least you know how to make a proper fist. Now, hit me." He held up a padded catcher's mitt thingy that I'd seen in boxing movies.

I eyed up the mitt and threw a punch like I did for the Tae Bo work out. "Heaw!" It made a nice sounding thwack. Rick's arm absorbed the shock and barely moved.

"Not bad. Now, first lesson, when you are punching, I want you to punch through the target." He must have noticed my confused look because he continued, "Have you ever played golf?"

"No, but I've watched it on TV."

"Okay, when the pros are teeing off for a drive, you start with the backswing coming fully up behind." He demonstrated. "Then down, connecting with the ball, but they don't stop there. They finish the swing, pulling it forward."

"Yes. I get it. I've seen *Tin Cup*. If you don't swing through, it looks unfinished, and you may not get enough power to get the ball as far as you want."

"Exactly." He seemed pleased. "Same with a punch. Pull back, then hit me as though you are pushing that fist through the target."

"Okay. Got it. More power." I screwed up my mouth, concentrated on the pad, looked past it to Rick's shoulder, and, channeling my inner golf goddess, I pulled my arm back and let it fly. *Crunch*. Using another golf term not seen on the pro circuit, I whiffed, completely missing the pad. And, swinging too high, my fist connected with his jaw.

He recoiled and grunted.

"Holy shit. I'm sorry, are you okay? Crap, I guess I should have warned you, my aim isn't the best. Do you need some ice? Do you want me to go find Jin? I didn't break it, did I?"

He rubbed his jaw and watched me as I babbled. "Not bad, Cardinal. You put the power of your arm and shoulder into it."

"I'm really sorry. Maybe you should put on one of those boxing helmets. Are you going to charge me extra for hitting you?"

"The helmet isn't a bad idea until we get your aim corrected. However, I suspect you've made my staff's night with that sucker punch. I don't doubt they're laughing their asses off at my expense."

"I'm not sure. Does Jin know how to laugh?"

At that, Rick busted up. It was better than watching an *SNL* cast member break character. The smile transformed his face into something less dangerous, almost inviting, and I finally relaxed. Rick added some more padding to his body, and we continued the punching lessons. At the bottom of the hour, he added some kicking, teaching me to aim for the knees and shinbone. Of course, the knee to the groin, a well-known woman's defense, we also practiced. With Rick in body padding and the family jewels encased and properly insulated, we only did that exercise twice. Rick assuring me after the second time that a kick to the balls was a skill I didn't need additional practice for. At least, not on a live target.

At the end of the night, I put a finger to his reddened jaw, and he hid a slight wince. "I told you we should have had Jin bring you some ice," I said with consternation. "I have a feeling it'll be bruised by morning."

"Maybe." He handed me a clean white towel and a bottle of water. "The Tae Bo has served you well. You did good work tonight."

I tossed the towel over my shoulder and sucked down half the water in a few quick gulps. "Thanks," I said, coming up for air. "When is my next lesson?"

"I'll email you some dates and times."

The door opened and Joshua lumbered into the gym. "Angus tracked down the shell company." He held out a sheet of paper for Rick.

"You're sure?" Rick's brows heightened.

"As sure as Angus can be."

"Well, Cardinal," he said as he turned to me, "the owner of your waterfront house is—"

"Wait, let me guess," I interrupted, "J & P Pharmaceuticals."

"No, Teason Medical."

"Huh." My confidence drooped. "That's not what I was expecting. You're sure it was Teason?"

"So it would seem."

"Isn't their headquarters located in Jersey?"

"I believe so."

"Huh. They are one of the big pharmaceutical companies. The question is, why do they own a home down there?"

"The paperwork didn't specify."

"And you're sure there wasn't a poker game on Thursday?"

"I can double-check."

"Do, please. If Finley wasn't there for the card game, then considering our last conversation, I want to know what the hell he was doing down there." Like a Tetris board, the blocks began falling in place, and I didn't like the design they were making. Nor did I care for those pesky holes of outstanding questions now filling my brain.

"You need to be careful." Joshua crossed his arms.

"Oh, I will. Don't worry about me." That quip drew deep frowns from the pair. "Hey, I know how to defend myself now." I flashed a grin to lighten the mood.

Neither face changed.

"You're an amateur, no match for a pro," Josh asserted.

Cheekily, I taunted, "Try me."

Josh had always treated me with offhand amusement and occasional concern. A flash of irritation flared across his features, and, before I knew what happened, he had me pinned on the mat, my ears ringing.

"Jeez," I wheezed.

He pulled my body into a sitting position. "Breathe in slowly. It'll come back. There you go. That's it. Don't panic."

Finally, the fish-like gasping stopped as the blessed, sweat-sock-and-forest-scented oxygen refilled my lungs. *In and out. In and out.* The mantra repeated. I'd never had the wind knocked out of me before. The experience was deeply disturbing, and one I never wanted to repeat.

I glanced past his shoulder to Rick. "You were taking it easy on me."

"I was teaching you. An attacker won't be teaching. Josh gave you a tiny taste of what a professional like Rivkin can do. You're not dealing with a street thug that you can evade by smacking him over the head with your purse. We'll practice more defensive, attack and evasion tactics at our next session, and work on your reaction time."

A trail of water strewed across the mat from the bottle that had flown out of my hand when Josh took me down.

"I'm not cleaning that up." I pointed to the mess.

Rick crouched to eye level. "Cardinal, whatever you're into, I don't like the looks of it."

Finally, I'm not the only one with misgivings scratching at my conscience.

"I want you to share this information with your FBI friend, and stop nosing around. You need to leave it to the professionals."

Where had I heard that before? Were Rick and Mike connected via ESP? "Sure thing."

"Why don't you call him now?" Josh's muscles rippled as he stood and held out a hand to help me. I stared at those stout digits, a bit afraid of the easy-going blond bear. Even though I knew Josh had been a former SEAL, I never expected he would use that kind of violence against me. Lesson learned.

"Now?"

"No time like the present," Rick agreed.

Giving in, I allowed Josh to pull me to my feet. "Next time, you'll be ready." He gave my hand a reassuring squeeze before releasing it. "Now make that call."

"Fine." I retrieved the cell out of my handbag lying on the edge of the mat. As expected, the phone call went straight to voicemail. "Hi, Mike, it's K.C. Listen, there's been a development in the case that I think you should know about. Call me." I hung up and turned to the men. "Happy?"

"How long before he normally returns your calls?" Rick asked.

I shrugged. "He's currently out of town, on assignment."

Rick's brows caterpillared together. "When does he get back?"

"No idea. Could be tomorrow. Could be in two weeks."

The men shared a look.

Joshua shifted. "Do you have another FBI contact?"

"I suppose I could figure out how to contact Director McGill. I believe I have his card at home."

"And he is . . ."

"The lead for the taskforce on Harper's case. You think this is time sensitive?"

"Not sure. It seems squirrelly," Rick admitted.

"I feel it too. So does Rodrigo."

Rick pinched his chin. "Rodrigo?"

"My coworker. We were together when we saw Karen Ferngull leave that house. She used to work for J & P Pharmaceuticals. She's currently deputy secretary at HHS. It's the reason why I wanted you to check it out."

Another look passed between the two.

Joshua turned back to me. "Did she see you?"

"I don't think so. Why? What's that look?"

"Nothing." Rick rubbed the towel across his face. "Just . . . be careful. When are you getting the alarm system installed?"

"I have meetings with the two companies you recommended on Thursday and Friday."

"Good. Joshua will show you out."

Jin waited in the hall when we exited, a ten-dollar bill pinched between his first and middle fingers.

"Told you." Josh smirked and snatched it.

I stopped in my tracks. "What's this all about?"

Jin delivered one of his signature frowns. "I made a bet that you'd land a hit on Josh."

"Wait a minute. So, you planned that take down? Was it some kind of joke?"

"No joke. Part of your training. Jin thought you'd land a sucker punch, like you did Rick. He played the odds against your naiveite and inexperience and lost. I also played on your trust in me." Josh threw the comments over his shoulder as he headed toward the door.

My mouth flattened, and eyes went into squint mode as I glared at his back. Jin's frown disappeared and he winked. I had to do a quick jog to catch up behind Josh.

"Never bet against me, my friend."

It was a dirty trick I hadn't pulled since my middle school years, when it had been in fashion. As he picked up his right foot, I swept it, so his boot got caught behind his left calf. Generally, the ploy would only make the walker stumble a little bit and look clumsy. But the cheap shot in the gym and bet with Jin at my expense had my blood boiling. It only took a little push from behind and down went Josh with an "oof", his hands flailing as they reached out to break his fall. Adults fall a lot harder than a skinny middle school kid. I winced as his palms smacked to the ground and may have felt a teensy bit of regret as Josh's angry eyes flashed at me.

Jin's bark of laughter filled the hallway, temporarily distracting the two of us. The mirth made his long scar, from eye to chin, scrunch and pucker, but the sound of delight and even, white teeth offset the ugliness of the mark.

I danced away from Josh's grasping fingers and scooped up the tenner that had flown from his hand when he fell. "I believe this belongs to Jin."

The gym door flew open and Rick stepped out, taking in Jin's amusement and Josh on the floor. "What's going on?"

Lickety-split the tenner disappeared in my bra. "Testing a

theory. I was wrong, Jin *does* know how *to* laugh."

Jin staggered against the wall at that.

I offered my hand to Josh who'd gotten to his knees by now. "Shall we call it even?" I murmured.

He glanced back at his buddy hooting like a wild dingo, and I witnessed a genuine grin splay across his features. "Even." He took my hand and climbed to his feet.

Really, Jin's laughter was like none I'd heard before, and I couldn't help giggling along with it. Soon Josh joined in. Rick watched our merriment with crossed arms and bemusement.

Finally, the chortling dissipated and Jin pointed at me. "You're okay, Cardinal," he said before disappearing behind one of the nondescript doors lining the hall.

With a shaking head, Rick returned to the gym, and a few minutes later Josh held the driver's side door of my car for me.

Turning before climbing inside, I pulled the money out of my bra. "Give this back to Jin."

"Keep it. You earned it."

My brows rose. "For taking you off guard?"

"For making Jin laugh. In the two years I've worked with him, I haven't heard so much as a snigger. As a matter of fact, you managed to make every man in this building smile, and not just in appreciation of your ass. That doesn't happen often."

"Glad I could be of service," I said drily.

His face turned serious. "Take care of yourself, Karina."

I hesitated getting in. "What aren't you and Rick telling me?"

"I don't know what you're talking about."

"You shared a look."

"We don't like Rivkin mixed up in all of this."

"You think Finley's and Harper's deaths are related?"

"Do you?"

"I do now." I slid into the front seat and grabbed the door.

Josh held it open. "You have my number?"

"I've got your card back at the house."

"Put it in your phone."

"Okey doke." I pulled at the door, but Josh held it fast.

"Now."

I fished the phone out of my purse. "Here, put it in yourself."

"And call McGill." He handed it back.

"Thanks, Josh. I appreciate your concern."

My drive home was uneventful. I didn't call McGill that night. Instead, I left a note to do it in the morning, after I'd slept on it and came up with the perfect excuse for having gone down to the scene of the accident where another elected official died. And, maybe, after I spoke with Jessica.

Chapter Twenty-one

The incessant, eerie sing-song of the *X-Files* theme woke me at half past midnight. The spooky music had my heart jackhammering into overdrive, until I realized it was my cell phone. I'd recently given the ringtone to Mike's number. We were both *X-Files* fans, and since Mike was an FBI agent . . .

I stubbed my toe on the way into the kitchen where the phone charged; cursing, I swore to change the ringtone in the morning.

I bypassed polite greetings, still half-asleep. "What? What's wrong? Are you okay?"

"Am *I* okay?" Mike's voice bordered on irate. "What the hell is going on up there? Damn it, K.C. When I left, you promised me you'd stop this asinine and dangerous snooping. And tonight, as I'm about to fall into bed, I get your message that there's been a 'development in the case.' A case *you're* not supposed to be anywhere near, by the way. Key-rist, I need to hire a damn babysitter to sit on you, so you stop making harebrained decisions. Now what have you gotten yourself into?"

While he lectured, I fell into a prone position on the couch and pulled a blanket over my legs.

"Naftali Rivkin." My statement had the desired effect.

Mike stopped mid-ass-chew. "How do you know that name?"

"I know that's Jablonski's real name."

"Who have you been talking to?"

"Someone who doesn't mince words and can tell me the truth because he's not bound by stupid FBI uber-super-secret clearance bullshit. And if you don't want to listen to what I have to say, I'm happy to have *my* lawyer call *your* boss in the morning to explain why you should damn well listen," I snapped. The abrupt wake-up and subsequent ass-chewing made me a little cranky.

Silence.

"I woke you. Didn't I?"

"It's past midnight here. Of course, you woke me."

"I'm sorry," he apologized. "Go back to bed. We'll talk in the morning."

"No." I rubbed my eyes. "I'm up now. We might as well talk."

I launched into Rodrigo's and my adventures on the way to IKEA, and Silverthorne's stop-by to tell me about Naftali Rivkin. Mike remained silent throughout.

"So, you've been talking to Navy boy." I knew Mike didn't have the best opinion of Silverthorne. He believed they worked in the gray areas of the law.

He was likely correct. Whatever the case, I trusted them. Not that I advocated for lawlessness. However, unlike Mike, as a lawyer, I knew that justice wasn't always served in black and white, but rather worked in the shadows of gray. Sometimes you had to walk that fine line. It's why the CIA hired spies, and companies like Silverthorne existed. However, I didn't want to antagonize Mike, so I changed the subject. "Did you know about the house owned by Troika Star?"

"We're looking into all the homes in the area."

"Did you know it's owned by a major pharmaceutical company?"

"No, I didn't. Where did blondie get his information?"

"No idea. Why?"

"The holding companies were offshore, and the only way he could've gotten the information is by hacking into bank files or having someone on the inside."

"Uh, I wouldn't know anything about that."

"This is exactly why I don't like you playing with these guys. Everything they do is underhanded."

"How is the Harper case coming? Did you get your man?"

Even though I couldn't see him, I could hear the ruminations skittering around his head as he decided what to say. I rolled to my side and waited.

"What I can tell you is this . . . we are close—very close—to capturing the person I believe is responsible for Harper's pacemaker hack."

"Good for you. Maybe he can shed some light on Finley's death as well."

"K.C., Finley's driver had drugs in his system."

"He took them, or someone drugged him?"

"We're not sure. The body was mangled beyond recognition."

"Oh, lord. Was he married?"

"Yes, with kids."

"How awful." My mind went back to my discussion with Rick. "I just don't believe it, Mike. My Silverthorne contact said he was very professional. Never drank on the job. I doubt he would do drugs. What about the car? Had it been tampered with? Do you have a clear reason why the gates didn't go down?"

"We haven't gotten the full reports yet."

"What are they waiting for?"

"K.C., this takes time. There are a number of fingers in the pot."

"You should tell McGill about Troika Star. Someone needs to look into that."

"Even if we do find out that Finley was there, it may lead nowhere. Nevertheless, I'll talk to McGill and have someone look into it."

"Thank you."

"You know what's strange about Finley? We never found his cell phone. It wasn't on the body, and so far, they haven't found it in the car."

"So, like Harper, you can't trace the text messages or call logs."

"We got a warrant for the texts and call logs from both of them."

"And did they share a number?"

"Many. But there was one . . . from a burner phone that we can't place."

"That's it? One number?"

"Only one. Is there anything else you needed to tell me?"

"I'm meeting with two different home security companies this week."

"Good. Anything else?"

"No."

"I'd better let you go. My morning just got a little earlier."

"Mike . . ."

"Yes?"

"I don't know if this take-down is dangerous, or what, but . . . stay safe. Don't do something stupid and heroic. Okay? Come back safe."

"I won't. And you either, for that matter."

"If the FBI is on the case, I'm off of it."

A windy sigh blew at me from afar. "Sleep well, K.C."

"You too."

I pulled the blanket up to my chin and fell asleep on the couch.

Chapter Twenty-two

During the main course, I spied Karen Ferngull across the room and made a mental note to swing by her table to speak with her. My mind debated different opening lines as I stared. She looked . . . pale. I think she'd lost weight just since Friday, perhaps mourning Nick's loss of affections. Senator Kollingwoods took the podium to provide the keynote address at the monthly Women in Business luncheon. Karen gave a little jump, grabbed her phone, and began madly tapping on it. With a furtive glance around the room, she quickly gathered her materials and slipped out through the emergency exit, practically plowing down a server on her way out.

I considered following when a finger tap on my shoulder stopped me. Wincing pain shot down the side of my neck as I rotated. I should have returned to bed last night, instead, I woke up with a stiff back and painful crick. "Hi, Tesha," I whispered as she slid into the empty chair on my right.

Senator Kollingwoods spoke passionately about the power of women mentoring other women to rise in the ranks amongst the male-dominated business culture. Everyone agreed with her, but one could argue she was singing to the choir. While her speech hummed along, I stared at the chocolate mousse confection the waiter placed in front of me. It took every ounce of willpower to keep from picking up the fork. I didn't need the delectable but empty calories ending up on my hips. LaTesha had no such qualms and dug in. I stared enviously.

Finally, the senator wound down, and LaTesha, licking the last bit of mousse from her fork, turned to me. "Been a while. What's new?"

I waited for the woman on my left to gather her things and leave before answering, "Oh, you know, work stuff, lobbying, fundraisers . . . being a suspect for murder." I murmured the last under my breath.

The frown doubled her toffee-colored chin. "Have they found Harper's killer?"

"Not yet." I shoved the plate away and rubbed my neck.

"What's wrong?"

"Fell asleep on the couch. Paying for it this morning. Do you know a good massage therapist?"

"I do, as a matter of fact. I'll text you." She picked up her phone to find the contact. "So, nothing new on Harper?"

"Nothing of interest. I'm still waiting to hear, myself. Tell me, what do you know about Karen Ferngull?"

"Deputy Secretary of HHS? Some say she slept her way into the position, although I don't believe it. Others think she bribed her way into it. Either way, you and I both know she's not looking out for the nation's healthcare, she's looking out for the corporations. Not a surprise, considering where she comes from."

"You mean J & P?"

LaTesha put her phone down. "Well, that, of course. But, long and short, it's nepotism. Her stepbrother, Lars Dillon, is one of the president's financial lawyers."

"Really? I don't recall reading about that."

"Saw it in a Newsweek article. It came out about the same time as one of the North Korean missile tests last year. It got overshadowed. Besides, the media circus focused on the secretary's confirmation, not the underlings."

My phone dinged with a meeting reminder. "Girlfriend, I'd love to stay and chat longer, but I've got an important meeting at the office. I need to head out now to make it on time."

"I want to hear more. Text me when you've got an open lunch hour." She rose with me and we hugged.

Twenty minutes later, I slipped silently into the back of the conference room. Hasina had already started and was discussing the strides we'd made with the state legislature initiatives. My lateness meant that I missed out on seating, and I stood with four other officemates, massaging my stiff neck. Rotating my head from side-to-side, I realized Rodrigo was absent. Subtly, I pulled out my phone and texted him.

You're missing the staff meeting. Where r u?

Don't worry. Call me when you get out.

Two hours later, my toes had gone numb and the meeting finally wrapped. I dialed Rodrigo on the way to my office. He picked up on the second ring.

"Hey, how are you feeling? Cathy said you called in sick."

"I'm down here at the Troika Star house."

"You're *what?*" I closed my office door and flopped down on the guest chair. "Are you out of your mind? You missed a staff meeting to surveille the house? We have a quarterly board meeting and committee meetings coming up. Hasina is stressed beyond the max, and she'd fire you on the spot if she found out you were playing hooky to do a little amateur investigation. What is *wrong* with you?"

"Karen Ferngull showed up about fifteen minutes ago, and two other men arrived five minutes ago."

After my conversation with the Silverthorne guys, not to mention the midnight call with Mike, I wasn't so sure Rodrigo's little stakeout was a good idea. I needed to convince him to leave. Who knew what kind of trouble he'd get into if someone in that house found him loitering?

"Rodrigo, I spoke with my FBI friend. It's really not a good idea for you to stay there. The FBI is working on the case, and you'll only get in the way. And, if Karen finds out, she could bring you up on stalking charges."

"Fine, when the FBI shows up, I'll give them my notes. I'm sure they'll appreciate my help."

"Notes? How long have you been there?" I demanded.

"I got down here around noon today."

I picked up on the slight intonation. "*Today?*"

". . . I may have been here last night for a few hours," he admitted.

Clearly, my coworker was not going to be persuaded over the phone. I pressed fingers against my temples to ward off the growing headache. "I'm coming down. Stay by your phone."

My watch read twenty past four. I-95 rush hour traffic would be in full swing. It'd be faster for me to catch a southbound train, but I only had ten minutes before the Virginia Railway Express rolled into the station. Shutting down my computer and scooping up my handbag, I powered out of the office, practically jogged to the station, while cursing myself for wearing pumps today. Not only were my feet sore from standing the entire meeting, the heels would now be in tatters from the concrete. Luckily, the train ran five minutes late, and I had time to catch my breath before its arrival. Blessedly, with a groan of relief, I collapsed in an empty seat at the back of the car. When we reached the Lorton station, I texted Rodrigo.

> *Pick me up at the Rippon VRE station in fifteen minutes.*
>
> *Get an Uber.*
>
> *Check your map. It's only five minutes from where you are.*

I might miss something.

You won't miss anything.

No response.

Rodrigo?

After a lengthy pause, his answer popped up on my waiting screen.

I just ordered you an Uber. Virginia plates, NUC-6400, your driver's name is Szingo. Here's his photo. He's been given directions to my location. Be safe. Check the plate before you get in. See you in a few.

I ground my teeth.

At five-fifteen, Szingo dropped me off behind Rodrigo's green Forrester. He was parked half a dozen houses down, facing our target. Karen's BMW was parked on the street. In the driveway sat a black Charger and a gray Cadillac.

I slammed the passenger side door. "Anything?"

"Nothing yet." A pair of binoculars hung around Rodrigo's neck and he sucked on one of the two bottles of water sitting in the cupholders. A spiral notebook and pen sat on the dash next to a half-eaten orange bag of BBQ potato chips.

I kicked aside an empty, refillable, red Big Gulp mug. "Did you already drink an entire Big Gulp? Isn't that a little risky, considering there aren't any bathrooms nearby?"

"That is the bathroom."

"Eww!" I pulled my knees to my chest.

"Don't worry. I haven't used it. I've been rationing the water."

"What on earth are you thinking, Rodrigo? What do you think you're going to find?" I demanded.

"Maybe nothing."

My face twisted.

"I know, I know, it's almost a compulsion." He went back

to his binoculars.

Putting on my best stern voice, I lectured, "This borders on irresponsibility. We've got a lot of work to do before the meetings."

"Pshaw. Hasina has a lot of work to do." He pulled up the binoculars. "I sent in our report last night."

My mouth dropped open. "*Rodrigo!* That was a draft. There are a few more points I needed to add."

"Forget it. Nobody reads all those over-bloated reports. We'll be lucky if they skim the one-page synopsis. Even Hasina doesn't read *everything*."

"How do you know?"

"I once accidentally repeated a full paragraph of information. Nobody said a word."

"That's sloppy. It's not the way I work."

"I get it, okay? You're Ms. Lawyer-perfectionist. Relax, if you're that concerned, just make your updates and send it back to Hasina. Tell her I sent it before you had a chance to finish your edits. She'll understand." He smiled and popped a chip in his mouth.

"You're killing me . . ." More temple rubbing ensued.

Another chip followed the first and Rodrigo's crunching filled the car. The haunting *X-Files* theme resonated loudly enough to drown out his chomping.

"Shh. Don't say a word." I held up a warning finger.

Rodrigo paused mid-chew.

"Well, hello, Sunshine," I greeted. "I didn't expect to be hear from you so soon. Did you talk to McGill?"

"Hello, Karina." Mike's voice sounded stiff.

Uh, oh, it's never good when Mike calls me Karina. Now what did I do?

"What are you up to?" he asked in a carefully measured tone.

"Like, right now? Ah . . . this and that. You know, boring work stuff," I lied.

"And by work stuff, that includes sitting in a car with whom I can only suppose is your equally inquisitive officemate, outside the house I specifically told you not to go back to."

My head whipped around; pain sliced down my spine. "Ow. How did you know? Where are you?"

"Me? I am in New Orleans doing my job. My question is, why aren't you at *your* job? Where you should be!"

"New Orleans?" Mike must be pretty upset. Heretofore, he hadn't revealed his location. "Then how . . . ?"

My gaze rested on a white panel van sitting in the driveway of the empty house for sale, the same house Rodrigo and I had used as cover last week. Black lettering along the side of the van read *PWC Electric*. I covered the receiver with my hand and whispered, "How long has that van been sitting there?"

Rodrigo shrugged. "It's been here as long as I have."

"It doesn't matter *how* I know. What matters—" Mike grit out.

"White van. Electric company logo on it," I interrupted. "Apparently, my information was important enough to put a team on it."

An exasperated breath blew across the phone line. "It's one tech guy. McGill ordered it this morning. Our guy saw you get in the car a few minutes ago and called McGill. Leon called me. This is no joking matter. You and your buddy need to leave. *Now.*"

"Or what?"

"Or . . . I'll have you arrested."

It took me a moment to digest his threat. "Nah."

"I beg your pardon?" he snarled.

"I don't think the tech in that van is going to blow his cover to arrest the two average folks sitting here, minding our own business."

"Who said he would do the arresting?"

"What do you mean . . . Oh, I get it," I said, catching on. "You'll send the cops."

"Do you feel like hanging out in a holding cell for the night?"

I sucked in a breath. "You wouldn't."

"Listen," he ground out, and I could feel the tension across the line. "I'm in the middle of a sting which is going to go down any minute. If I have to send the cops to throw you in the clink for a night for my own peace of mind, I will do it in a heartbeat. *Capisce?*"

"Fine, you don't have to go all caveman on me. We'll go quietly. I didn't want to stay here anyway."

"I'm leaving word with the agent in the van. If you're not gone in five minutes . . ." he threatened.

"I get it. I get it."

He hung up without a goodbye.

Rodrigo finished chewing and swallowed. "That doesn't sound good."

"We need to leave. They're watching the house."

Rodrigo's shoulders slumped. "Seriously? The FBI gets all the fun."

"If we don't go, they'll send around a blue and white to arrest us."

"Arrest us for what?"

I shrugged. "Who knows. Peeping Toms?" I pointed to the binoculars. "Drugs. Theft. They'll make something up, and we'll spend the rest of the night trying to straighten it out. Trust me, it won't be worth . . ."

A bearded man wearing athleisure, dark sunglasses, and a ball cap got into the Charger, backed it out of the driveway, and parked in front of Karen's car. He then climbed into Karen's

BMW, fired it up, and drove into the open garage. The door rumbled down behind him. A moment later, a tall African-American man wearing a three-piece suit exited through the front door and got into the Caddy. My coworker and I ducked down in our seats as he drove away.

We shared a look.

"I guess Karen's gettin' some action tonight." Rodrigo made a suggestive gesture.

I rolled my eyes. "Men are pigs."

We scooted back up in our seats. Rodrigo started the car and rolled away from the curb. I made the peace sign with my fingers at the white van as we drove past.

Chapter Twenty-three

MIKE

"All clear. She's leaving now," Sean, the tech in the van, reported.

"Thanks."

"If they return?"

Mike sighed and rubbed his eyes. It wasn't out of the realm of possibility that K.C. would be stubborn enough to return, and considering the FBI had put the house on the watch list, he didn't want her anywhere near it. "If they come back, send the police out for a neighborhood drive-by. Seeing the cops should oust them."

"Roger that."

Mike turned his private cell off and walked back into room 122, where two agents hovered around a set of computer screens, visually checking the hotel's security camera feeds, along with the FBI's own cameras they'd installed yesterday. In half an hour, LadyBlue and NKBarbie would meet in the Regency room, a lounge area hosted by one of the big security companies that offered refreshments, cookies, Wi-Fi, comfortable couches, and chairs for guests to kick back and log on in between sessions. Two agents were already installed in the lounge—one female greeting guests at the hostess table as they arrived, and a male agent played Minecraft on a computer near an orange couch where LadyBlue would sit when she arrived. A handful of other guests were scattered around the room.

"Any changes?" Mike scanned the various monitors.

"Nothing yet." Amir sat in front of one of the screens, sucking a lollipop.

"Shayna, it's time," Mike told the undercover agent.

Shayna, a young blonde with a nose ring, wearing Converse sneakers, jeans, and a Metallica T-shirt, drew on a beat-up, red backpack.

Amir held out a black box to Mike that contained two tiny wireless earbuds and put on a pair of headphones.

Mike, wearing business casual slacks and a polo, took his earpiece and tucked it in place. "Check, one. Check."

"You're good," said Amir.

Shayna reached for the second earpiece and ran her sound check.

The conference brought professional security specialists and IT techies from around the nation. It also brought Blackhat hackers, some who had legit jobs and others who didn't. You watched what you said and to whom, because you really didn't know what type of person might be sitting next to you at a panel session or workshop. It was the type of conference where most people paid in cash instead of credit cards and never used the hotel's free, open Wi-Fi. Therefore, people visited the Regency lounge because it offered secured Wi-Fi.

Mike, a black laptop briefcase in hand, entered the room.

The agent at the hostess table smiled at him. Her nametag read AMY, which was not far from her real name of Ashley. "Good afternoon, do you have a reservation?"

"Yes. Michael Brandt."

"I see you've prepaid for one hour. Every additional hour is twenty-five dollars. We take cash or credit. Here is your password for the Wi-Fi, Mr. Brandt." She handed him the information and gestured. "You can use station twelve, over there. And help yourself to the refreshment table."

"Thank you, Amy." Mike took the paper from his colleague

and moved into position at a chair near one of the exits.

Shayna arrived a minute later, repeated the charade, got a cup of coffee, and took up a position opposite the orange couch.

They didn't have long to wait before a blue-haired woman wearing a Chicago Cubs ballcap, white jeans, and black T-shirt arrived. Her eyes darted around the room. When Amy addressed her, she dropped her phone and fumbled to pick it up.

"Sorry, sorry, butterfingers," LadyBlue mumbled. "What did you say?"

"Don't worry, honey. You just need some coffee," Amy said with her sweet southern drawl. "Do you have a reservation?"

"Oh, right. Yeah, I have a confirmation number here on my phone." LadyBlue tapped her cell. "It's nine-two-one-th-th-thrree-fffour," she stuttered.

"That's our girl. Finnegan confirm," Amir said over the coms.

Mike scratched his left ear.

"We have confirmation."

LadyBlue dropped the phone again.

"And she's a bundle of nerves," Shayna murmured.

Mike put a prop phone to his ear and spoke, "Ashley, see if you can calm her down."

Ashley turned her beauty pageant smile on LadyBlue, leaned forward, and whispered, "Just act natural. We've got you covered. Stay calm and remember the sign. Once you give it, your part is over." She switched to a normal voice and passed a piece of paper to LadyBlue. "You can sit at station sixteen. It's that orange couch, over there."

LadyBlue took up residence at her assigned seat and her thumbs went to town, tapping away on her phone. Contrary to what Hollywood would have you believe, a lot of investigative work involved sitting around and waiting. It was not a job for impatient people. LadyBlue's leg bounced in constant rhythm as the minute hand slid past the hour. One of the patrons left. Five minutes. A woman in a red suit arrived and checked in. Ten minutes. LadyBlue's leg continued to bounce and her thumbs worked the phone at warp speed. Fifteen minutes.

"He's late," Amir stated the obvious.

"Give it time," Mike murmured.

Another woman arrived in skintight leggings and a long peach blouse and began asking Ashley questions about the lounge. As Ashley handed the woman a flyer explaining the fee structure and hours, a heavy-set man arrived, wearing tan cargo pants, a black T-shirt, flip-flops, and a blue Tampa Bay Devil Rays ballcap. He moved past Ashley's table, searching the crowd for a moment before zeroing in on LadyBlue.

"Everyone on alert. We may have our target," Mike mumbled.

He stopped at the orange couch. "LadyBlue, right?"

The leg stopped bouncing and she stood. "You're late. I'd almost given up on you." She took off her Cubs cap.

"That's the signal. Move in!" Amir cried.

In moments, both NKBarbie and LadyBlue were removed from the lounge in handcuffs. They were put in separate vehicles. LadyBlue, not wishing to be revealed as the informant, requested to be arrested along with NKBarbie, whose real name turned out to be Jethro Finster, from Mississippi. Mike had LadyBlue released at the airport with her bags and a first-class plane ticket to Boston, compliments of the FBI.

Meanwhile, NKBarbie had the pleasure of being escorted to an FBI holding facility at the regional field office. Agents confiscated everything in Finster's hotel chamber, including the laptop he'd locked in the room safe.

Mike had put a lot of effort into catching this guy. He

prayed it would pay off. An hour later, he and Amir packed the last bit of surveillance equipment away. Snapping the locks shut, he loaded the heavy case on the luggage cart.

"I think that's the last," Amir said.

"Shayna has Finster's laptop and is heading to the field office," Mike reminded him.

"Want me to start working on it?"

Mike produced a wan smile. It would take hours to break through Finster's computer security. "You did good today, Amir. Get something to eat first."

"I know a great place to get Crawfish Étoufée. Want me to pick up an order for you?"

"Sounds good. I'll meet you at the office. I'm just going to do one more sweep of the hotel and check my messages." He pulled out his cell phone.

"See you there." Amir pushed the loaded cart down the hall toward the elevators.

Chapter Twenty-four

I expected Rodrigo to head back to the highway so we could go home; instead, he turned the corner and stopped a block away, out of sight from the Troika Star house and FBI van.

"What are you doing?" I asked.

"Nothing. I just want to see if Black Charger sticks around."

"Did you see anyone else in the house?"

"No."

"If they're doing what you think, he's probably in for the night. Now, I'm starving, so let's get something to eat on the way home."

Rodrigo passed me the chips and the unopened water bottle. "Here. An appetizer."

"Rodrigo, c'mon, I'm starting to get hangry," I whined. I wasn't that hungry, but frankly, I didn't want to test Mike. I think I'd pushed his limits for the day and didn't doubt he'd follow through with his threat.

However, my colleague seemed unfazed by my plea. "Just a few more minutes. Don't worry, they can't see us."

I shifted, checking the street . . . drummed my fingers . . . ran arguments through my head that might convince Rodrigo to get moving and came up with nothing more than what I'd already said.

"Fine," I huffed, "you can sit here and play your games. You're on your own. If they arrest you, don't call me." I grabbed my phone and opened the Uber app.

"*Get down!*" Rodrigo's seat whipped backward.

I had a bad feeling and followed suit. A moment later, the FBI's white utility van passed us, going at a fast clip. We waited in our reclined position, with mirror faces of fear and horror, to see if he would come back. After a minute, I prairie-dogged my head to take a look around and found nothing out of the ordinary—no van, no cops, no swat team bearing down on us.

"He's gone. I think it's safe to come up for air. The guy in the van must not have noticed us." It seemed we had dodged a bullet.

"Wonder where he was going in such a hurry." Rodrigo's seat popped upright.

"Maybe he didn't bring his mammoth Slurpee cup to use as a bathroom." Fear laced my response with sarcasm. "Whatever the case, that was a close call. And it's not out of the realm of possibility he did see us and is sending local PD. I'd rather not get another call from my friendly neighborhood fed. In other words, let's get the hell outta here while the gettin' is good."

"Okay, okay. You're right. That was a close call." He started the car and checked the rearview mirror. "Well, I'll be damned."

I turned to see what he was looking at. Karen's white BMW paused at the stop sign, turned, and rolled up the street toward us. As it passed, my gaze met the unnerving, eerie blue stare of the driver.

Even though the ballcap was still in place and the dark beard hid the defining characteristics of his face, he hadn't replaced the sunglasses.

I'll never forget those spooky eyes as long as I live.

"That's not Karen." Rodrigo glanced at me. "You look like you just saw a ghost."

To my horror, the BMW's brake lights came on. The car crept to a halt at the stop sign ahead of us and remained there.

My heart jolted into action. "Get us out of here. *NOW!*"

Rodrigo must have felt my panic because he jerked the car into gear and it jumped forward.

"Don't stop! Go around, go around!" I hollered.

Rodrigo buzzed around Karen's car.

Silver metal flashed in the sunlight. "*Gun!*" I yelled, pulling on the seat release again and falling backward.

Rodrigo, in a panic, swerved, hitting the opposite curb. The passenger side mirror shattered. "What was that?"

"Bullet! *Go! Go!*" I planted a hand on Rodrigo's knee and pushed his foot to the floor.

We careened around the corner and out of the neighborhood. He blew through the stop sign at the T-intersection and bounced us over the train tracks. Thank the lord there wasn't a train coming.

"It's too bad that FBI guy left."

No joke.

I dialed Mike's number, but it went straight to voicemail. "Mike! It's Jablonski! Rivkin! Whatever his name is. He just left the house in Karen Ferngull's car. The FBI van left. He's got a gun with a silencer and shot out the side mirror of our car and he's following—watch out for—" I shouted.

Rodrigo zipped around a slow-moving minivan, just barely missing an oncoming car. The phone flew out of my hands as he whipped back into the correct lane.

Gripping the "Oh Shit" handle, I said with slow deliberation, "It doesn't help if we get killed in a car accident."

"We're fine. Everything's okay," Rodrigo assured me through his teeth.

Well, if we get pulled over by a cop, at least Rivkin will leave us alone.

"Want to tell me why this guy is shooting at us?"

"Me. He's shooting at me." My hand searched blindly for the phone on the floor behind Rodrigo's seat. "His name is

Naftali Rivkin. Ex-Mossad. He broke into my home to steal Senator Harper's phone. He posed as a Capitol police officer and is believed to have been part of the team that assassinated Harper. Intel said he'd left town."

Rodrigo processed that. "I guess intel was wrong."

"We just need to lose him. Once we do that—ah, got it" — my fingers captured their prey—"we'll figure out our next step."

"He's fallen back. He's not chasing us."

I glanced in the rearview mirror. Sure enough, Rivkin had fallen behind two cars and wasn't making an effort to pass them. We had to stop at the major intersection at Route 1. I kept my eyes on the mirror to make sure Rivkin didn't sneak out of his car. The light turned green, as did the light down the road.

"Punch it. Go around this slow poke. If we can get through the light and he doesn't make it, we can get on the highway and lose him."

Rodrigo followed my directions, revving forward through a break in the traffic, then cutting back into the lane in front of a semi to get onto the I-95 onramp. The light behind us turned red, but I couldn't see around the semi to determine if Rivkin made it.

The Subaru buzzed onto the highway. Rodrigo moved us to the far-left lane and put the lead out. The southbound traffic on the opposite side crept at sloth pace. Luckily, we were going north, against traffic, and the flow moved at a fast clip. A flash of white rolled into our lane three cars back.

"I think he's following us." Rodrigo voiced my fears. "What else do you know about this guy?"

"Rick said there's a price on his head."

"You're saying, this guy is like an assassin—"

"Wait a minute." I slapped my hand on the dash. "There's a price on his head."

"Uh, Karina, it's not like we're Dog, the Bounty Hunter. We

don't have the skills or know-how to take him down. Remember, right now . . . he's chasing us."

"No. But I might know someone who can." Relieved he'd forced me to put the number into my contacts, I phoned Joshua.

"Go for Joshua."

"Josh, guess who?"

"Karina? What's going on?"

"Didn't you say there was a price on Rivkin's head?"

"So to speak."

"What does that mean? Is there or isn't there?"

"Unofficially, the Israelis have a million-dollar bounty on him."

"Whoa." I checked the rearview mirror again. "If I bring him to you, will you cut us in on that?"

"Uh, Karina? Have you been drinking?"

"Rivkin is following me right now."

"Where are you?"

"We're on 95, heading north. We just passed over the Occoquan bridge."

"Jesus! There's too much between here and D.C. You'll never make it. I'm calling local PD to intercept you."

"No, wait, don't do that." The BMW remained three cars back in the line of sight, but not aggressively following. "I think . . . I think he's stalking us. He's driving a car that's not his own. He's waiting for us to make a move. Go home, or somewhere off the grid where there aren't any cameras. I don't think he's going to risk an accident on the highway."

"Hold on. I'll call you back in a minute."

"What are we doing?" Rodrigo shifted into the center lane to pass a slower car in the left lane. A minute later, Rivkin pulled the same move.

"Keep doing what you're doing. We don't want him to get

any closer, but we don't want to lose him either."

"Are you sure about that?"

"Just . . . wait." The phone rang. Caller ID read UNAVAILABLE. "Hello?"

"Josh said you had a lead on Rivkin," Rick drawled.

"You could say that. He's currently three, no, four cars back. We're heading north on 95. Just passed the Lorton exit."

"What's the plan?"

"I was hoping you could tell me."

"Are you okay? Is anyone hurt?"

"Just the sideview mirror. My copilot is doing a surprisingly good job. You want to collect the bounty on his head? Or should I call the cops?"

"Hold on a minute."

I stared at the gridlock on the opposite side of the highway, while absentmindedly humming a tune.

"Are you singing *Dirty Deeds Done Dirt Cheap*?" Rodrigo asked.

"I guess I am."

"Huh." His eyes stared straight ahead, and his fingers wrapped so tightly around the wheel that his knuckles had turned white.

"You're doing great, pal. It'll all be over soon," I assured him.

"Cardinal?" Rick growled.

"I'm here. I'm putting you on speaker." I held the phone out between the two of us. "Okay, go ahead."

"Jin is near Edsall Road."

"We haven't hit Springfield yet," Rodrigo said.

"That's fine. What kind of car are you driving?"

I gave him a description of Rodrigo's and Karen's cars. "I don't know Karen's license number, but it's a D.C. plate."

"BA-3261," my colleague rattled off. "I wrote it down in my

surveillance notebook."

"Good. Jin will find you."

"Then what?" I asked.

"You're going to lead him into a trap."

"Great . . . I've always wanted to be bait," Rodrigo drawled.

"We can always send the police if you're not comfortable with this," Rick said.

I eyed my pilot. Sweat stains spread beneath his armpits. The stress was starting to wear on him. "Hold on a sec." I pressed the mute button. "Rodrigo, Rick can send in the police and end this immediately. Rivkin may or may not get away, but it won't be up to us. But, he's got a million-dollar price on his head. If you want a piece of that . . ."

He didn't speak for a minute. "Bait it is."

I unmuted the phone. "It's on. Tell us what you want us to do. We're a few miles from Springfield."

"Take the I-395 lanes. Jin will be with you in a minute."

Our little Subaru entered what is known as the Springfield Mixing Bowl, where I-95, I-395, and I-495 (a.k.a. the Capital Beltway) all combined, along with a couple of local lanes. We passed beneath a handful of highflying exit and entrance ramps, keeping an eye on the multitude of overhead signs to make sure we were in the correct lane for I-395 and didn't end up heading toward Maryland. While Rodrigo navigated the mess, I watched our tail to make sure Rivkin still followed. Finally, we came out underneath the last flyover.

"We're through the Mixing Bowl," I told Rick. "The Edsall Road signs are just ahead, and Rivkin has moved into the center lane, three cars back."

Rick smoothly directed, "Move into the center lane. You want to make sure he's behind you and doesn't pull up next to you."

Rodrigo cut off a guy in a yellow Volkswagen Beetle in the

center lane and received the blast of a horn for his efforts. "Oops." He hunched his shoulders in embarrassment.

The car zipped into the left lane. Rodrigo didn't glance over as the driver passed us with his middle finger up. Incidents of road rage were common in the D.C. area. It was best not to engage—especially when being followed by a homicidal maniac.

"Okay, Jin's got you. He's behind Rivkin."

"Where do we go from here?" I craned my neck to see if I could figure out which car was Jin's. "I can't see him."

"Don't worry, he's there. Stay on until the Glebe Road exit."

A couple more miles and the Glebe Road signs came into view. "We're almost there."

"Jin's moved in front of Rivkin and will make the exit with you."

Sure enough, a black sedan wheeled up behind us. Large aviator sunglasses and a black ballcap hid his features, but knowing he was right behind us gave me a small sense of relief. We were the first car stopped at the red light at the bottom of the exit ramp.

"Be ready to go. When the light turns green, I want you to move ahead quickly. Jin's going to stall Rivkin. Stay in the right lane and turn right at the next light."

The honking started as we took our right. Rick continued to guide us until we turned into a warehouse district. Rivkin was still behind us but we lost sight of him on and off as we made each turn following the directions Rick rattled off.

"You're doing great. You're almost there," Rick assured us. "Take the next right and at the end of the row of warehouses come to a stop."

"Uh, Rick? You just backed us into a dead end." A concrete wall rose ahead of us.

"Forget this," Rodrigo mumbled, shifting into reverse.

"Don't panic! And no matter what, stay in the car," Rick

barked.

"Wait." I placed a hand on Rodrigo's shoulder.

The BMW nosed around the corner and moved in for the kill. Garage doors on our left and right flew open and two large, black SUVs shot out, effectively trapping Rivkin in front and back. They also blocked our view. Shots rang out.

"Get down! Get down!" someone shouted.

Rodrigo and I slunk down in our seats, popping our heads up like prairie dogs to check on the show. Men in black tactical gear, carrying assault weapons, piled out of the SUV on the side closest to us. One of them tossed something over the roof of the SUV toward the BMW. *Pow!* They moved single file around the back of the car. There was scuffling, two quick shots, a shout, then not much of anything.

Rodrigo and I waited.

And waited.

His eyes wide like saucers, he asked, "Do you think they got him?"

"I don't know. Stay here. I'll go find out." I rolled out of the car, and in a crouched position, ran up to the big SUV. The windows were darkened, so I couldn't see a thing, but I heard the quiet murmur of male voices. Inching my way to the rear end of the vehicle, I peeked around the side. Rivkin lay face down on the ground, trussed up with zip ties like a calf at a roping contest. Half a dozen men stood about, relaxed, while Rick rifled through a wallet.

"Check the trunk," he directed.

A guy I didn't know ducked into the car and popped the trunk latch. Jin opened the rear lid.

"Is he dead?" I asked. All heads, except Rick's, turned to me.

"Nope. Hit him with the stun gun. He'll be coming around in a minute," Josh answered. "You and your friend okay?"

I nodded. "What do we do now? To whom do we turn him over to collect the bounty?"

"Uh-oh, boss, you better see this," Jin said from behind the car.

"What is it?" Rick finally looked up from the wallet.

"Dead lady," Jin replied.

A hand flew to my mouth.

"I bet it's Karen," said a voice in my ear.

"Aiyee!" I yelped, nearly jumping out of my skin. Rodrigo hadn't followed my direction to stay in the car and snuck up behind me on cat feet. It also didn't help that my emotions were amped up from the thrill ride. Irritated eyeballs were on me again. "Sorry, sorry. Just startled."

Rick and Josh trotted to the back of the BMW; Jin stepped aside. Neither said anything, but I could tell by the frowns that they didn't like what they saw. Rodrigo headed their way and I followed, only to be barred by Jin's whip-fast arm.

"You don't want to see that," he assured me.

"I don't?"

He shook his head but allowed Rodrigo to pass. It must have been a man thing and I was about to get pissy, when Rodrigo, getting a gander at the woman in the trunk, blanched, turned away, and promptly vomited on the front wheel of the SUV.

My gaze met Jin's. "Bullet to the head?"

"Garrote. Sliced her windpipe."

My face turned into the one Lucille Ball used to give on *I Love Lucy* when she finds out her harebrained scheme has gone bad. No wonder poor Rodrigo lost his stakeout snacks.

A Hispanic guy I didn't recognize took pity on my coworker and handed him an olive-green bandana.

"Is it Karen?" I asked.

Rodrigo nodded, wiping his face.

"Where do you think he was planning on dumping her?"

Jin shrugged. "Who knows. You two probably changed his plans."

A cold shiver ran down my spine. Rodrigo and I could have been stuffed in with her. What was eminently clear, now that we had a dead body, was we couldn't just hand Rivkin over to the Israelis to collect the bounty on his head.

I let out a deep sigh. "Hey, guys, I hate to say this, but I've got to call in the feds. We can't just hand him over."

"Not with a dead body on our hands," Rick agreed.

"Does that mean we won't get the reward?" Rodrigo asked with the teensiest bit of whine in his voice.

I understood where he was coming from. Who couldn't use a piece of that million-dollar reward? "Probably." I pulled the phone out of my suit pants pocket and mumbled, "Mike is going to be so pissed at me."

He still hadn't returned my panicked call from earlier, and I decided I wasn't in the mood to get yelled at again. So I dialed my lawyer instead.

"Jessica? It's Karina Cardinal, can you give me the number for Director McGill?" Foolishly, I'd failed to add him to my contacts.

"What are you into now?" she asked on high alert.

"Wellll . . . I'm here with a couple of security specialists and we've captured the guy who we believe broke into my apartment. Oh, and . . . there . . . is a deadwomaninhistrunk," I mumbled quickly.

Jessica took a beat. "Did you just say, 'there is a dead woman in the trunk?'"

I stared at the ground, rubbing my temples. "Uh-huh."

"Give me your location. I'll contact Leon."

"Thanks." I turned to Jin. "Address?"

Rick rattled it off before anyone else could speak, and I

repeated it to Jessica.

"Are you safe?" she asked.

"Well, I've got one, two, three . . . lots of burly men with assault rifles, my coworker, and Rivkin is cuffed and drooling on the ground. I think I'm good."

"Who the hell is Rivkin? You know what . . . never mind. You can explain when I get there."

"Oh, there's no need for you . . ." She hung up before I could finish. I pocketed the phone. "Well, boys, seems like the FBI is on its way. If there's anyone who doesn't want to be here when they show up, you better leave now."

Rick pointed to three of his men, and they piled into the SUV behind the BMW. Then he closed the trunk.

"Do you need to leave too?" I asked Rick.

He made a swirling motion with his finger and pointed at the Hispanic guy in the SUV driver's seat. The big black truck rolled out. "I'll stick around for this one."

Rivkin showed signs of life. Josh took pity on him and, grabbing his collar, moved him into a sitting position against the car. There was a burn mark on his neck and wet patch around his crotch. The stun gun must have made him pee his pants.

I snapped my fingers in front of his closed eyes. "Hey, remember me?"

The lids opened.

"Who do you work for?" I asked.

Nothing.

"We know you were part of the plot to assassinate Harper. Finley too. What did you do? Mess with his car? Drug his driver?"

That ghostly, pale gaze stared at me. Josh kicked his foot. "The lady asked you a question."

"You're wasting your time," Rick said. "He's trained Mossad. You could torture him for a week and he wouldn't crack. The FBI will get nothing out of him."

"Not unless they make you a deal? Right?" I crouched down to his level. "You know the FBI had a surveillance van watching the house. They've got photos of you. Rodrigo and I are also witnesses. They'll be sending in a team. Right now, I bet you're wondering if you cleaned it properly. What about your clothes? Is there DNA evidence on them? Were you planning on burying your kit with Karen?"

He didn't bat a lash.

"Who paid you?"

"You have no idea what you've gotten into," he said with a distinct accent. The few words I'd heard him say after Harper's death had been said with a nasal midwestern accent and held no resemblance to this deep, rugged voice. "These people have long arms."

I knew I should leave him alone and let the feds deal with him. But Harper was personal to me, and I wanted answers. "You killed a senator and a congressman. I think I have a pretty good idea what's going on. What I'm trying to figure out, are you willing to deal, or will you go down for your bosses?"

He said something in a language I didn't understand, and he said it with such venom, I had a feeling he cursed me.

Fearful he might spit, I hopped back. "Anyone get that?"

"He doesn't have a boss. He's an independent contractor," Rick explained.

"Let me guess, Hebrew?" I glanced up.

"Yes," Rick said.

"Rick, what happens if we tell the Israeli intelligence where he is? Can they get to him?"

He rubbed his chin in consideration. "I give him forty-eight hours once the feds put him in prison."

"Do we still get the reward?"

"Hm," he mused, pursing his lips, "I imagine I can work

something out with my contacts."

Rivkin took the news rather well. Or maybe he didn't. I couldn't tell through his stone-faced expression.

"Hey, Rivkin or Jablonski, what's your real name? Is it even Naftali Rivkin?"

No reaction.

"Forget it, I'm going to call you Creepy Eyes. Listen up, I'm sure there will be a deal with the feds." I kicked his foot. "But what you've got to realize, there's a different deal right now. And I would guess it'll only be on the table for a few more minutes before our FBI friends show up."

Rick must have seen where I was going, because he put his hands on his knees and looked Rivkin in the eye. "What the lady is saying, none of us work for law enforcement." He indicated the men standing around. "Like you, we're independent contractors, and we work for whoever pays the most. Right now, your head is worth a cool mil. That's a nice bit of change. Like you, *I* have connections."

"What do you want?" Rivkin's gaze turned to icicles.

Rick rotated his head to me, and, crouching back down to Rivkin's level, I picked up where he left off. "Answers. You were part of the hit squad on Harper?"

He nodded.

"And you broke into my house for the phone?"

He nodded.

"Why? What's on it?"

He shrugged.

"You don't know why you broke in my house to retrieve the phone?"

"The clients wanted the phone. I didn't ask why. It's called compartmentalization."

"Do you still have it?"

"Destroyed."

I'd been afraid of that. "And your clients are . . ."

"Troika Star."

"Teason is Troika Star?"

"Teason is the tip of the iceberg."

"What do you mean by that?"

"Tip. Of. The. Iceberg," he repeated with deliberation.

"What did Karen have to do with it? Is she part of Troika Star?"

He tilted his head toward the trunk. "She was."

I couldn't help the recoil. "You murdered your employer?"

"She became a liability."

"She got cold feet?"

"Something like that."

"Why Harper? Why Finley?"

He gave a disinterested shrug. "Ask them."

"Them, who?"

"My clients."

"That's what I'm trying to get to. *Who* are your clients? Who hired you?"

A lazy grin spread across his face. "Follow the money."

Clearly Rivkin was speaking in circles. I tried a different tactic. "Who's the hacker?"

Another shrug. "I didn't hire him."

"But you know him? You know who he is?"

"Never seen him in my life."

Another dead end. "Why did you kill Harper in the tunnels? Was it to set me up? Make me a suspect?"

"You flatter yourself. Up until a few days ago, I had no idea who you were."

"Wrong place, wrong time?"

"I'd say so."

"I see, it wasn't personal. Just business?"

He didn't respond.

"And what did you plan to do with Rodrigo and me today? More business?"

"No." He threw off his nonchalance like a blanket and delivered an evil grin that sought to enhance the uncanniness of those eyes.

I sucked in a breath.

"*You* have become a nuisance. Believe me, it is personal, and it will be very painful."

Before I could react to the hatred and evil, Joshua punched him. There was a crunching noise, the back of his head slammed against the car and blood poured from his nose. He didn't make a peep.

"Enough questions." Rick pulled me to my feet as a black sedan rolled into the alley.

Chapter Twenty-five

Director McGill arrived first, but it didn't take long for our tight alleyway to fill up with law enforcement. As soon as we explained to McGill that Rivkin had followed us from the Troika Star house, he called in a team to sweep the place. Apparently, the guy in the van was only providing exterior surveillance, he'd been ordered to follow the Cadillac and is why he left in a hurry to catch up to it. They hadn't gotten any warrants for listening devices inside, so Karen's murder had not been caught on tape.

When someone asked how Rivkin got the bloody nose, Rick replied, "He tripped and fell."

The FBI looked skeptical, but nobody bothered to correct him.

We leaned against the SUV, arranged like some ragtag police lineup—Rick at one end, Jessica next to him in a red power suit, me in my stained navy pants suit, Rodrigo in jeans and sweaty madras shirt, Josh and Jin still wearing tactical gear—while FBI agents bustled around taking photos and gathering evidence.

Upon arrival, Jessica declared all of us her clients, and would only allow us to tell the bare bones of facts. Any agent asking questions—McGill had sent a few our way—had been shooed away by a single word and a flick of Jessica's wrist. I knew our silence would only take us so far. Soon enough, we'd have to tell the story. Now we watched the show and waited.

The *X-Files* sang out.

"Isn't that your FBI friend?" Rodrigo pointed to the phone in my hand, which I stared at as if it was an adder ready to strike. "You should get that."

"Maybe later." I sent him to voicemail. I had an inkling our next conversation wasn't going to be pretty.

I should have known he wouldn't leave it be. A minute later, an FBI agent with a blonde ponytail and aviator sunglasses came over to me.

"Are you Karina Cardinal?" she asked in a no-nonsense way.

"That would be me."

"This is for you." She passed me her cell phone.

My stomach knotted. "Hello?"

"K.C.?"

"Hey, Mike, what's up?"

"Not much. I got your message," he said in a monotone voice.

"Oh, riiiight." I pressed two fingers against my temple. "You can disregard it. Everything is fine. We're all fine." I tried to convey nonchalance.

"So, I understand." There was hardness to his response.

Divert! Divert! my mind screamed. "Did you get your man?"

"As a matter of fact, I did. We're transporting him home tonight."

"Good for you," I injected jovially.

Mike seemed to be waiting for me to say something more.

I didn't give him the satisfaction.

He finally broke the quiet. "And, you? Anything new to report?"

"Not really."

"Nothing?" It's amazing how much sarcasm can be infused into one word.

"Oh, you want to know about Rivkin?"

"You're testing my patience." I'm pretty sure he spoke through gritted teeth.

"Well, I'm here with a bunch of FBI agents, Rodrigo, my lawyer Jessica—you remember meeting her at my house—right? Also, Rick and Josh, from Silverthorne—your favorite security specialists."

Jin, three people down, leaned forward and cocked his head at me.

"Oh, and Jin too. He helped us trap Rivkin as he stalked us down the highway." Jin gave me a thumbs-up which I returned. "I'm sorry to be the one to tell you, there's been another murder. Karen Ferngull is dead. Rivkin garroted—garroted . . . is that the right word? Anyway, he did her in. I didn't see it, but apparently it was pretty gross. Rodrigo lost his lunch." I got a sock to the shoulder for that one.

What? I mouthed at my coworker.

Mike made a choking sound.

"TMI? Don't worry, the ME has already tagged and bagged her. Considering Rodrigo's reaction, I didn't watch. The rest of the team is scurrying around like squirrels, photographing, collecting evidence . . . you know the drill. I think we're also waiting for a wrecker to come for the car. It'll undoubtedly be sent back to some forensics lab. But I'm sure you know that too. We're just waiting for everyone to clear out. Basically, our cars are trapped until they do."

"K.C.—"

"Any who," I continued, ignoring the warning in his voice. "Your boys already took Rivkin away, for interrogation purposes, I imagine. Did I forget anything?"

I looked left and right. Everyone stared straight ahead except my officemate.

"Did you tell him Rivkin shot out my passenger mirror?" Rodrigo piped up. "Who's going to pay for that? Will the FBI cover it?"

"Rodrigo wants to know if the FBI will pay for his busted mirror? The one that Rivkin shot out."

Silence.

"Mike? Are you still there? Will the FBI reimburse Rodrigo for his mirror?"

"Those are like three hundred dollars to fix," Rodrigo spoke into the mouthpiece.

More nothing.

"Mike? Hello? You haven't stroked out, have you?"

"Please pass the phone back to Agent Reinhart."

"You mean the blonde?"

"Yes."

"Okey doke. Good talk." I let out a sharp whistle—Agent Reinhart hadn't gone too far—and wiggled the phone when I caught her attention. "He wants a word."

She took the cell. "Hello? Yes. . . . No. . . . Uh-huh. . . . I see. No, we didn't. I'm on it."

Lucky for me, the phone went back into her pocket. I guess Mike didn't have anything more to say to me right now. I wasn't looking forward to the next time we spoke.

"Which one of you is Rodrigo?" she asked.

Three of us pointed to my coworker.

"I understand your side mirror was shot?"

"Yes, it was," Rodrigo said proudly.

"Show me."

He left our questionable cast of characters to show Reinhart the Subaru's broken mirror. "Can you fix it?"

"I'm an FBI agent, not an auto mechanic. It needs to be entered into evidence."

"What does that mean?" His voice faded as they went around the SUV and I didn't hear her answer.

We all heard Rodrigo's response: "*What? NO! Not my car!*"

I suspected Agent Reinhart just told Rodrigo his vehicle was going to be impounded for evidence.

Jessica sighed and pushed herself away from the SUV. "I'd better go help him. Not a word." She pointed at all of us.

I checked our lineup. Rick sported his normal straight face, but Josh was shaking from holding his laughter, and Jin had broken into a wide grin.

"Don't laugh now, Jin. We wouldn't want to ruin a hot streak. Not within hours of your last outburst."

"*You can't take my baby! Karina! This is all your fault!*" Rodrigo hollered.

An unguarded chuckle escaped from Jin.

"Damnit." Josh pulled his wallet out and passed a twenty to Rick's outstretched hand.

I tutted, "I told you not to bet against me, my friend."

Rick shook his head. "I pity Agent Finnegan."

Much to his distress and Jessica's ire, another wrecker came to take Rodrigo's car away. Jessica negotiated with the FBI, and we were allowed to retrieve our personal belongings after it had all been photographed. I didn't understand the necessity for taking Rodrigo's car, and I began to wonder if this was simply Mike's way of getting back at us for disregarding his request. Though that seemed a bit petty.

I lost track of time. Full darkness descended, and the moon peeked over the rooftops before FBI cars began rolling out. Finally, Director McGill approached our motley group.

"We need statements from each one of you," he said.

My stomach rumbled. It'd been awhile since my last meal, and Rodrigo's stakeout snacks went with the wrecker. I'll admit, I regretted declining his generous offer to share the BBQ chips hours ago. "Do you think we could do it over a Big Mac and fries? I'm starving."

"Director McGill, my clients have had a trying day. Perhaps

we could take statements in the morning."

"Jess—Ms. Williams, as I'm sure you're aware, witness statements immediately after an incident are vital."

"Fine. But, they need some food, and we'll do this all at once. We're not splitting them up and playing FBI interrogation tactics. Remember, my clients are the heroes here. They've helped capture an international fugitive."

Leon didn't look happy about that, but he conceded.

Rodrigo and I rode in Jessica's car, while the Silverthorne boys followed in the SUV, to an FBI facility in Crystal City, Virginia. They got us sub sandwiches and chips and put us in a nice conference room with cushy swivel chairs. Much better than the gray interrogation cell I'd been fearing. We shared the day's events as they played out chronologically. McGill occasionally interjected with clarification questions. It turned out Rick's lawyer was in Bermuda, so Jessica remained as his attorney. He basically spoke for his crew using short sentences without much elaboration. Rick wasn't known for lengthy exposition. He might have left out the part where there were other men as part of the take down. I tried to keep it short and sweet. On the other hand, Rodrigo, better known for expansive descriptions, had to be quelled a few times by a simple look from Jessica. One might call it a glare. I mentioned the only real piece of information that Rivkin gave us—Troika Star was the tip of the iceberg, and there seemed to be a conspiracy afoot when it came to Harper's and Finley's death.

My testimony was duly recorded with a head nod and surprisingly little interest, as though I'd just told them crows are black. Either the FBI already knew those little bits, or they didn't deem it important to the investigation. I preferred to believe the former.

"Well, I think that wraps it up." Leon finally closed his handwritten notes into a file folder, the two other agents in the room did the same.

"What will happen to Rivkin?" I asked.

"We'll interrogate him. Try to find out what he knows."

"Trained Mossad?" I rolled my eyes. "Ha. He won't crack. You'll have to make him a deal."

"Don't worry, Ms. Cardinal. We've got things under control."

"I'm saying, he knows. He knows who's responsible. You need to do whatever it takes to make him tell you." I pounded the table in frustration.

Leon's brows drew together, Josh's head shook ever so slightly, and Jessica turned her hard stare on me.

I drew back. "Never mind. I'm sure you've got this in the bag. I apologize. It's been . . . a long day."

"Indeed, it has." My lawyer wheeled her chair back and rose. "Since we're through here, I think it's time my clients got some rest."

We gathered our things. Josh offered to give me and Rodrigo a lift. Rodrigo took him up on it, but Jessica insisted, since I lived in the opposite direction, she could take me home. I suspected she had some words of wisdom to impart.

As soon as we exited the underground parking garage, she started, "What did Rivkin tell you?"

"I don't know what you mean."

"Someone punched him before the FBI showed up. What did he say?"

"That he wanted to kill me. It wasn't a job for him. He made it personal. I think I kind of . . . grated on his nerves."

"Karina . . ." She brought the car to a stop at a red light. "How do you get yourself into these messes?"

"I've no idea."

Her brows rose in disbelief.

"Seriously, I promised Mike I was out of it. It was Rodrigo.

He pulled me back in," I said in my best Michael Corleone impression.

My lawyer simply stared with brows raised.

"Hey, it can't be that bad. We just apprehended an international criminal."

The light turned green and she returned her attention to the road. "That's what concerns me."

I had no adequate response. Instead, I directed her to my office so I could pick up my car. Fortunately, rush hour had long since passed and the uncomfortable ride only lasted a few minutes.

Chapter Twenty-six

I dropped my purse and computer bag by the door, kicked off my ruined pumps in the hallway, and collapsed on the couch. Any sort of adrenaline coursing through my veins from all the excitement had long worn off, leaving me physically drained. Unfortunately, the passage of time hadn't had the same effect on my mind, and it took awhile before the relative peace of my apartment worked like a balm to quiet the stormy thoughts.

We had captured a professional assassin. A killer. Murderer. That felt good. I knew, tomorrow, I'd go back to work and carry on with the mundane day-to-day. Thank heavens. Catching bad guys was stressful. And a little dangerous.

Of course, there was that last bit of information that Rivkin didn't supply, which was going to drive me nuts. "*Follow the money.*" Clearly, there was a conspiracy surrounding Finley's and Harper's murders, and I was dying to get to the root cause. I had Teason and J & P. Who else made up the motley group of murderers? Were these companies so concerned about the *possibility* of legislation that would cut into their profit margins that they'd kill for it? Or was there something more? Something deeper? I wondered if the FBI would get what they wanted out of Rivkin. Or, maybe the guy Mike apprehended would confess.

My phone blinked a calendar reminder at me. I'd scheduled the first appointment with a security company at seven, before work. It was past midnight, too late to call and cancel, so I dragged myself through the shower and fell into my fluffy bed, utterly beat.

I must have forgotten to set my alarm because the *X-Files* ringtone woke me at half past six. I'd also forgotten to charge my phone, and the little red bar blinked at me.

"Morning," I mumbled. "If you're going to yell at me, could we table it until lunch?"

"Rivkin's dead."

I shot upright, all thoughts of returning to sleep gone. "What? What do you mean, he's dead? What happened?"

"He was in a holding cell. Someone got to him. Slit his throat. Guard found him this morning."

"Who was it?" I shoved a wad of hair out of my eyes. "There must be cameras."

"Working on it."

"Was it an inside job?"

"I hope not. But it's not out of the realm of possibility."

"Do you think the Israelis got to him?"

"Also a possibility."

Considering Rivkin's last words to me, I confess, I wasn't completely brokenhearted over the fact that he was gone. Had he ever escaped . . . well, I wouldn't have slept again.

"Jeez. What about your hacker? Is he still alive?"

"We have him at—"

The cell cut out. "Damn it." I reached over to my bedside table to retrieve the landline and dial Mike back.

"K.C.?"

"Sorry, my cell died. What were you saying about the hacker?"

"He's safe at a different location, and we've put a double guard on him."

"Has he talked?"

"Not yet. We're letting him stew for a bit."

"Don't let him marinate too long. This is dirty. I mean, pig-in-shit dirty. Rivkin said to follow the money. Karen and Teason Pharmaceuticals are definitely in on it. This isn't some hate crime due to immigration policy."

"We're checking all the avenues."

I ignored his interruption. "Rivkin told us they were only the tip of the iceberg. I got the feeling there was more and connected to someone big. You need to get answers out of the computer nerd. I'm telling you this goes deep."

"I'm working on it. Are you okay?"

"Me? I'm fine. Why?"

"Why? You're kidding, right?"

"Oh, you mean yesterday's business. Yeah, we're all safe. Although, it wasn't very nice for the FBI to take Rodrigo's car just because of one little bullet hole. It's not like his car had a dead body in it."

"I'll see" —Mike let out a big yawn— "what I can do to get it released."

"Thanks. What about you? You sound tired. Any difficulties getting your man?"

"No. The take down was textbook. Couldn't have gone any smoother."

"Great."

"Yes, great. Yesterday would have been a great day. Except for the message you left."

I thought back to my panic. "Ah, right. Terribly sorry about that. I was a bit worked up."

"If I was an older man, a message like that would've given me a heart attack."

"Look on the bright side. You're still a young man."

"It aged me a dozen years."

"Don't be so dramatic."

"Would you like me to replay it for you?"

"Uh, no." I had no interest in reliving those desperate moments. They'd snuck unpleasantly into my dreams last night. "Listen, I've got to go. I have a security company arriving in fifteen minutes and I'm not dressed yet. Can I call you later?"

"I'll call you around lunch."

He rang off and I scrambled around to get dressed and put on makeup, praying the security guy would show up a tad late. He, of course, arrived five minutes early. I liked what he proposed. The price was right, and they could get the system put in on Saturday. I signed on the dotted line and escorted the guy out the door by eight thirty.

On my way to work, I phoned Rick. He answered on the second ring.

"Rivkin's dead," I said.

"What happened?"

"Someone got past security. Slit his throat." I saw no need to sugarcoat it, figuring Rick, being a man of few words, would appreciate my brevity.

He didn't respond.

There must have been an accident, traffic crawled particularly slowly this morning. "Rick, I know we made threats last night . . . you didn't, uh, happen to mention to your Israeli friends that the FBI had Rivkin in custody, did you?"

"No, I didn't. However, I alerted my contact that we had a lead on Rivkin. Karen's murder made it into the local news. Also, that the FBI had a suspect in custody . . ."

"You think they put two-and-two together?"

"Possibly. I can think of a number of people who would want Rivkin silenced. However, I find it more likely the Israelis would take a diplomatic approach to get him back."

"The Israeli government, yes. But, Mossad? There must have been some angry folks when Rivkin flipped. Maybe a rogue operation?"

"I can't say."

"Let me know if you hear anything."

"Sure."

Rick tended to play his hand close to the vest, the way he said that one syllable made me doubt I'd hear back from him on this matter. I changed the subject. "By the way, I hired one of the companies you recommended. They gave me a discount when I mentioned your name."

"Good. I sent you a date and time for your next self-defense class. I'm leaving town. Jin offered to work with you."

"Jin? Are you sure? Not Josh?"

"Not Josh."

"O-kay." I tried not to sound too reticent.

"Don't worry. Jin's taken a shine to you."

"Great."

"Also, he lost the coin toss." With that parting shot, Rick hung up.

Traffic came to a complete standstill. Sirens whined and lights flashed in the distance. I wasn't too worried; my first appointment of the day was a conference call that didn't start until nine thirty. The digital clock on my car's dash read 8:40. Still plenty of time to make it.

My cell rang. "Hello."

"Is this Karina Cardinal?"

"Yes, it is. Who is this?"

"My name is Joe Brock."

Why does that name sound familiar?

"I'm a journalist with *The Washington Post*."

That would be why. I didn't know Joe Brock personally but had certainly read a number of his recent stories about the long-fingered Russian influence on our last election. "What can I do for you, Joe?"

"I was hoping we could meet today."

"Why?"

"To talk about Senator Harper's death."

"I have nothing to say."

"What about Karen Ferngull?"

"What about her?" Traffic finally started moving.

"What do you know about her death?"

"What do you know about it?"

"Ms. Cardinal, can I call you Karina?"

"You may call me Ms. Cardinal." For the most part, I held reporters in high regard, however past experiences left me reticent to speak with them.

"This morning a flash drive showed up on my desk. A note was attached that read, 'In case of my death, deliver to Joe Brock at *The Washington Post.*' Her death was on the morning news."

I couldn't help the slight gasp that escaped. "What's on the drive?"

"Well, I'd like to talk with you about that."

"Why me? Am I on it?"

He hesitated. "No. But, your name keeps popping up on my radar. Harper's death and now Karen's."

As much as I disliked having to talk to the press, it occurred to me that Joe might have some of the answers I sought on that drive. "Fine. I don't have my calendar in front of me. Let me call you back in thirty minutes to set a time and place."

"I'll be waiting."

Rodrigo's cube stood empty when I arrived. After checking the kitchen and coming up empty, I phoned him. It went straight to voicemail. Then I spent ten minutes agitatedly pacing from my office to his cube. When he finally arrived, I pounced. "Rodrigo, my office."

My face must have betrayed my anxiety because he didn't

even bother dropping his crossbody computer satchel at his desk before following me to my office.

"Shut the door. I only have ten minutes before my conference call."

"What's wrong?" He gripped the back of the guest chair.

I didn't bother to sit either. "All sorts of things." I gave him a rundown of my morning conversations with Mike, Rick, and Joe Brock. "I think we should meet with this reporter."

"We?"

"He might be able to give us more information. And I'm dying to know what's on that flash drive. Aren't you?"

He paced the small bit of real estate in my office. "Okay, yes. I'm in. Where are we meeting?"

"I've got time at three thirty today. What about you?"

Rodrigo checked the calendar on his phone. "I can rearrange some things."

"Can you get us a private table at Alfonse's restaurant?"

"Yes, of course."

"I'll organize the rest. I'm in the city this afternoon, so I'll meet you there."

Once he left, I phoned the reporter. "I can meet you at three thirty. Côte du Rhône restaurant."

"I'll be there."

Now I had to figure out how to get one other person there who might be able to help put the puzzle pieces together, but who undoubtedly wasn't interested in meeting me.

Chapter Twenty-seven

Côte du Rhône was located on 18th Street, NW, between an Ethiopian and Chinese restaurant in the trendy Adams Morgan neighborhood. It served fine French cuisine, and at three thirty in the afternoon, between the lunch and dinner rushes, I figured customers would be light. As a matter of fact, when I walked in the door, only two white-clothed tables housed patrons.

I spotted a balding man of average height with a middle-aged paunch, wearing tan chinos, a white button down, and a brown polka dot tie hovering near the maître de station.

"Joe Brock?"

"Ms. Cardinal." We shook hands and I turned to the maître de. "Can you please escort this man to Rodrigo Alvarez's table? I'll join you in a minute, Mr. Brock."

He didn't question my actions and followed the tuxedoed host to a booth in the back of the restaurant where I could see the back of Rodrigo's head. The door swung open and the man in question arrived after all.

"I don't know what you're trying to pull here, lady. But, I don't take kindly to blackmail." Nick Ross's bird-of-prey features were even more forbidding than usual as they hovered above me.

"Not blackmail, Nick. Karen Ferngull is dead, and I believe you know more about what she was mixed up in than you're letting on."

"This is ridiculous. I'm leaving."

I seized his wrist, reminiscent of his breakup with Karen, the only difference being I wasn't infatuated with this callous man and my voice held none of her begging, but rather a quiet severity that brooked no arguments. "Her actions have led to the death of a senator and congressman, as well as her own, and almost mine. We're getting to the bottom of this. Now. Or, I tell the FBI all about your little affair, in addition to an intriguing conversation I overheard opening night of Turandot."

He visibly paled. "I had nothing to do with it."

"That's why we're meeting a reporter, rather than the FBI . . . today."

"A reporter," he hissed, "are you crazy?"

"No. The story is coming out, so you can either help control the message or be part of the bloody aftermath."

The maître de returned and watched us with open curiosity.

I released Nick. "Are you joining us, or not?"

His eyes narrowed. "After you, milady," he said with exaggerated gentility.

"No need to see us to the table," I told the inquisitive maître de, striding past his post.

Rodrigo and Joe stood when we arrived at the table. I made introductions and scooted inside the black velvet, circular booth between Joe and Nick, the latter sitting on the edge of his seat, as if ready to bolt at any moment. The location of the table and high back gave us the privacy I sought.

A waiter arrived to take our drink orders. No one was interested in allowing alcohol to loosen their tongue; everyone chose iced tea, and Rodrigo ordered some hors d'oeuvres for the table.

Joe flipped open a notebook and, shifting the candle aside, placed his phone in the center of the pristine white cloth. "I'd like to start with you, Ms. Cardinal."

"Actually, I think we'd all like to hear what you have to say. Maybe a little introduction as to what you're working on will get the conversation flowing."

Joe seemed disconcerted by my suggestions. "That's not how this works."

"I'm afraid if you want answers, today, that's how this works."

He glanced around the table and must have realized none of us would open up without something to go on. "Alright. As I'm sure the three of you are aware, global pharmaceuticals are a trillion-dollar industry. The International Trade Administration estimates it will grow to one point three trillion by 2020. Our aging population and rise in chronic diseases along with higher disposable incomes have been some of the reasons for its continued growth."

Rodrigo and I nodded. The numbers sounded right to me. Nick continued his impression of a bad-tempered vulture.

"For the past six months, I've been investigating a group of drug companies."

"What kind of investigation?" Rodrigo asked.

"Their political contributions, recent patents, R and D futures, stock prices . . . In addition, I've been watching the political climate surrounding the drug industry—Hill votes, new White House policies."

"And what have you found?"

"Some disturbing patterns."

"Were you investigating Karen?" Rodrigo asked and adjusted his tie.

"She was in the mix."

"And today, you said you'd received a flash drive from Karen," I put in.

Nick's frown deepened, but Rodrigo leaned forward, intrigued. "Ooh, spooky, she speaks from beyond the grave."

"Before I get into that, I'd like to ask you a few questions." He reached out to turn on the phone's recorder and poised his pen above the notebook.

Nick remained perched in position—his arms crossed and expression hostile. I began to fear he'd tell us nothing, so I reached over and tapped the cell's screen.

"Listen, Joe, I think it's best if we're off the record for right now."

Joe hid his disappointment and put the pen aside.

The waiter arrived with our appetizers—a plate of mussels, some sort of garlic sausage, and what looked distinctly like snails. I must have missed when Rodrigo ordered the escargot. He was also the only one who dug into the food, scooping a little bit of each offering onto his dish. After assuring our server we needed nothing more, Joe returned his attention to me.

"Where to start? Where to start?" I drummed my fingers. "I suppose my story begins with the death of Senator Harper. Before you ask, yes, I was in the tunnel with Harper when he passed. It has since been revealed to me that his pacemaker was hacked, causing it to go haywire and kill him."

"Wait a sec." Joe madly flipped through his well-used notepad. "Yes, here, Harper's pacemaker was made by Teason Medical."

That was news to me. "Teason Medical of Troika Star?"

"You know about Troika?"

"I do. They own a house near the train tracks where Finley was killed. What do you know about Troika Star?"

"We'll talk about that in a minute." He made a circular motion with his hand. "Let's get back to Harper. You said you were with him?"

"I provided CPR. A useless exercise, I found out later." I shook my head sadly.

"I've an idea why Harper," Joe continued, "but I can't

fathom Finley. Harper had been meddling in the drug industry for the past year. Turning more and more against the large companies. He even voted in favor of the—"

"—'Buy Your Pills from Canada' bill," I finished for him.

"Yes. Over the years, Harper's taken thousands from the drug companies, although on his last campaign there was a distinct fall off."

"You think they saw him as a traitor?" I asked.

"That's my guess," Joe confirmed.

"They saw him as a danger," Nick grumbled. "He'd been gaining support for the legislation he wanted to introduce."

Joe's gaze speared Ross. "What legislation?"

Nick shifted. "A new government pharmaceutical price modulating bill."

Surprise flashed across his features. "Harper?"

"What's more, Finley was in on it as well." Rodrigo supplied.

"Yes, but we don't know if they actually killed Finley. The final reports aren't in yet." I sipped my iced tea.

"According to my source at the NTSB," the reporter explained, "the crossing gates were tampered with. And the ME found remnants of ketamine in the driver's system."

Ketamine! A minute detail Mike failed to tell me.

"Ketamine? Isn't that the date rape drug?" Rodrigo asked.

"Yes, you are correct, my friend." I continued to watch Joe as I spoke. "What about the congressman? Why didn't he get out of the car? Did they tie him down? Drug him too?"

"The congressman's blood alcohol level was point two-five," Joe responded.

I whistled and directed my question at Nick. "Was the congressman a heavy drinker?"

He pursed his lips and shook his head. "Only socially."

"So, what? They force fed him drinks?"

"Or just gave him a couple of really strong ones." Rodrigo chewed the side of his mouth.

"Wow, I never knew Karen had it in her. A real black widow, that one." I directed the cutting jibe at Nick.

"She didn't. If it weren't for you, the congressman would still be alive!" he spat back at me.

I reared back, placing a hand to my chest. "Me? How on earth can you blame me?"

"Everything was fine. After Harper passed, Finley gave up on his grand plans to stick it to the pharmaceutical industry. Then you came along with all your talk about honoring his grandchild. Your hoity-toity speech in the hotel room actually got to him. The old man, one of the most level-headed conservatives in Congress, was swayed by your ridiculously passionate call to arms. Making a difference." Nick snorted. "He latched on like a tick ready to feed. They knew he had influence and feared he'd wield it to pass the bill."

"And knowing this, *you* ran to Karen. To what? Tell Mommy?" I taunted nastily.

"I mentioned it might be back on. But it was Finley who did it. I heard him talking to Ari over the phone that afternoon."

"Ari? Ari, who?" I held up my palms in confusion.

"Ari Punjab."

"Ari is head of R and D at Comstock Medical. They're based in New Jersey," Rodrigo explained to Joe with a smug smile.

"I think they invited him down to the house to try and negotiate with him. Get him to back off." Nick fidgeted with his spoon, tapping it on the table.

"And when he didn't . . ."

Nick tossed the spoon aside and shook his head.

Joe shifted forward. "So, let me get this straight, the murders were a conspiracy, to stop the possibility of a bill?"

"Finley had the votes. At least he said he had them. That's what he told Ari." Nick rubbed his eyes.

"Even so," I scoffed, "it's such a stretch. I'm having a real difficult time reconciling killing two members of Congress over a bill that had yet to be proposed. There's got to be something more. Joe, what has your investigation found?"

"Actually, it makes complete sense, and it's the piece I've been missing." Joe went back to his notepad. "Last year, prescription drugs brought in almost three hundred billion in domestic sales alone. Only fifty billion in international exports. America is funding the pharmaceutical industry, and it will only increase as the baby boomers continue to age. Too many European and Asian governments manage pricing, and America is footing the bill. If we pass price controls, the industry profits will shrivel by billions."

"I told you. Remember, at the theater?" Rodrigo put some more appetizers on his plate. "Seriously, you all should try some of this. The garlic mussels are to die for."

I ignored Rodrigo's jibe and his offer of food. "I hadn't read the latest numbers; they are bigger than I thought."

"Back to the conspiracy theory here; we're saying it was Karen, Ari, and someone from Teason Medical? They are Troika Star? Why them? What's the connection?" Rodrigo slurped up a snail.

"Hardly." Joe tapped the pen against his notebook. "It's more."

"How many more?" I asked.

"Troika Star is a conglomerate of five pharmaceutical companies and includes multiple executives at those companies."

All eyes turned to the reporter.

"And you can prove that?" Nick chimed in.

"Karen's flash drive provides bank account numbers and

screenshots of an account with regular deposits from J & P, Comstock, Orlando, Teason, and Maceret. The account has over forty-five million in it."

Rivkin's words came back to me— *"tip of the iceberg"* and *"follow the money."* All five of those companies fell into the top ten pharmaceutical companies in the world.

Joe continued, "There were over two hundred emails outlining a strategy to put politicians in place at the highest levels who would enact and continue to uphold laws that maximize company and industry profits."

We digested the information with varied expressions of shock.

"My God, how many years has it been going on?" I asked.

"So far, we've found emails dating back to 2008."

"Ten years?" Nick said in disbelief.

"They can't *all* be a part of the conspiracy to the assassinations." I rubbed my temples. "Someone's conscience would have gotten the better of them."

"One of them did," Rodrigo said, "Karen."

"True," I muttered.

"I'm still culling through the emails. From what I can tell, Karen, Ari, Jamichael Teason, Brett Culligan at Orlando, and Vanya Didi at Maceret were put in charge of the fund."

"Oh my god!" Rodrigo cried. "I just realized who the guy in the Caddy was, Jamichael Teason. I remember him from a fundraiser I attended last year."

"Did you know?" I aimed my accusing question at Nick.

"*No,*" he denied.

I delivered a skeptical frown.

"Look, I knew, before Karen took the job at HHS, that she was under tremendous pressure to make sure J & P was as profitable as it could be. She always referenced her stockholders, though. As any executive does. I only began to realize that she was mixed up in something more after Harper. And then . . . when Finley . . ." His shoulders sank with guilt.

I left him alone, returning my attention to Joe. "Did the deposits come from company accounts or private accounts?"

"Almost all of them are shell companies that can be traced back to pharmaceutical executives or the company itself. However, there were three from private accounts. One from Ari. One from Jamichael Teason's father, Michael. . . ."

"And the last?"

"Lars Dillon."

Nick and I sucked wind.

Rodrigo leaned in. "Who is Lars Dillon?"

"Lars is Karen's stepbrother. He's also one of the president's private financial lawyers. Probably one of the reasons Karen got the job at HHS." I turned back to Joe. "Are you saying this goes all the way to the White House?"

"I'm not saying anything. I'm telling you what's on the drive."

I had no doubt Joe knew he was sitting on an explosive story. It was also a dangerous story. "You need to pass that information to the FBI."

Joe didn't respond.

My gaze cruised the table, taking in each man. I began to realize the knowledge we each shared filled in the holes—the gaps—in the story. And the picture it created dripped in blood. I'd been feeling pretty comfortable with Rivkin dead. But here, Joe was telling us that a large group of powerful men and women were willing to purchase an assassin for hire to get rid of a senator and congressman based on a possibility. We were merely ants beneath their colossal boot.

I popped my head above the booth to make sure no one was within hearing distance before speaking. "Joe, I get it. You're in the midst of uncovering a massive conspiracy that might go all the way to the president. I'm assuming your editor is thrilled and safely sitting on the flash drive. However, if this meeting were to get out, before you publish, it puts us all in danger. You don't understand the type of people Troika Star has hired. We're sitting ducks. The hacker was able to kill Harper with the pacemaker *in his own body*. And it sounds like he was able to hack the CSX train lines. The assassin they hired was a disgraced Mossad agent with a million-dollar price on his head. A forty-five-million-dollar slush fund will go a long way to buying a couple of fly-by-night killers to take out the four of us."

"That's why I need you to go on record. Once I publish, we're all safe."

I wasn't so sure about that. Nick and I exchanged wary glances. However, Rodrigo had no inhibitions. "I'll go on record. You can quote me. Here, I brought my notes from the stakeout yesterday." He pulled half a dozen tatty pages from his suit pocket.

"Wait a minute." I planted my hand on the paper and stared at Nick. "We have no choice. We've got to do this."

He gave a sharp nod. "With conditions."

"Okay, Joe. We'll go on record as anonymous sources. None of us wants a damn parade of reporters hounding us for the next month. Got it?"

"Agreed." Joe turned on the cell's recorder and flipped to a fresh page of notes. "Mr. Ross, let's start with you and your relationship to Karen."

I judged Nick's testimony mildly forthcoming, Rodrigo, an open book, and I . . . well, I told most of my story. I kept the fact the FBI was sweating the hacker under wraps. Joe would have to obtain that information from someone else. We were closing in on half past five when Joe finally wrapped our meeting. The dinner rush had begun, and we all became concerned about listening ears. Shockingly, Nick picked up the tab for the table. Rodrigo and Joe offered to pitch in, but I didn't make a peep.

It's the least he can do.

"I'm going to say goodbye to Alfonse before I head out. See you at work tomorrow." Rodrigo waved and headed into the kitchen area.

Before scooting my way out of the booth, I offered to pass the flash drive on to the FBI for Joe.

Those hazel-brown eyes studied me for a minute. "I'll take it under consideration."

"Please do. Once you publish, you know they'll be knocking at your door for it anyway. Why don't we work something out?"

He gave the briefest of nods. "I'll talk to my editor. In the meantime, I'm going to stay here and finish up my notes."

Nick and I walked out together. A clammy mist kissed my face, and the smell of damp concrete rose to greet me. I pulled my hood up on my raincoat as I headed toward the Metro station.

Nick paused my steps with the slightest touch to my shoulder. "I know what you must think of me."

"*I* know *you* know more than you're saying. *Talk* to the FBI. Make this right, Nick. Then it won't matter what I think of you."

"I'm sorry you and your friend were put in danger. I didn't know." Those harsh features softened with contriteness.

"Or maybe you didn't want to know." I couldn't help pushing the needle deeper.

He stared down at the wet sidewalk. "Maybe so."

"She was in love with you, you know."

"She was infatuated," he returned.

"She was married." A fact the four of us danced around in our discussion with Joe. However, I hadn't forgotten that sometime last night, a man up in New Jersey was given some terrible news about a woman he loved. Once the story got out, the ramifications of her crimes would make his life hell. I wondered if he knew about his wife, or if he was simply the unwitting husband in this debacle.

Nick stared into the distance. "I know. Believe it or not, *she* pursued *me*. After we started the affair, I tried to break it off. . . . She told me her husband had a mistress too. Then I didn't care, knowing she was using me to get back at him. Somewhere along the way . . ."

"Somewhere along the way–?"

His hooded gaze returned to mine. "She became infatuated with the excitement of sneaking around. At least, that's what I told myself. Now I wonder if she stayed simply to garner information about the congressman from me."

"And you willingly . . . spilled the beans."

Nick cringed.

Men! Always thinking with their dicks. "Make it right." I strode away without a backward glance.

Chapter Twenty-eight

Friday came and went with no bombshell headlines. Nothing under Joe Brock's byline. All day, I felt antsy and on edge, waiting for the other shoe to drop. I worried the greedy conspirators would get wind of the investigation or Joe Brock's exclusive, and they'd empty the bank accounts, closing up shop and removing all the evidence before the FBI could investigate.

Mike left a brief message on my cell while I attended. a fundraiser. Saturday, the security company arrived at eight o'clock sharp, and I left my own message on Mike's phone letting him know the system was being installed. At nine, Mrs. Thundermuffin, wearing a peach turban and emerald green caftan, knocked at my door.

"Good morning, Mrs. Thundermuffin. What can I do for you?"

"Hello, dearie. I heard some noise and wanted to make sure everything was alright."

"Everything is fine. I've decided not to get surround sound and chose instead to have a security system installed." I opened the door wide, so she should see the installer working on the keypad in the front hall.

"I don't blame you. A smart call indeed." She leaned in close and whispered, "Those surround sound folks seemed a little dodgy to me."

"I think you're right." If I had to guess, Mrs. Thundermuffin knew the parade of people in my apartment, the last time we met, were not surround sound installers. "Would you like to come in for a cup of coffee?"

"Oh, no, thank you. It's time to take Mr. Tibbs out for a walk. I just wanted to make sure you were okay. Ever since that incident in the stairwell, I realized we must be vigilant in looking out for each other. I wouldn't want anything like that to happen in our building again. Especially not to you." She might be a bit strange, but Mrs. Thundermuffin's heart was in the right place.

"You're right, Mrs. Thundermuffin. We do need to watch out for dangerous characters. Would you like the phone number of the security company for your own apartment?"

"Yes, I think so."

I wrote the number down on a piece of paper, and, clutching it in her veiny hand, my petite neighbor tottered away on her Hollywood-style feathered mules. She wore some wacky outfits, but I'd kill for a pair of mules like that. The next time I saw her, I'd have to ask where she purchased them.

Around one, the installers packed up their gear and left. I hadn't heard back from Mike, so I called again.

This time he answered with a grumpy, "Hello."

"Did I wake you?"

"Yeah. I've been up half the night."

"Getting a confession from your hacker, I hope."

"No."

"Could you tell me if he did?"

"No. He lawyered up."

"I'm not surprised. You'll have to make him a deal if you want him to talk."

"I know."

"And?"

My question met with a deep sigh.

"You've already made a deal," I said.

"He wants to sweeten the pot."

"I'll bet." My mind, of course, lingered around the conversation with Joe. Even if I told Mike what I knew, there was still too much conjecture. None of us had actually seen the USB drive. We were all going on what Joe had told us. I could tell Mike about the drive, but I was fairly sure the paper would stonewall until they were ready to print. Also, Joe seemed to be a good guy. I didn't want to double cross him by throwing him into the FBI's lap. I wanted him to give up the drive on his own, without forcing his hand. However, my antsy subconscious hadn't rested since my meeting with Joe and something had to be done.

"Do you have enough to hold him?"

"Oh, yes, we've got DNA evidence on the threats to Congress and a link to another unrelated hack into the State Department website. But I don't have enough to tie him to Harper's murder."

"How did you get the DNA?"

"He licked the envelope."

"Rookie move." I tapped a finger on my chin, pondering how to approach Joe.

"Enough about the case. Did you get your security system installed?"

"What? Oh. Yes, the guys came this morning."

"And?"

"It seems fine. I'll have to get used to turning it on before I leave the apartment or go to bed."

"That's the most important part."

"Mike—"

"Yes?"

"Don't sweeten the pot."

"What?"

"Don't make the deal with your hacker. Not yet."

"It's not really my call."

"I know. But . . . tell them you're working another angle and you'll have more hard evidence on the hacker soon."

"K.C., I can't lie to my employers. Amir and I were up half the night working the hacker's laptop, but so far, we've come up with nothing. We can't even get in. We're down to one more password try. If we don't get it right, I'm afraid he's set up the entire hard drive to melt down. Same with his cell phone. A search of his home has revealed nothing but a small arsenal of legally obtained firearms and a hell of a lot of porn."

"Rivkin said to follow the money. Have you determined how he was paid?"

"Not yet. We're going on the assumption it was Bitcoin on the darknet."

"Which means you'll never be able to trace it."

"Precisely."

"What if I told you I might be on to something?"

"K.C.," his voice held that warning tone, "what are you into now? Does this have something to do with Silverthorne?"

"For once, no, it doesn't. I need you to trust me. See if you can buy twenty-four hours."

"What have you done?"

"Mike, please . . . I've done nothing. And I know this is hard for you because of what's happened. But I think I'm in a position to help. Trust me." I drew out the last two words.

"I'm so exhausted, I can't think straight. Fine, I trust you. I'll tell Leon to keep our hacker on ice for another twenty-four hours. Maybe a miracle will happen and the passcode will be revealed to me in a shining ray of light."

"Get some rest. I'll be in touch soon."

Chapter Twenty-nine

I left a message on Joe's cell and anxiously paced the apartment, waiting for him to call back. When the phone rang, I didn't even bother looking at the caller ID before answering.

"Joe?"

"What? Hello? Rina? It's Jillian."

"Oh, hey, Jilly. What's up?"

"Well, I haven't heard from you in a few weeks. I was wondering if you wanted to go shopping or to the movies with me this afternoon?"

My sister lived in Falls Church, about twenty minutes away, without traffic. Normally, I'd take her up on a shopping trip just to get my mind off waiting for Joe to call me back. Which could be longer than I'd anticipated. However, Jillian had gotten tangled up in my past adventure, and I had no interest dragging her into the latest one. I also didn't want an audience when Joe called, especially not one as smart as my sister.

"Unfortunately, I've already got plans."

"With Mike?"

Well, my plans sort of had something to do with Mike. "Yup."

"How are things going with you two? I mean, is it weird moving past the friendship phase into a relationship?"

"Um, I'm not sure I can say we've moved into the next phase." I paced into the kitchen and absently cleaned the kitchen counters. "We're kind of stuck."

"Uh-oh."

"What do you mean by that?"

"Well, you're going to have to move forward. You certainly can't move back. And you can't stay in the waiting place. So, forward is the only move to make. Right?"

"Yeah." I had to agree.

"You're sexually attracted to him? Right?"

"Yes." *No doubt.*

"Then what are you two waiting for?"

"It's complicated." I tossed the sponge into the sink.

"Pshaw. It's always complicated with you. So, uncomplicate it, and take that man to bed," she admonished.

"If only it could be that easy."

"Oh, for crying out loud. You all call *me* the drama queen."

"Wha—"

"No. Don't deny it. I know you and Tyler used to call me the drama queen. I'll admit, there were some embarrassing teenage years to back that up. But, really, for you and Mike it should be easy. You're already best friends. I've seen him around you. He'd take a bullet for you. Now get your shit together and move it along. Otherwise, you're just marking time."

I didn't respond, and she added, "You know, you're not getting any younger."

I rolled my eyes. "Thank you for pointing that out, dearest sister."

"Well, I'm just saying, don't wait too long or you'll miss the moment."

"He's not a shooting star. There will be other moments."

"Nuh-uh. Not like this one. Trust me. I know."

"Because you and Tony are in love? Instead of the drama queen, you're now the queen of love?"

"Don't be a brat. What Tony and I have is different. Ours was more like lightning. A love at first sight. What you and Mike have is a developed relationship that needs a push to move it into more."

"Okay, Jilly. I understand what you're saying. I'll work on it."

"See that you do. And say hi to Mike for me."

"Will do. Take care."

As much guff as I gave my sister, she had a point. When this stupid case wrapped, it was time to kiss or get off the pot, so to speak.

Speaking of the pot . . .

Of course, the phone rang the moment I sat down on it. This time I checked caller ID.

"Joe?"

"Ms. Cardinal. You called."

"Yes, and call me Karina. Listen, I need you to turn over the USB drive to the FBI."

"We will."

"When?"

"Soon."

I blew up my bangs. "When do you plan to publish?"

"Monday."

"I have something to tell you, off the record." I waited for him to acknowledge.

"Off the record, what have you got?"

"The FBI has a suspect in custody, but they need Karen's financial files to make the case and anything in her emails that might implicate him."

"That's very interesting. But making the FBI's case is not my job."

My little hamster brain began running on the wheel. "What if I can get you an exclusive?"

"Keep talking."

"What if . . . you can work together? What if, in addition to the story, you can report on FBI raids to arrest these turkeys?"

"I don't know. The television media is already sniffing around the story."

"You don't want to get scooped. I get it. But, there is more going on than a good story. It's putting away a conspiracy of murderers."

"I know what's at stake here. My job is to report the news. Not make the FBI's case for them."

"They're going to get the information from you anyway. Why not help them now? And they would owe you. You'd have a chip to cash."

He paused before answering. "I like your thinking, but I'm not convinced."

"Joe . . . I'm trying to help everyone here, so I'll lay it out for you. Three murders have happened, and I am both morally and legally bound to tell law enforcement what I know. If I tell them what you've got, they'll come after you, and if you don't give it to them, they'll slap you with obstruction of justice. That will become the story. You're sitting on a key piece of evidence, and you know it. Your boss knows it. I'm trying to do what's right by you, and in the name of justice."

"You make a compelling argument. What's your plan?"

"A negotiation that benefits both you and the FBI and brings down Troika Star. I can set up a meeting."

"When?"

I did some fast thinking. "Tonight, at five."

"Where?"

"Your office."

"See you then."

****

At five on the dot, Mike and I spun through the rotating front door of *The Washington Post* offices on K Street, a modern building the paper moved to in 2015, full of glass windows, black ergonomic chairs that contrasted with the white walls, and cubes for the journalists. It was a vast difference from the days of Woodward and Bernstein, when *The Post* was housed in an antique edifice with low ceilings striped by fluorescent lights, dingy carpet, and desks crammed practically on top of each other, built by the Graham empire.

"I don't know what you've got up your sleeve here, K.C. I've got no authority or plans to leak information to the media regarding the case," Mike warned.

"I don't expect you to. What I'm hoping for is a conversation that creates a win-win for everyone."

Joe's Nikes squeaked as he crossed the marbled foyer. Mike and I were both dressed casually in slacks and polos. However, Joe seemed to have rolled into work wearing yesterday's clothes—baggy jeans and a rumpled Washington Nationals jersey.

"Joe Brock, I'd like you to meet Agent Michael Finnegan."

The men shook hands.

"Follow me." Joe made a jerking motion with his head.

We took the elevator to the upper levels of the executive offices, and Joe led us down the hall to a room with more glass and a shiny conference table. Two men rose as we entered. I recognized the bearded *Washington Post* executive editor, and the man who stood next to him in a sharply tailored designer suit could only be one of their lawyers. A thick manila file rested in front of one of the empty chairs. After the introductions were made, Joe took the seat behind the folder.

I decided to get the ball rolling. "Joe, you know why we're here. Let's talk about Karen Ferngull's flash drive."

The lawyer blustered for a few minutes, spouting a bunch of

legal jargon at Mike and declaring this meeting a bad idea. He was silenced by the prominent editor. "Joe and I are aware of your feelings, Marcus. With that being said, I'd like to turn the conversation over to Joe."

Joe began with information he'd provided at Friday's meeting. However, as I suspected, the reporter had been holding out on us at the restaurant, he was sitting on so much more. Over a thousand emails were spread across the drive. It was a treasure trove of information on the level of Lewinskygate. His team had been working day and night researching the materials. As a gift of good faith, Joe's manila file held a packet of a hundred printed and highlighted emails and text messages. They implicated key players at the five pharmaceuticals and provided information about the hiring of NKBarbie and Naftali Rivkin on the darknet—how they were contacted, how much they were paid, and where the payments went. Rivkin was paid in diamonds, whereas, NKBarbie had chosen Bitcoin, as Mike suspected. However, emails sent to Karen identified Jamichael Teason as the mastermind behind Harper's murder.

Frankly, I couldn't believe these folks would be so stupid as to put all of it in writing. However, with so many players, perhaps the emails were the insurance they carried against each other. They must have realized, when Karen made threats—started bucking the system—that she had all the dirt she needed to put a dozen of the players behind bars for life.

Even though he hid it well, I could see Mike couldn't believe his luck. The meeting devolved into a discussion about deadlines, deals for exclusives, front page news, etcetera. I, now as useful as the potted plant in the corner, barely spoke during the meeting. The men hashed out their agreements while I watched like "an Egyptian Sphinx", as Mike framed it when we finally left the marbled halls of *The Post* at half past nine.

On our way out, Mike called Leon. "You'd better wake up Judge DeLawerence. We're going to need some warrants."

It was clear he wouldn't be getting much sleep tonight. He gave me an absentminded kiss when we reached my car before hurrying off to his own vehicle with the phone attached to his ear.

Chapter Thirty

Monday morning, I awoke to the sound of hammering on my front door. I checked the peephole and found Rodrigo on the other side.

"Karina, wake up! Let me in!" His knuckles continued banging.

I considered ignoring him and walking back to my snuggly, warm bed, but he was making such a racket, I worried he'd wake the neighbors.

"What is it?" I demanded grumpily, pulling the door open. The high-pitched beeping of my new system reminded me I had thirty seconds to turn it off before we had a full-on, ear-splitting alarm. "Just a minute." I punched in the code and found Rodrigo standing at my shoulder. "Come on in. Make yourself at home," I harrumphed.

"Have you seen it?" He waved a newspaper in my face.

"Seen what? What the hell time is it?" I yawned.

"Quarter to six."

"As in, five forty-five?"

"Five forty-three, to be exact," he said, glancing at his phone.

"How the hell did you get in the building?"

"One of your neighbors, heading out for a jog, held the door open for me."

"Christ! This better be good, Rodrigo, or I swear I'll chop you up in tiny little pieces and shove you down my disposal."

He scrutinized me for a moment. "You need a cup of coffee."

"Screw a cup. I need to open a vein and mainline it through an IV."

"Where's your kitchen?"

I didn't deign to answer; instead, I stumbled to the couch, flopped down on it, and closed my eyes. Rodrigo must have found the kitchen and the coffeemaker on his own, because a few minutes later, the scent of the lifesaving brew wafted past my olfactory senses.

He retrieved the largest mug in the cabinet, one I usually used as a soup bowl, and brought it over where I remained in a supine semi-coma. "Here, drink this. You'll feel more like yourself in a jiffy."

"What if I don't want to feel more like myself? What if I want to return to my relaxing slumber and pretend my coworker didn't invade my home at five in the morning?"

"Karen's emails are the front page of this morning's *Post.*"

His statement brought me to consciousness better than any cup of coffee could. I snatched the paper from his hands.

The sordid story splashed across *The Post*'s headlines, along with names of the conspirators and the murders of Finley, Harper, and Karen Ferngull. I took the mammoth cup from Rodrigo as my eyes zipped across the page.

"Did you know about this?" he asked me.

"Yes."

"Yes? Seriously? Did you talk with Joe again? Without me?" He sounded hurt, but I couldn't muster up an apology or sympathy at this ungodly hour.

"And the FBI." I sipped the brew and grimaced, glancing at the black liquid for the first time. "Could you add some cream and sugar?"

The paper got a whole lot more than one article out of Karen's emails and the Troika Star conspiracy, and, in my opinion, Joe Brock should be nominated for a Pulitzer. Rodrigo splayed the different sections of the paper across the coffee table, and we each took a page of the thin newsprint, eagerly reading the in-depth reporting.

At seven, Rodrigo turned on the television. I juggled reading the paper and watching, in my robe and slippers, as Sam Cactus reported the story. The network ran live footage of the FBI raiding Lars Dillon's Manhattan law firm, escorting him out of the building. The FBI arrested Jamichael Teason at his home as he backed out of the driveway in his Cadillac. Rodrigo and I high-fived, congratulating ourselves, as if we'd singlehandedly solved the case. Stupid, I know. But the euphoria of seeing the FBI get their man/men/women was on par with winning the Super Bowl.

By the time eight rolled around, I reluctantly headed to the shower, admonishing Rodrigo to keep watching and let me know if anything new happened. I tuned in to a news radio channel on the way to work, eagerly listening for new information that I hadn't already read in *The Post* or heard on TV. The day brought more raids and more information. The twenty-four hour news networks barely reported on anything else. Everyone in the office was as consumed by the story as Rodrigo and I, so our rabid curiosity didn't seem out of place to our colleagues. He spent a good portion of the day in my office with his laptop, scanning the internet for breaking articles and rereading the old ones.

It started as a whisper, but soon, work colleagues who found out I'd been with Harper the day he died began creeping into my office. Rodrigo happily filled them in on the big story. They came and sat or stood against the walls, gossiping like it was a day at their local beauty salon. Barely any work got accomplished. I thanked the heavens Hasina was out of town until mid-week. By four thirty, I gave up pretending to work and suggested we all head to a local bar for drinks. The day ended with me driving a happy, drunk Rodrigo home.

News of the amounts of dirty pharmaceutical company money going into politicians' pockets came out on Tuesday and the public went into an uproar. Social media lit up like wild fire, and #congressionaldrugmules was trending before noon. One congressman's home office in Illinois had a Molotov cocktail thrown through the front window. By Friday, both the House and Senate introduced new bills with bipartisan sponsorship. They focused on sweeping federal oversight on the pharmaceutical industry, which included setting price caps and modulating costs on specialty medications for chronic conditions. It was called the Harper-Finley Bill. Harper was right, S46 paled in comparison.

One thing stood out to me and was mentioned by only a handful of reporters—the president's Twitter account remained unexpectedly silent. Our tweeter-in-chief had nothing to say for himself, allowing his press secretary to decry this awful crime on behalf of the administration.

The silence lasted until Wednesday, when a tabloid splashed the headline "WHITE HOUSE CONNECTED TO D.C. MURDERS" on its front page. The headline was picked up by a local news station, and then its national affiliate. A fiery tweet storm raged down.

The flash drive turned into a gold mine for the FBI; arrests were made and indictments handed down. Rivkin was right—once the feds had Karen's accounts, all they had to do was follow the money . . . and the emails.

During one of our few and hurried conversations that week, Mike told me the hacker in custody didn't get his plea deal. The

FBI didn't need it. The case would undoubtedly do wonders for Mike's career. I predicted he'd be looking at a promotion before too long, and I was thrilled for him.

My talk with Jillian about my relationship with Mike stayed with me. Generally, it would come to mind at night as the day's stresses floated away and I lay alone in bed. Jilly was right, we needed to move forward. But how? Dozens of imaginary conversations with Mike ran through my brain, each one filled with deep, drawn-out confessions that you read about in sappy romance stories. All of which I could see in my mind's eye, none of which I believed would actually come out of my mouth, or his for that matter. Until one scenario came to me that seemed so simple and unencumbered, I knew it would work. Finally, two weeks after the story broke, things calmed down and we found time to meet for dinner. He texted he'd pick me up for our date at seven.

****

Mike arrived ten minutes late. I didn't mind. Neither did he, when I opened the door wearing a gossamer robe with a matching negligee, and a pair of feathered mules (à la Mrs. Thundermuffin).

His eyes bulged, and a strange squeak came out.

"First, a glass of champagne to celebrate solving the case." I drew him into the apartment and handed him a flute filled with the bubbly.

He sucked down the glass in one gulp and placed it on a side table.

"Okay, I guess we'll do the toasting later." I took his hand. "Mike, I've been giving this a lot of thought. My sister says it's time for us to move this relationship forward. And she's right. We've been dancing around a sexual liaison for too long now.

Do you want to move the relationship forward?"

He nodded with the look of an excited puppy.

"Then follow me." I crooked a finger and cat-walked to the bedroom.

Karina's next adventure will be hitting bookshelves in 2019. If you are interested in learning about upcoming Karina Cardinal mysteries, join Ellen's newsletter at *ellenbutler.net.*

Author's Note

The idea for *Fatal Legislation* came to me when I saw an ad, on TV, for a pacemaker recall, due to the fact it could be hacked. Immediately, my writer's mind thought, "What an excellent way to kill someone. I've got to write a Karina Cardinal adventure about that!" So, if you were wondering how realistic killing someone via pacemaker would be, sadly it is a viable option. As I delved deeper into my research, I found out exactly how vulnerable our culture is to the dangers of hacking. Technology running on Wi-Fi systems, such as smart appliances and virtual assistants are at particular risk. Security measures can be taken and software improved, but there is always some hacker around the corner trying new ways to access these everyday items.

My time at the American Academy of Physician Assistants helped form the pharmaceutical industry conspiracy. In the 1990s, the FDA rolled back pharmaceutical regulations; the new regulations allowed drug companies the ability to advertise direct to consumers. I remember having a long conversation with a group of Physician Assistants from work, and they were *not* in favor of these rollbacks. They felt marketing prescriptive drugs directly to consumers would be dangerous. What was the result of the FDA rollbacks? Drug companies dumped millions into advertising and patients began hounding doctors for medication they'd seen on TV or in magazines. For the first time in history prescription drugs were put on public display in direct competition to each other in the same manner toilet paper brands compete. From 1990 to 2000, the United States saw an increase of consumer prescription drug expenditures jump from $40.3 billion to $121 billion and up to $205.3 billion in 2005. The largest 15-year increase in pharmaceutical history.

Furthermore, the pharmaceutical industry statistics in the

novel are not fictional, they come from real data. According to The Center for Responsive Politics, "The pharmaceutical industry, which has about two lobbyists for every member of Congress, spent $152 million on influencing legislation in 2016." The Guardian wrote an article titled, *How big pharma's money-and its politicians-feed the opioid crisis,* where it states, "drug companies also contributed more than $20 million directly to political campaigns." In the book, Karina refers to a bill she calls, "Buy your drugs from Canada," it was proposed by Democrats in 2016 and had support from a handful of Republicans. The legislation didn't pass, because the pharmaceutical lobby did its job well. Two other truths in the novel: 1) America is paying the offset of other countries who do control their pharmaceutical industry pricing, and 2) Hunter Syndrome is a real condition. The annual cost for an American consumer of the drug Elaprase is approximately $500,000/year. Sadly, it is not the most expensive drug on the market.

Acknowledgements

I'd like to thank the following people for their time, ideas, suggestions, and clarifications that helped create Karina's latest adventure.

To Matt Fine, a high school friend, who helped me create some interesting plot points around the FBI investigation. I am thankful you continue to provide your time and expertise. And, speaking of law enforcement, David Swinson, formerly of the D.C. Police Department, provided help defining the different roles each department of law enforcement would play, should a senator be murdered on Capitol grounds. Your knowledge, kindness, and support surrounding this story is greatly appreciated. I also want to thank two of my former American Academy of Physician Assistant (AAPA) colleagues, Marilyn Fitzgerald and Sandy Harding. Our hours long lunch provided plot points and character development which I hope you'll recognize as you read. Thanks to my editor, Emily, for pointing out a plot hole that was in desperate need of fixing.

To my high school friend, Nancy Green, who had the unfortunate experience of seeing her husband almost die from a pacemaker gone bad—luckily, he survived—I would personally like to thank you for providing such honest, and, what must be, heart-wrenching details of the incident. Your information allowed me to make my fictional senator's death as realistic as possible. I'd also like to thank intern Danny Duong, from Senator Tim Kaine's office, for escorting me through the tunnel systems under the Capitol and Senate office buildings. My time on the Hill happened pre-9/11, and the tunnels have changed quite a bit, to include, new paint, bright lights, cameras, restricted access, and the improvement of drywall over the creepy plumbing and steam pipes. Finally, I'd like to thank my friends and family for all their loving support as I continue through this writing journey. Larry Geib provided information from his decades of climbing experience for Karina's break-in, and I especially appreciated my husband sharing his cyber security expertise for this novel.

About the Author

Ellen Butler is a bestselling novelist writing critically acclaimed suspense thrillers, and award-winning romance. Ellen holds a Master's Degree in Public Administration and Policy, and her history includes a long list of writing for dry, but illuminating, professional newsletters and windy papers on public policy. She is a member of International Thriller Writers, Sisters in Crime, and the OSS Society. She lives in the Virginia suburbs of Washington, D.C. with her husband and two children.

You can find Ellen at:

Website ~ *www.EllenButler.net*

Facebook ~ *www.facebook.com/EllenButlerBooks*

Twitter ~ *@EButlerBooks*

Instagram ~ *@ebutlerbooks*

Goodreads ~ *www.goodreads.com/EllenButlerBooks*

Guided Reading Questions for Book Clubs
Available on Ellen's Website
EllenButler.net

Novels by Ellen Butler

Suspense/Thriller
Isabella's Painting (Karina Cardinal Mystery Book 1)
The Brass Compass
Poplar Place

Contemporary Romance
Heart of Design (Love, California Style Book 1)
Planning for Love (Love, California Style Book 2)
Art of Affection (Love California Style Book 3)
Second Chance Christmas

Isabella's Painting

Peeling back layers of lies could save a masterpiece...or reveal a killer.

After a long week lobbying on Capitol Hill, all Karina Cardinal wants to do is chill with Netflix and her boyfriend, Patrick Dunne. Instead, she's slipping her aching feet into red stilettos for his parents' annual holiday bash. When she accidentally interrupts Patrick's father in his study, her embarrassment is tempered by suspicion that Martin Dunne and his dapper, secretive guest are hiding something. Maybe the painting she barely glimpses right before it disappears behind a secret panel.

An internet search raises her curiosity to full-blown alarm. If she's right, Martin is in possession of a stolen masterpiece. Infamous because everyone close to it has turned up dead. As in Mafia-style-execution dead. As she's chewing over which instinct to follow—back off while she still can, or dig deeper for the truth—she crosses paths with FBI agent Mike Finnegan. An old friend and not-quite flame from her college days. When she looks into his warm, mocha eyes, she's tempted to tell him everything.

Trouble is, she's already being watched. And the next move she makes could destroy innocent lives...including her own.

The Brass Compass

Can she elude the enemy?

A beautiful American spy flees into the night. On her own, she must live by her wits to evade capture and make it to the safety of the Allied forces.

Lily Saint James grew up traveling the European continent, learning languages as she went. In 1938, her mother's abrupt death brings her back home to Washington, D.C., and after the bombing of Pearl Harbor, Lily comes to the attention of the Office of Strategic Services (OSS). Her knowledge of German, French, and Italian makes her the perfect OSS Agent, and her quick thinking places her as a nanny in the household of an important German Army Colonel, where she is able to gather intelligence for the Allies. After her marketplace contact goes missing, she makes a late-night trip to her secondary contact only to find him under interrogation by the SS. When he commits suicide, she flees into the frigid winter night carrying false identification papers that are now dangerous and a mini film cartridge with vital strategic information. In order to survive, Lily must make it out of Germany, into the hands of Allied-controlled France, through a path fraught with peril.

Poplar Place

Will demons from a former life destroy her tranquility?

The sleepy, small town of Denton, South Carolina, possesses the tranquil life Cara Baker craves, but will she be able to keep trouble from following her?

Newly minted librarian, Cara Baker, effectively cuts ties with her tumultuous life as a Pittsburgh District Attorney and moves down to South Carolina, where she embraces the peaceful, laid-back style of small town living. Everything seems to be falling into place when Cara finds the perfect house to round out her new plans. Well ... perfect except for the immovable hermit living on the top floor. She throws caution to the wind and buys the fabulous house—hermit and all—without meeting him. Eventually, by wooing her reclusive renter with notes and mouthwatering meals, he caves and invites her up to the apartment. Preconceived notions are blown out of the water, when she finds he isn't the Mr. Mole she envisioned.

Unfortunately, phone calls from the FBI bring Cara's summer idyll to an abrupt halt, as the past she fled catches up putting her in danger.

Made in the USA
Middletown, DE
08 October 2022

12224107R00172